RAVE REVIEWS

"Tim Lebbon move[...] me remember how rich [...] —Jack Ketchum, be[...] *[...]dom*

"Lebbon is a genuinely masterful writer…[with] fresh ideas, shimmering prose, and often terrifying scenarios."
—*Rue Morgue*

"Lebbon is quite simply the most exciting new name in horror in years."
—*SFX Magazine*

FACE
"Intense and affecting, *Face* will seize and hold your attention from the opening paragraph to the end. A writer blessed with extraordinary gifts, Lebbon's chief talents lie in exploring the darker moments of everyday life…. A true disciple of the dark, Lebbon's imagery wrings true fear from his audience."
—*Hellnotes*

"Lebbon's novel will reward the careful reader with insights as well as gooseflesh."
—*Publishers Weekly*

"Lebbon draws the reader into this nightmare to experience the horror with his characters. Lebbon taps into our universal fear of the unknown, the unseen, keeping this reader looking over her shoulder to catch that slight movement of shadow glimpsed out of the corner of her eye."
—*CelebrityCafe.com*

THE NATURE OF BALANCE
"Beautifully written and mysterious, *The Nature of Balance* will put some readers in the mind of the great Arthur Machen. But with more blood and guts."
—Richard Laymon, bestselling author of *To Wake the Dead*

"Vibrant, exploding with imagery, Tim Lebbon takes you on a white-knuckle ride of uncompromising horror. This is storytelling at its best."
—Simon Clark, author of *Vampyrrhic*

WRITTEN IN BLOOD

Cain had to leave. This attic had been a refuge, a sanctuary for the crippled old man, and the difficulty he must have faced getting in here made it feel even more special. By leaving the room as it was after his death, the landlord had revealed the true extent of the invasion into Vlad's life. And much as Cain suddenly felt empathy for that victimised man, he did not feel that he should be here. This was a private place, made more so by its user's death.

Scrawled in blood on the floor at Cain's feet, six words: *They know I'm going to tell.*

Those claw marks on the door? Cain thought. *What put them here? And why?*

His answer stared him in the face as he turned to leave. Above the door hung an old photograph of Vlad in all his glory, swinging from a trapeze with one hand and waving to the photographer with the other. He was young, fit, full of life, and his smile promised nothing of his grim, lonely demise.

Across the picture were the words: *They're going to kill me tonight.*

Other *Leisure* books by Tim Lebbon:

FEARS UNNAMED
FACE
THE NATURE OF BALANCE

DESOLATION

TIM LEBBON

LEISURE BOOKS NEW YORK CITY

For my childhood friend.

A LEISURE BOOK®

March 2005

Published by

Dorchester Publishing Co., Inc.
200 Madison Avenue
New York, NY 10016

ISBN 0-8439-5428-0

The name "Leisure Books" and the stylized "L" with design are trademarks of Dorchester Publishing Co., Inc.

Printed in the United States of America.

DESOLATION

Chapter One
Nowhere

Cain had few possessions, even fewer memories, and no family. Nowhere seemed a perfect place to begin his new life.

The taxi dropped him at the curbside and left him sitting on his suitcase, several plastic carrier bags scattered around his feet like bloated dead pigeons, real birds chattering from gutters and telephone lines, irate at his intrusion. He turned to the wooden chest beside him on the pavement and grabbed its handle, hardly surprised when he found he could lift one end from the ground with ease. Its weight seemed to vary with his own moods. Today, he was happy to be here.

The street sign announced itself as *Endless Crescent*, but some wit had daubed *Nowhere* across the name in bright blue paint, ironic vandalism that would likely confuse more than amuse. Such skewed intelligence was hardly in evidence in other graffiti that decorated walls along the street, occasional proclamations such as "Darren woz yer," and "Mandy has a wet pussy," and "Follow me for the Way." Some of the perpetrators had imagined themselves as artists, the vandalism taking on colors and shades and shapes that were meant to bestow individuality. Such ego was a nonsense, as the work was always done in secret. Cain stared at one of the names sprayed across the side of a garage in great green swaths, "Kelvin," the tails of the *K* turned up into crude wings, the dot of the *i* a hooded eye, comical when it was intended to be threatening. He wondered where Kelvin was now, what he was doing, and whether he even knew himself.

Someone had once tried planting trees in an attempt to turn Endless Crescent into an avenue, but their efforts had led nowhere. Thin stumps protruded from squares of removed paving slabs, snapped off at waist height or lower, kicked and scarred, and blackened with dog piss and rot. The ground around them held more life, weeds sprouting as if in mockery of the trees' doomed attempts at existence.

The houses in the street were all large, an unusual mix of modern and Victorian, mostly three-storys, and over half of them had been converted into flats. The unmistakable signature of student accommodation marked some: open windows blaring a heady mixture of rock and dance music, bikes chained to garden fences like dangerous pets, uncurtained windows displaying half a dozen scenes of domesticity gone awry. Most of the houses were in a good state of repair, though one or two looked as if they should have been condemned years before. Indeed, one house directly across the street from where Cain sat seemed to have been surrendered back to the wilds. Its render had blown and been shed right across the front facade, and its windows were smashed, boarded up from the inside. The front garden was a riot of weeds and unkempt rosebushes. Cain could see the house's nameplate bolted to the wall beside the corrugated iron front door: HEAVEN. A joke, surely. He closed his eyes and shook his head, and when he looked again the sign still read the same.

A shout sounded from somewhere out of sight, a woman's shrill voice calling some missing kid in for lunch. Perhaps it had been missing for months and the woman tried this every day, hoping that continued normality would bring her child scampering back to her from whatever unknown distance it had traveled.

Cain looked down at his feet. Narrowing his field of vision helped him to calm his nerves. He shifted slightly and the suitcase flexed beneath him, threatening to burst open and spill his clothes across the street like fabric guts. He should go. He should stand and drag his possessions along to Number 13, his new home, his new life, or so he had been told. *It's time to stand on your own two feet*, the Face had said, handing him another pill.

Two children ran along the street, laughing and swearing, and laughing again at their secret rebellion. To Cain they seemed easily old enough to be in school, and too young to be out on their own. They stopped a few feet from him and sized him up, their eyes far too mature for their age.

All Cain could remember of his own childhood were the dreams.

"Hey, mister!" the taller of the two kids said. "You wearing that coat for a bet?"

Cain glanced down at the duffel coat, up at the sky, the sun burning its way through a haze of clouds. "It was cold where I came from," he said.

"Where's that, then, the fuckin' Arctic?" the short kid said, and they both laughed.

"No, not that far away," Cain said, trying to remember the name of the home, but there were only feelings and sensations—rough sheets on his bed, sterile decor, dirty floors—and the Face and Voice giving him advice and pills, food and comfort.

"I like your new sitting room," the tall kid said. "Where are we, then, in your kitchen? Where you going to sleep, in the box?"

Cain smiled. "It's a chest," he said, "and I'm sure I'd never fit in there."

"Bet I would," the short kid said.

"I'm sure you would."

The three fell silent for a few seconds, a silence loaded with something uncomfortable that Cain could not quite pin down. Had he issued a slight threat? Had the kids perceived it that way? Or were *they* threatening *him?*

"I've just moved here," he said, "from somewhere else."

"The fuckin' Arctic!" the kids said in unison, giggling at their humor.

"Shouldn't you two be in school?"

They looked uncomfortable at that, avoiding his eyes, kicking at a crushed tin can, and giving the

4

street another note to its urban theme. Cain wondered if the sounds around him made up the whole, or whether the street would have been exactly the same without them. He doubted that. Tin can rattling, distant music blaring, mothers shouting, a dog barking, cars grumbling, kids screaming, pans crashing, doors slamming . . . He was somewhere unique, a place set apart from anywhere else by its own distinct sounds, sights, and smells. He tried not to sense too much.

"There," Cain said. "That's my new place. At least, a part of it is." He reached into his jacket pocket and pulled out the letter of introduction, already crinkled and grubby from many readings. *Afresh Respite Home, Tall Stennington,* the letterhead read, and he knew where he was from.

The kids looked to where he was pointing and laughed, punching and grappling each other as they turned and ran away from Cain. "So you're another fuckin' nutter, then!" the tall one shouted over his shoulder, running faster as if to escape the words.

"What?" Cain stood from his suitcase. But the kids slipped into a lane between two houses and were lost to him, leaving behind only an echo in his mind . . . *another fuckin' nutter* . . . "We'll see," Cain said. He looped his finger through the carrier bag handles, lifted the suitcase, hefted the chest with his other hand—it still felt very light, almost empty, and he could move it by dragging one end along the ground—and approached Number 13 Endless Crescent. "We'll see."

The front gate swung open when Cain nudged

it with his knee, and he was able to negotiate his way through and kick it shut behind him without having to put anything down. There was a path and a planting bed and that was it; no lawn, no graveled area. The plants were waist-high and lush, their leaves dark green, big, spiked, like something from a rain forest instead of a suburban front garden in South Wales. And although there was variety here, all the plants must have belonged to the same family. Some leaves were larger than others, a slightly different shape, an alternative shade of dark green, but they were all spiked, with bright orange flowers hidden down at the leaf stems as if hiding away from the sun instead of seeking it. The many bees harvesting their pollen were fat, heavy, and lazy, providing a low background drone. It was strange, but Cain did not know why. The only other garden he knew was at the Afresh Respite Home, and that had consisted of a huge, square lawn with a few random shrubs at its edges and a summer house in one corner. Functional and easily maintained, with nowhere for mad folk to hide.

As he approached the front door, Cain realized that the garden was louder than the street. Leaves whispered in a slight breeze, bees bumbled from one flower to the next, and down beneath the waist-high canopy something was scurrying around in the shade. Birds, perhaps. Or mice. But all these sounds were somehow louder than the occasional car passing beyond the gate, the woman still calling her child's name in vain, the music polluting the summer day from open windows. It was as if coming through the gate had moved him on a great distance.

For the first time Cain felt truly alarmed at being out here on his own, away from what he knew. He had been thrilled when the Face told him it was time to leave, invigorated, proud of his soon-to-be independence. Although his father's death and much of Cain's existence from before were little more than dreams—like the memory of a book read long ago, someone else's life and experiences—he felt strong and fit and ready to begin again. He *knew* he was ready, he was certain of it . . . and yet he craved that Face and that soothing Voice. The cool hand on his brow. The calm void of drug-induced sleep.

Natural sleep was when it hit him the most. Then, so the Voice had said, Cain's mind tried to compensate for his lack of memories by creating false ones. *Never trust them,* he had said, *they lie, and dreaming is going to hinder your recovering mind as much as aid it.* Cain had his doubts, but the Voice knew what it was on about, he was *qualified.* Cain shook his jacket and heard the comforting rattle of pills. *Here,* the Voice had said quietly just as Cain was leaving, *don't tell . . . but take these. They'll help you to settle in with only reality as your bedfellow.*

"Help you?"

Cain spun around, letting out an involuntary squeal.

"Whoops, sorry!" The man in the doorway held up both hands and stepped back into the house. "Didn't mean to spook you."

"I'm not spooked," Cain said. Strange choice of words. "Just a bit startled. Sorry. I was admiring the garden."

"Ah yeah, the plants. They look a bit severe, but they keep people to the path." The man came forward again, down the small front door step so that he was on a level with Cain. He was only Cain's height, but something about his bearing made him appear taller.

"I'm here for the flat," Cain said. "I have this." He handed over the crumpled letter from Afresh, and the kids' parting shot echoed once more in his mind, *another fuckin' nutter . . .*

The man opened the letter, smoothed it several times as if the creases contained hidden messages. There were none—Cain had read it a hundred times on the way here—but still he was nervous at what would be found.

"That seems fine," the man said. "I've had the flat ready for a couple of days, wasn't sure when to expect you. Come on in and I'll show you up."

"That's it?" Cain said. It all felt so easy.

The man gave him a frank up-and-down inspection, as if looking for scars or something less visible. "As I said, I've been expecting you. The people who sent you appear to be very good payers, and everything's sorted. I'm not going to make anything hard for you with the deal I have with them. You stay here for a whole year, I get paid. You do a bunk at the end of the first week and disappear, I still get a year's money. Not bad, eh?"

"Not bad," Cain said, impressed, confused, flattered at the Home's confidence in him.

"I'm Peter," the man said, holding out his hand.

"Cain."

"Pleased to meet you, Cain. First name? Last?"

"Just Cain. It's easier to remember."

Silence hung heavy for a few seconds, backed by buzzing bees and rustling beneath the plants that kept people to the path.

"So what happened? The letter says you're been in the Home for quite a while."

"My father died."

Peter raised his eyebrows, expecting more.

Cain frowned, looked down, and he could remember nothing.

"No worries, just me being nosy," Peter said. "Never could keep my nose out of other people's business. Comes with being a landlord, I guess. Come on in."

Cain heard something in Peter's voice that told him he would be questioned again later. How would the landlord take the answer?

I don't really know what happened to me, Cain would have to say. *My father died, but before that there was only loneliness, and time, so much time. I don't remember much of it except in dreams. And most of those are bad.* Would Peter want someone without a past in his building, good deal or not?

Peter took the suitcase and left Cain with his carrier bags and the chest. Cain hefted the latter up over the front door step, and for the briefest instant it felt heavy, heavier than was possible, as if suddenly filled with lead. He grunted and let the chest hit the floor, then tried again. It slid easily across the quarry-tiled lobby.

"Hot day," Peter said. "You warm in that coat?"

"It was cold where I came from."

"Tall Stennington?" Peter headed for the staircase, head tilted slightly awaiting the answer, but Cain offered none. The landlord dropped the suitcase unceremoniously at the foot of the stairs, then turned around and grinned at Cain where he struggled with the chest.

"No lift, I'm afraid," Peter said. "Almost had one put in a couple of years back for a guy who lived on the second floor. He used a wheelchair, so I'd have got a grant from the council. Then I could have charged more because I'd have been disabled access compliant. But he didn't need it in the end."

"Did you give him a flat down here?"

"No, he died." Peter stared at Cain, obviously expecting a reaction. But Cain was not surprised at the revelation. It hardly seemed important. *People die,* he thought, and his own lack of concern chilled him.

"So where's my flat?" he asked, glancing up the staircase. The lobby and stairs were wide, bright, and airy. The walls had been decorated a pale yellow, and over time they had been scuffed and chipped from people walking up and down, apparently leaning against the wall for support. The vinyl flooring was the same color. *Lovely,* he thought.

"He was killed. They found him on Rich Common with half his stomach eaten."

Cain frowned, shook his head, avoided Peter's gaze. "How do they know it was eaten?"

"Sorry?"

"How do they know?"

10

Peter shrugged. "Teeth marks, I suppose."

"Right," Cain said. This fool was trying his best to be antagonistic. All Cain wanted right now was to see his room, make it his own for the future, unpack, lie down and spend his first night in . . . *ages. Ages*, he thought. *It's been ages since I slept free.*

"Room five, attic room," Peter said, suddenly bright and casual again. "Come on, I'll give you a hand with that!" He grabbed for the chest handle, and for a second Cain was going to lash out. *Leave me alone!* he thought, but it made no sense, and by the time he realized that Peter had lifted the chest and started climbing. It thumped from tread to tread. The tapping Cain thought he heard in accompaniment must surely have been an echo.

"Come on!" Peter said, pausing on the sixth stair, looking down at Cain and smiling. "And don't mind me. I'm a bit morbid at times. Watch too much shit on TV." He laughed as he started up again.

Cain hefted his suitcase and carrier bags and followed his new landlord. "So who else lives here?" he asked.

"Ah yes," Peter said, paused on the first floor landing. "I should have given you the tour. Oh well, maybe later. There are a few things I need to show you—laundry room in the basement, fire escape, alarm board, postboxes, that sort of stuff. But for now . . . well, who else lives here." He looked at Cain and smiled again. Then he giggled.

"What is it?"

"Well, mate, you're sharing a house with some odd folk, that's for sure."

Another fuckin' weirdo, the kid had said. "Odd? How so?"

"Where to begin?" Peter said. "Follow me up and I'll talk you through your new neighbors."

Cain felt uncomfortable at the thought of Peter describing his neighbors out here on the stairs and landings. Any of them could be listening, and he did not want their opinions of him to be tainted by what their mutual landlord had to say. But no doors cracked open, no shadows revealed lurking residents, and he thought that maybe they were all out. At work, perhaps. Or wherever it was they went during the day. Freedom was not something Cain was used to, and he could not imagine anyone not taking full advantage of it.

"Ground floor," Peter said, "Flat One. Sister Josephine. Don't ask me if that's her real name. Bit of all right beneath her habit, I reckon, but as I've never seen her not wearing it—*never*—I wouldn't know. She thinks she's a bit special."

"What's a nun doing living here?"

"Who said she's a nun?"

"Well, her name . . ."

"Yeah, but I just said don't ask."

They walked along the first-floor landing, past two doors, heading for the flight of stairs to the second floor. The idea of inhabiting a dead man's flat did not disturb Cain as much as it should. *At least I'm out,* he thought. Peter dropped the chest, glanced at his hand as if in pain, folded his arms and nodded at the closed doors.

"All strange," he whispered. "It's the number of the house attracts them. Number 13. Some streets don't have it at all, you ever noticed that? Evens on one side, they're fine, but odd numbers . . . seven, nine, eleven, fifteen . . . mad, eh? Surely number fifteen would really be thirteen, so it'd be just as fucked up?"

"I've heard some buildings miss out their thirteenth floor," Cain said.

"Ah yes, but do they? Maybe the floors are all there, home to government agencies or alien corporations. Ever thought of that?"

"Not really," Cain said, although he had read books containing that theory many times. He had no idea whether Peter was serious with any of this, or just testing him, dangling bait of various tastes and textures to see what he bit. Odd folk, thirteenth floor, a nun who may or may not be. The landlord seemed just as strange. His face was old before its time—he looked fifty, whereas Cain was certain he was no older than thirty-five—and the lines and crags in his skin hid true meaning like an abstract poem. It would need deciphering, concentration. Cain would need to *know* it.

"Well, don't forget it," Peter said. He laughed again. He seemed to do that a lot, although Cain had yet to hear true humor there. Perhaps after so long in the Home he had become inured against wit.

"So who's here?" Cain asked. The door he had just passed held a number 4, while the one next to him held a vertical word *Three,* the *T* hanging askew from where a screw had popped free.

"Well, maybe we should get you to your room first," Peter said, glancing at Flat Three, at Cain, then back at the door.

I'm too tired for this, Cain thought, *too confused, too overawed. I need to sit in my new home and take out my book and read.* He had read *The Glamour* a dozen times already, but he never tired of it, always found new messages hidden between chapters, beneath lines, behind paragraphs of exquisite prose and mysterious metaphor. On the surface the book was about invisibility, and Cain could relate. He felt so unseen by the world.

"Yes, maybe that is best," Cain agreed. He moved past Peter and headed up the flight of stairs to his attic room.

"Oh!" Peter uttered behind him, but Cain had taken the lead. He reached a small landing with two doors leading off, one marked "Flat Five," the other bearing only long, deep scratches for its entire height, as if something large and fearsome had tried to get through. Unnerved, he waited for the landlord to reach him.

"Flat Five," Peter said as he reached the landing, panting with the effort of hauling the chest. "Cain! Not such an odd fellow, perhaps." He laughed again as he took out a key and unlocked the door, dragging the chest through. He looked at it as if it could contain proof of all the lies he had so recently uttered.

Cain stood on the threshold for a few moments, unsure of what was about to happen. Was his life really starting afresh? Were all the bad times behind him? Would those memories—those torturous dreams of being hurt and alone—ever fade away to give him the peace he craved? He felt the lump of the pill bottle in his jacket pocket, and remembered the Voice's secret smile as it had pressed them into his palm. *Avoidance,* Cain thought. *I can go on avoiding the truth forever. But that doesn't mean it isn't always there, just as my father is always there. He hurt me, but he loved me. That's what the Face and Voice said. I have to come to terms with the fact that he simply didn't know what love was.*

"Nice views," he heard Peter say from somewhere in the flat. Cain stared down at the chest where it sat just inside the door. *I'm in there already,* he thought. *I beat myself in.*

"You can see the cathedral to the east, and north are the mountains outside the city. Wintertime, you can see snow on them from here."

"This is my new home," Cain whispered, not loud enough for Peter to hear. "I can do what I want in here." He leaned through the door without setting foot inside, and rested his right hand on the chest. The wood felt warm, but that must have been the weather. "And I'll never be alone again."

"Cain?" Peter said, emerging from a room on the left. "You need a hand?"

Cain forced a smile, and then surprised himself by realizing that force was not required. "Please," he said. "I don't have much stuff, but sometimes it's heavy."

"No problem." Peter lifted one end of the chest and dragged it through the hallway. "I'll put this in the living room."

Cain entered his new home and closed the door behind him.

The hallway was large and bright, lit by a roof

light. It was painted entirely white, and hung with contrasting black and gray landscape paintings, surreal, beautiful scenes of dead trees reaching ragged fingers for the viewer. The floor was a pale timber, scored here and there with deep scratches. Three doors led off from the hallway, and Cain was stunned at the scope of his new home. At Afresh he had lived in one room—bed, settee, books, small bathroom leading off to one side. Here, faced with three doors, he felt a sudden rush of panic. What if he got lost?

The second door on his left swung inward again and Peter peered out. "Like it?"

Cain could not speak. His throat felt hot and hard, and he was afraid that if he opened his mouth he would cry. He had cried a lot in his life, but he did not wish to shed tears in front of Peter. He could not say why. Perhaps now, alone in the world, he did not want to appear weak.

"I chose the pictures myself," Peter said. "I love dead trees. They're so filled with expression. It's as if shedding their leaves opens them up to view. What do you think? Do you like dead trees?"

Cain glanced at one of the pictures and nodded.

"Forgive the scratches," Peter continued, tapping the floor with one foot. "Vlad used to tear the tires from his wheelchair wheels just to make as much noise as he could."

"Vlad?"

"The dead guy. An old Russian circus performer, so he said. Broke his back falling from the trapeze. Vicious, horrible bastard he was. Nickname."

Cain wanted to explore his home, but something

kept him motionless. He was a tree waiting to be swayed by a breeze, and the breeze was his own freedom. He had not yet fully grasped it. His father was still there in the background, a shadow standing beside him, holding him still and not for a second allowing him to bend. *Pure Sight,* a voice whispered, and it was not the Voice. It must have been his father muttering in his mind, come to haunt him now that there was a home to haunt.

But that was plain crazy.

He's dead and gone, Cain thought, and behind one of the dead tree pictures he saw his own terrified reflection.

"So can I have the tour?" Cain asked.

"Absolutely! You'll love this place, Cain, believe me. I've never been to Afresh, but I've been places similar. And not to belittle it, but . . . well, you'll be free here. Never alone."

Cain frowned at that—*How does he know!?*—but followed Peter through the door on the right.

"Bedroom. Big, bright, great views, it even has a small balcony facing out into the back garden."

"It's nice," Cain said. And then he smiled at his understatement. Nice? It was *luxurious.* The bed was a large double, white sheets and duvet already folded back. The iron bedstead was glossy black, setting off the cream of the walls and carpet. The sloping ceiling was dotted with a dozen inset lights. One entire wall was composed of glass sliding doors, leading out onto a balcony with decorative wrought-iron railings and potted plants softening its harsh lines. Fine net curtains were held back from the windows by metal hooks, affording a view out onto the large back garden and the houses in the next street. The sun was just striking the windows, splashing the floor and already moving in toward the bed.

"It's fantastic," Cain said.

Peter shrugged. "Thanks. New carpet. Vlad wore out the old one. There's a TV in the cupboard there, remote's on the bedside table."

"Where's the bathroom?"

"En suite. Let me show you."

The bathroom was small but perfect, containing a shower stall as well as a bath and lit, like the hallway, by a roof light.

Peter took Cain back through the hall and into the living room. This was furnished with various pieces of new furniture, none of it exceptionally expensive but all tasteful and functional. The kitchen was open plan, separated from view by a flowering plant climbing a network of stainless-steel wires. The units were glass-fronted, displaying a whole range of cooking and eating utensils, and one cupboard contained a welcome pack of food: tea bags, biscuits, bread, sugar, rice, pasta, some jars of sauce. A door led out to the hallway. And there were more paintings, this time stark representations of animals set against muddy brown backgrounds. Nothing detailed or intricate, just a few white brush strokes revealing enough form and shape to identify. It took Cain until the third painting to realize that they were all depictions of extinct animals.

The living space was large enough to accommodate a dining suite as well, which sat below the wide dormer window facing the street. The walls held yet more paintings, but if they were by the same artist as the others, he or she was extremely adaptable. These images were more abstract, mostly constructed of many-angled shapes interconnecting or hovering within a hairsbreadth of touching, all of them black-and-white.

Through the large window Cain saw the cathedral as promised, and in the distance he could make out the mountain between office blocks and chimneys. He would sit here and eat breakfast, letting the early-morning sun stream in to keep his toast warm. Perhaps the window would be open, letting in birdsong from where birds would roost on the roof around him. He would be alone, but alone with his new life. At Afresh he was never really alone, but he had felt empty and useless. Here, free, he would be able to revel in his own company.

The dreams, he thought, *the dreams might still be there.* But he would face them. Standing in his new living room, he promised himself that he would not take a sleeping pill tonight. The Voice had given them to help, but now it was time for Cain to help himself. He had spent far too long since his father's death relying on other people to take care of him.

"It's wonderful," he said. "I never expected it to be like this."

"Well, I admit the outside is a bit of a mess," Peter said.

"No, no, I just never thought I'd have somewhere like this. *Live* somewhere wonderful like this. Such a blank canvas." Cain trailed off, aware that he sounded like a child in a toy shop.

"I've done a lot of work on it," Peter said. "Vlad left it in a hell of a shape. Contentious old bastard."

"How did he live here?"

"Sorry?"

"How did he survive? The stairs? The cupboards on the wall in the kitchen? The shower? You said he had a wheelchair."

For a second—an instant so brief that Cain may have imagined it between blinks—Peter seemed enraged. But then he smiled that humorless smile again and shrugged.

"Well, I helped him. He paid me. Up the stairs, down the stairs. He could stand, just, when he really wanted to, and in time he may have been able to journey up on his own. But most of the time he chose to stay in the chair. He was . . . awkward."

"Eaten, you say?"

Peter raised his eyebrows. "So it's said. Strange . . . they never even found his wheelchair."

Cain walked back through to his bedroom, opened the sliding doors, and stood on the balcony. He glanced down into the garden, hoping to see some of the other residents down there, but it was home only to insects, birds, and bees. The garden itself was somewhat wild, but weeds were kept down and paths and paved areas were well maintained. It looked like a place where he could be at peace. Sit and read. Enjoy being alive. Even at Afresh that was something he had never done.

"I like it," he said.

Peter had followed him through and was standing at his back. "Good. I'm pleased. And I'm glad my talk of Vlad didn't put you off. And anyway, it's not as if he actually *died* here."

Cain turned around. "It wouldn't have bothered me if he had."

Peter's smile faltered just for an instant, and Cain was pleased. *You're your own man now*, the Voice had said. *Time to make your mark on the world.*

Peter left him the front door key and a phone number to call if there were problems. And when the landlord closed the door behind him, Cain ran from room to room, in and out, kitchen living room hallway bedroom bathroom, back again, filling the flat with himself so that it came to know him.

He opened the dormer window above the dining table and, leaning out, watched Peter cross the street. The landlord stood on the pavement for a few seconds, chatting with two children who may or may not have been the ones from earlier. And then he walked into the unkempt garden of the house named *Heaven*, prized the corrugated iron front door to one side, and vanished within.

Cain went to the shops. There were a lot of things he needed, and he had the money that Afresh had given him to start out on his own. There was a bank account, his father's money sitting there waiting to be claimed—he had not died a poor man—but for now, Cain did not wish to dwell on such affairs. He had a new life to find first. Then he could pick up the loose ends of his past, confront them, and end them.

He did not see anyone on his way downstairs. He passed by Flat One, wondering whether Sister Josephine was praying in there even now. He had passed Flats Two, Three, and Four with no idea of who was inside, and after Peter's allusion that every occupant was odd, Cain found the silence strangely loaded. There were peepholes in each door, and he wondered who was watching him pass by, the lens distorting him into someone new. Perhaps he would knock on Heaven's door on the way back from the shops, ask Peter the truth.

He left the house.

The front garden fell silent to mark his passing, whether in reverence or disdain Cain could not tell. Probably neither, though ignorance was worse. As he closed the gate the spiky bushes rustled, the bees began to hum, and he was back in Endless Crescent again. The vandalized sign now read wrong; he was not Nowhere. For the first time in his life, he was somewhere he truly wanted to be.

He bought a bottle of wine, an Indian takeaway meal, and a packet of fruit jellies. He planned an evening of indulgence to mark the start of his new life. He felt that was more positive than celebrating the end of the past.

The past . . .

Cain's father had never been good to him, though perhaps he was too mad to be truly bad. He had seen Cain as a project, his own subject for experimentation. Cain had tried his best to block those many terrible memories, and they had receded into his dreams, driven underground by his efforts at Afresh. The physical evidence of his past—the impossibility of what had happened to him—was locked away in the chest. He would never open it again, but he knew that he could never lose it completely. Having independence was another step toward creating a whole new life for himself.

Still, those dreams.

Walking back from the shops, Cain took time to really assess the neighborhood. The buildings were a surprising mix of styles and periods, ranging from Victorian town houses—much like the one housing his new flat—to brand-new modern executive homes; five bedrooms, large gardens, and four-wheel-drives in the double garage. There were clutches of council houses mixed in with unique self-built homes. A terraced street backed onto a court of luxury apartments. It gave the whole area a surreal atmosphere, as if it had never known itself, nor what it wanted to be. A young businessman in a sharp suit walked along the pavement, talking into a hands-free telephone wrapped onto his ear. Cain nodded, but the suit was too busy to reciprocate. Minutes later, a gang of youths approached and asked if he had a light. Cain shook his head, unnerved, and they drifted off with a polite "Thanks, mate." Halfway home, he decided to sit and watch people pass by. He used to enjoy doing this at Afresh, but there the strollers were mostly mad.

He found himself outside a small park—little more than a fenced-in area of grass and shrubs, and some tattered play equipment—and sat on a bench dedicated to "Dear Jack." The takeaway meal was going cold, but he had a microwave, and besides, the air this afternoon smelled so much fresher knowing he did not have to return to Afresh that evening. No more day passes, no more weekly evaluations, no more prodding and poking, no more trial journeys, no more mornings with the Face smiling down as he woke up, no more evenings with the Voice asking how he was, where had he been, whom had he seen. His time spent at Afresh since his father's death—years, though he had lost track of just how many—was a good time in his memory. He had been treated well and, for the first time in his life, allowed to join in with the community. Interaction was good, they were always told. Whether he had actually *wanted* to join in, he was still not sure.

The street where he sat was quiet, salubrious, well kept. The few houses facing the park were all slightly different, extended and renovated versions of the same original plan. The cars in their driveways were new, high-performance models. His father's house had been a little larger than any of these, isolated out in the country. That's where they had found Cain.

A man went by walking his dog. Cain smiled, and the man averted his eyes and hurried on, tugging the dog on its leash so that its nails skittered across the pavement. Cain opened his fruit jellies and started eating. He had developed a liking for them at Afresh, and they were still the only sweet he remembered ever having tried.

A woman approached, searching through her

handbag, muttering to herself and cursing, quietly at first and then louder. A few steps away from Cain, she dropped her bag. Its contents spewed across the pavement; lipsticks rolled, tissues fluttered, notebooks and pens and purse collided and stuttered into the gutter. A mobile phone spun on its end and then hit the ground with a crack.

"Fuck!" The woman squatted and began gathering her belongings. She did not appear to be aware of Cain's presence.

"Need some help?" he asked.

"Shit!" She jerked upright and almost fell over backward, eyes wide and startled, and her thoughts were a stew of nasty, vile images, ideas that should have driven Cain away, but they were seen and experienced by another part of him.

"Get away from me!" she said.

"I was only offering to help." He went to kneel down, reaching out for a lipstick that had rolled his way.

"I said get away! I don't need any help, not from you!" The woman hurriedly gathered her things and shoved them in her bag, pocketing the phone after a cursory glance at its cracked face.

"Really, I'm only trying to help." Cain felt stupidly ashamed, as if this woman's reaction were his fault, not her own. The need to explain himself was annoying, but he did not want her thinking bad of him. Not that vileness, that pure *viciousness* which scored her eyes from the inside out, unpleasant in the extreme.

She stood and stared at Cain for a moment, and he was sure that she was about to apologize, offer tales of missed meetings and lost phone numbers, an empty apology that may at least make him feel a little better. But her face did not change. A big car cruised by, adding a roar to her voice.

"Keep . . . the fuck . . . *away from me!*" She hurried away the way she had come, not glancing around once. Cain watched her go, and it was like saying good-bye to a bad smell. His mind cleared, the taint of her thoughts—expressed through her eyes, her voice, her stance surely, how else could he know?—burned away by the afternoon sun.

"Well, someone needs to work on her manners," he muttered. A bird landed on the railing behind him and sang its agreement. Cain turned slowly, careful not to scare it away, and he listened to its song, watching its chest vibrate with each warble until it flew into the park.

Back at the house, the other residents still kept to themselves. Cain stood in the downstairs lobby for a while, listening, hoping that one of them would emerge from a flat or come home from work and meet him. He wanted them to accept him, to know that he was living here now, a part of the house's small community. He still felt strangely unwelcome, as if the house would reject him at any moment. Perhaps it was the silence—he hated silence—and the crazy idea that seconds before he had entered the front door there had been TVs blaring, laughter, doors slamming as people moved from one flat to another, mixing and mingling and being involved in one another's lives. And yet he also remembered a story he had read once, in which everyone in a block of flats was so reclusive that they ignored a brutal murder in their own courtyard. For them, everything was somebody else's problem.

The lobby was still. If this was the heart of the house, his entering had caused it to miss a beat.

He started upstairs, and halfway to the first-floor landing he paused as something annoyed his ear. Shaking his head, scratching with his finger, swallowing hard, none of these cleared the sensation. It was as if a fly had flown in and was hovering against his eardrum. He moved on, and two stairs later realized that he was hearing music.

Cain paused. The sound came from so far away that it must surely be outside the house, beyond the street, aimless. He held his breath, expecting the music to recede as a car moved away, but it was still there. He moved up to the landing, stood outside Flat Four, and knew that the music was coming from inside. He could almost see the timber in the door shimmering and shifting as it transmitted the sound, becoming fluid under such relaxing notes. It was pan pipe music, the type the Face would play at Afresh to calm someone gone wild. The music of the elements; soulful, soothing, evocative. There was no particular tune, no identifiable melody, but it held an allure that bade Cain stay and listen. He remained on the landing with his Indian meal cooling in the bag, bottle of wine in his other hand, dusky sun shining through the landing window and lighting dust motes dancing to the music. The pipes continued. Cain began to think about energy and how it formed, the subtle vibration of the universe all around him, how matter did not matter, and that was not his way of thinking at all.

The music stopped. He shook his head again, this time trying to recapture the tickling against his eardrums. There was a thump from inside Flat Four—a door slamming, perhaps—and then total silence once more.

Cain walked up to his flat, glancing at the scored door next to his before entering. That was a heavy door, and those were deep scratches. He would ask Peter about them tomorrow. There was much that Peter had yet to reveal. But time was on Cain's side—time was *his* now—and with freedom the likes of which he had never known beckoning, there was no reason to rush things at all.

Occasionally, when Cain knew things he should not, he tried to attribute it to nothing more than observation. Anything else was too frightening. He had read a lot since his father's death, fiction and nonfiction, and sometimes he could close his eyes and read people like an open book.

Chapter Two
Silence

His father has not allowed him to talk for over a week.

The room is utterly silent. The door remains closed, apart from when his father comes in with a meal or to remove the toilet bucket. Then the lights flicker on and off as a signal for Cain to wear his earplugs. They are the same set he has been using for a week, and they are filthy, smelly, greasy. But he cannot open his mouth to tell his father about them, because if he does there will be trouble. Before putting him in the room his father warned him of this, and though the "trouble" was unspecified, Cain knows what it will be. He has experienced such trouble before.

He looks down at himself and is surprised to see that he is a small boy. His mind has aged, expanded by his years of reading at Afresh, used to dwelling on the cruelties of time and contemplating what his life may become. But the body here now is small, unformed, weak. The arms are thin. The legs are scrawny. It looks as though he has not exercised in months. He raises his hand and stares at it for a long time. He finds the scar on his left thumb, put there when he lost his temper at Afresh and punched out a window to let in birdsong. But he was eighteen when that happened. The hand he is looking at now belongs to a little boy, and the scar is a pale reflection of its original. This hand has never punched anyone in anger, never laid itself across a woman's breast, never clasped himself in secret pleasure. Cain wishes for a mirror, but touching his face is enough to convince him that he is a grown mind in the memory of his small boy's body.

The knowledge leaves him strangely flat. His childhood is nothing to covet. He is here, in this room, and somewhere out there his father's life continues. Somewhere farther out there, real life works its way through time, passing hours and minutes, days and hours, in whatever cycle nature or God has set it upon.

In here only silence, and time frozen in place.

Cain opens his mouth to wake up his dreaming self, but a noise like an air-raid siren blasts into his skull. He screams and the siren roars again, a brief, unbelievably loud burst of white noise right inside his head. This time he does not scream, but as he clasps his small hands to his ears and leans forward—he is sure there will be blood, his eardrums feel hot and tingling—he utters an unintentional whine of pain.

The siren explodes again.

Cain bites his tongue while the pain slowly ebbs away. He stays hunched over, staring at the concrete floor, certain that there are eyes upon him. He should feel love in their gaze, but it is something far baser that prickles at the back of his neck. Though it is not malevolent, he does not care for it at all.

At Afresh he read many books about torture when he could get them. The Voice had decided that they were unsuitable reading, and Cain's argument that they had no right to hobble his intellectual development fell on deaf ears. The Face merely smiled and nodded in agreement, and then left the room filled with books on philosophy, history, and science. But another one of the patients smuggled books to Cain's room with his fresh bedding, and he immersed himself in what was one of the oldest of the Arts.

Torture had been around ever since humankind discovered its thumbs. Cain read of its use for spiritual fulfillment and enlightenment in ages past, and as a means for extracting information in more recent, so-called civilized times. There were books that detailed the psychological implications on both the tortured and torturer. Others concentrated on the more gruesome side of things, reveling in descriptions of dismemberment, eye-skewering, limb-chopping, genital-burning atrocities. Some writers considered torture from biblical times, while others posited that modern society was creating more monsters every day. Now, they suggested, rather than torture as ritual or for information, it was mostly practiced for pleasure.

And yet, through all his reading, Cain could ally none of it with what had happened to him. It had been torture, there was no doubt of that, but the reasons behind it were far less clear. He once read of a Russian self-mutilation cult that expressed love through pain. The idea was grotesque, the facts unbearable, the feel of the story awfully familiar.

None of this knowledge belongs in that small boy's head, and yet it is there, because the older Cain is dreaming this memory. He opens his mouth as if to talk, wincing against the expected siren, but it remains silent. His heart thumps in his chest, blood rushes through his ears, and he is terrified that if he concentrates long enough on these sounds, the siren will hear them as well.

The more he listens to his heart, the louder it becomes. At first it is little more than a sensation, a movement in his chest as familiar as breathing, and equally ignored. But then it changes from a sensation to a sound, louder, louder still, until he begins to suspect that his father is outside crashing his hand against the door. The room is empty of all but Cain—a good home to echoes—but loud though it is, something deadens this sound. It is as if there is something unseen with him in the room.

Cain closes his eyes and tries to quiet his runaway heart, but it grows even louder. He opens his eyes again, stands as silently as he can, paces the room. He hears a humming, but perhaps it is coming from him.

The lights flicker off and on.

"The old fuck's coming," a voice says. Cain—both the child Cain, petrified at his situation, and the adult dreamer even more scared at being back here—spins around to see who has spoken. But there is nothing in the room with him, no one else. Only a shadow where light should fall.

The door handle dips, and Cain reaches for the dirty ear plugs.

The crashing continued. Irregular, loud, hard enough to make pictures rattle on the walls. And then a shout joined in with the banging and Cain sat up in bed, sweating and disoriented.

Home, he thought, *I'm home, this is my home.* He reached for the bedside lamp as the shouting began to coalesce into some sort of sense.

"Noisy bastard! Shut up! Shut up, there are people trying to sleep in here. Sleep! Know what that is? Understand that? Or do we now have an insomniac in place of a wheelchair-bound fucking psycho?"

"I wasn't saying anything," Cain muttered, and his voice seemed so much louder than the shouting and banging. *I was completely silent,* he thought. *I had to be.*

The pounding ceased, and Cain sat frozen in his bed, waiting for the next round of abuse. The man was still outside his front door. There was no sure way Cain could know that, but he was certain. There had been no footsteps receding across the landing, perhaps that was how he knew. Or maybe the shouter's breathing was loud enough to make an impression, albeit subconscious.

Cain let out a breath he was not aware of holding, and there came a polite knocking at his front door.

"Can we talk?" the person asked. It was the

same voice as before; shame and guilt could not hide that certain weight, that timbre.

Cain stood from his bed and opened the door out into the hall. He half expected to see the front door crashed from its hinges, but it stood firm, unmoved by the appeal hanging behind it.

"Cain," the voice said. "Can we talk? I apologize for my abuse . . . though I assume by your silence that you've heeded me."

"You know my name?" Cain asked, and his voice carried farther than he had intended. No siren erupted around him, no torture for his eardrums.

"Peter told me," the voice said. "I'm sorry, I just wanted to know who I was sharing the house with now. After Vlad, I'm hoping it's someone approachable. And your shouting . . . it *was* very loud."

"Vlad wasn't approachable?"

"Oh, no," the person said, not elaborating.

Cain stood quietly for a few moments, surrounded by a sudden silence loaded with promise. He hated silence and tried to imagine anything to fill it. The banging and cursing had been bad, but better than nothing.

"Are you still there?" the voice asked.

Cain smiled. *Where would I go?* He went to the door and drew the chains and bolt, swinging it wide, having no idea who he was about to see and what they would do once the door was open. The voice had been manic a couple of minutes before. But Cain trusted his instincts, certain that he would reveal a smile.

He even had an idea of what the smile would look like. He shook his head at what he should not know.

"I'm George," said the man standing in the doorway, teeth bared in a grin bordering on a grimace. He held out his hand, and it was cold, clammy, shaking.

"I'm Cain," Cain said, "but then, you already knew that. How are you?"

"Yes, fine. I'm sorry for having to wake you."

"I'm the one that should be sorry," Cain said. "I've been disturbing your sleep."

Something passed across George's features. Cain could not convince himself that it was anger—yes, George had been hammering at the door just minutes earlier, but that seemed to have been a vastly different person—but it was something similar.

"Well, you *were* very loud," George said. His tongue flicked over his lips and he glanced down at Cain's sleeping attire. Shorts, T-shirt, and socks. Cain had become used to wearing socks to bed at Afresh, where a midnight trip to the toilet involved crossing a corridor with a quarry-tiled floor.

Was I really shouting? he thought. *Screaming myself awake from that dream of silence, perhaps? But the siren wouldn't have let me come awake. It wouldn't have allowed me to scream.* He shook his head, and for a second he wondered whether he was still asleep. Perhaps his father was watching this from somewhere, always out of sight just behind him no matter how quickly he turned around to see.

George put his hand to his mouth, belched, apologized profusely.

"What was I saying?" Cain asked, trying to hide his embarrassment.

"I'm not really sure," George said. "But you were raging at something. I heard you from all the way downstairs. The house swallowed your words, but the rage was there for sure."

The house swallowed your words.

"You're the first of the other residents I've met," Cain said.

"Really? No Whistler? He's usually first to welcome someone new."

"Whistler?"

George glanced around, then leaned in over the threshold of Cain's flat. "Flat Four. Always playing those damn pipes of his. Hence the nickname. Bit weird, if you ask me."

Must be the house number, Cain thought. George's eyes were wide, deep, reflecting golden lamplight spilling out of Cain's bedroom and seemingly amplifying it back at him. They were not the eyes of a quiet, meek man, though that seemed to be the image that George was attempting to portray. He was small and thin, weak-looking, shoulders slumped, hands clasping and unclasping by his sides . . . but his eyes seemed *hungry*.

That's what Cain had seen in his face. Hunger.

"I heard him earlier," Cain said. "When I was on the way upstairs this evening."

"You only heard him?" George asked, smiling that smirk again.

"Yes, his door was closed."

"Not what I meant." George shook his head. Cain was sure he glimpsed the man's tongue lolling from his open mouth.

"Look, I would invite you in, but—"

"Oh no, no!" George said, stepping back slightly. "It's the middle of the night, I know that. I just wanted to wake you up, make sure you were okay. Some dream you were having there."

"It must have been," Cain said, but his memory of the dream was silent. *No dream . . . a nightmare!*

"So I'll see you around, I guess. Maybe you can come down for a few drinks one evening? I'm in Flat Two."

"Next to the Sister?"

"Ah, I see Peter's told you about her, at least."

"She's as far as he got."

George smiled, laughed a little, looked down into the darkness of the staircase. "Yes, the Sister."

Cain was tempted, but he thought George had intended that. And now, with night's silence mimicking Cain's dream with its completeness, standing here talking to George felt suddenly wrong. Perhaps deep down Cain was always waiting for that siren to shatter his mind.

"Well, I'll see you around," Cain said. He smiled, George nodded, and he shut the door on the man from Flat Two.

Cain returned to his bed, turned off the light, and stared out the window. He had not drawn the curtains before retiring for the night, enjoying a strange thrill at being able to lie back and see the stars and moon spread across the sky. Starlight touching him made him feel very young.

The dream sat around him like an invisible cloak, its silence and lack of substance heavier than anything solid. He often felt like this when he woke up at night, whether or not he knew he had been dreaming, as if he were trapped in endless rock, his body and mind the only living things there, everything else inanimate. It would always take a while for him to crawl from the rock's grasp; sometimes by talking quietly to himself and listening to the echo coming in from farther and farther away, sometimes by chewing on a piece of fruit, *always* reminding himself that there was much more to things than just him. A smell would bring him around faster, but in Afresh the air had always been sterile and clean. Staring at something familiar would urge his senses to find themselves, but in the dead of night at Afresh there were no lights, and gazing into the dark would often make matters worse.

Here, Cain had freedom. He saw the light-speckled sky and the dream quickly faded away. Meeting George had already driven its memory down, but their brief exchange had little effect on the hollow echoes still haunting Cain's mind. It needed him to focus his own attention, rather than being a passive target of someone else's, to find release.

He stared out, and the skies stared back.

"We're all the stuff of the stars," he whispered. And even though his dream had almost gone, he cringed slightly as he awaited the siren's assault. When the silence continued, it felt safe to break it again. "We all come from the stars, father, and you never allowed for that. With so much history already inside me, how can I never feel, hear, speak? How, when I've got so much to tell?" Nothing answered him. For once he was comfortable in his own solitude, now that the dream was gone. As he continued gazing out at the clear night sky, he ran his hands over the blanket tangled around his legs, feeling its landscape and creating a hundred stories from every dip and ridge.

The next day was Cain's first full day of freedom. He was a man with responsibilities now, choices, and a potential that made him dizzy when he thought about it. Sitting at his dining table eating breakfast—dry toast and a cup of watered-down orange juice—the possibilities of the day seemed endless. There was so much he could do, and yet the idea that there was no one to tell him *what* to do was disconcerting. If he decided to curl up in bed and whimper himself back to sleep, the Face would not come in and urge him awake. If he remained seated at the table, pushing toast crumbs across its surface, losing himself in ambiguous memories of a past that was all dream and nightmare, the Voice would not whisper over his shoulder that the present mattered so much more.

He could look to the future and do his best to make a life. He could dwell on the past and let the future stretch away untouched. Or he could seize the day.

For the first time, the choice was truly his own.

He left the flat soon after breakfast. The building was silent—no pan pipes from Whistler, no praying from Sister Josephine's room—and Cain assumed that they had either left for work or were still asleep. It was so quiet that he clicked his fingers to check his hearing. Once he opened the front door, however, the busy sounds from outside flooded in to fill the lobby. He looked around to see if anything was annoyed at the intrusion, but the doors and walls stared blankly back at him.

He passed quickly through the garden and stood on the pavement beyond, looking across the road at the dilapidated house named Heaven. It seemed strange that a landlord would own such a well-maintained block of flats and yet live in a place like that. Cain had yet to see anyone else's accommodation, true, but once past the garden and inside, the whole of Number 13 felt well looked after. Heaven, on the other hand, was close to collapse. *Does Peter really live there?* Cain thought. *Or maybe he just went there yesterday for something else. Maybe there's a man living in there, a drug addict, and Peter helps him out now and then with some advice, a shoulder to cry on, a source of harsh words when they're needed.*

He enjoyed making up things about people. It camouflaged the uncomfortable fact that he sometimes knew more than he should.

Cain turned from the house and walked down the street, passing busy homes and quiet buildings, welcoming the sounds of people getting on with life. He glanced back once at Number 13, looked up at the roof window of his living room, and for a split second he saw a face in the window below his. He paused, blinked, and the face was gone. He moved slightly to the side, trying to make out whether he had merely seen a reflection or a sheen of dust catching the sun. But whatever he had seen did not return, and he could not make it reappear from sunlight or shadow. It was Flat Three facing out onto the road, and he realized that he still did not know who lived there. He knew of the nun, Whistler and George, but this flat was still a mystery. The windows were dark, not inviting his inspection. He could see no curtains or blinds. The flat may as well have been empty.

A few people passed him and he wondered whether any of them were from Flat Three. Peter had made vague promises about giving him the guided tour, telling him about the other occupants (*You're sharing a house with some odd folk*, he'd said), showing him the electric cupboard and laundry room. But Flat Three remained a mystery. Perhaps it always would. Cain had his share of secrets, some of which he knew, many he did not. Why should he be the only one?

A postman passed him by without a glance; there would be no letters for him. A man walking his dog nodded a curt greeting, and a woman dragging a child by the hand glanced up and offered a nervous smile, as if trying to forgive herself for her offspring's red wrist and wet eyes. A group of teenagers parted to let him through, offering polite "hello"s and throwing smirks at the corner of his eye. Cain returned the greetings and weathered the smirks, and he knew only what he saw. For that he was glad. When he sometimes knew *more* his father would have called it Pure Sight, but then the old man was mad.

Cain walked to the end of Endless Crescent,

wondering whether he was disobeying some unwritten law in doing so. He smiled. The Voice would have something to say about that. *Humor,* he had said, *is endemic, a fundamental part of us as humans, and you're the living proof of that. Shut away for so long, you can still find humor.*

At the end of the Crescent he faced a difficult decision. Turning left would take him back to the shops he had visited the previous day: a takeaway, a local grocer's, a newsagent's, a video and DVD rental store, a few others. If he turned right, the busy road wending that way would eventually guide him out of the suburbs and into the city proper. There was a lot of traffic here, and Cain winced at the noise. A horn blared and he pressed back against a garden wall, fearing that the siren would descend and deafen him from the inside. More cars streamed by. There would be hundreds of people shopping in the city, thousands, maybe more, all wearing colorful clothing and perfumes, chattering into mobile phones glued to their ears. The crowd would act as one unit, surrounding him and drawing him into itself, the city's defense mechanism spying an alien body. He could imagine the result—the bright clothes, the loudness, the taste of commerce, the sight of all those faces staring at him and knowing that he was nothing special—and as each new image presented itself, the siren threatened to shatter it into fragments. A butterfly fluttered by, and Cain thought of grabbing it in case it was part of his mind.

Left, quietness and safety and a place he had already been. Right, something unknown. He was free—away from Afresh and his father's skewed influence—and as the Voice had told him so often, his life was his own.

But that dream from last night still spoke to him. He turned left.

Sometimes Cain believed he had an original idea, something elemental and unique, something that could change things. But he was never confident enough to believe in it.

Chapter Three
Circus

They tried. After his father died and Cain went to Afresh, and the extent of his mistreatment slowly revealed itself, the Voice and the Face did their best to help him sense real life.

He was a teenager then, lost in his years, confused by his body and thoughts and everything around him. Ironically, in many areas he was as educated as anyone they had ever met. His father had allowed him access to an impressive library of reference books, which Cain read compulsively during those times when his father's research and experimentation led him elsewhere. He had also spent a long time educating Cain himself, because Pure Sight would never manifest in someone without extensive knowledge. So Cain's father had taught him numbers but not languages, because he said that the language of wisdom was universal. He had lectured in physics but not biology, because the flesh is weak. He had helped Cain understand the history of war, but never the tales of those who strove for peace, because chaos was the fundamental form of existence. And Cain had remained trapped in that old, rambling house in the country, forever denied the experience to complement his learning. He knew the great histories of Egypt, though he had never smelled the spice of its forbidden sands. He read of women and their beauty, though he had never seen a member of the opposite sex, not even his mother. He found endless cookery volumes celebrating feasts, banquets, the world's foods and wines, but his father fed him the most tasteless, insipid concoctions imaginable.

In one tome there were fifty essays written in celebration of Mozart. Cain was mesmerized. Such beauty and rapture in words, describing something so beyond his understanding. The only music he heard was the humming in the shadows, the tune that took years to progress from nothing to something he could never, ever forget. And that had been beyond his father's knowing.

So at Afresh they tried to bring him out of the deep, dark place his father had forced him into. And though their efforts were benign and designed only to help, for his first couple of years in the Home the siren had blasted Cain every single day. When he heard music, the siren erupted. If he tasted something new, it smashed the pleasure from him. If he looked at a painting, the siren's sheer violence bled the colors to gray. He slowly came to believe that it was no longer real, but that made it worse. It meant that it was inside him, and he had no concept of how he could ever purge it from his mind.

As the years went by so the siren receded, first in frequency and then in volume. It still found its voice from time to time, but Cain's understanding of his father—what he had done, how, and why— seemed to temper it somewhat, and its influence faded away into bad memories and nasty dreams.

They took him to a circus. At seventeen he was older than most of the children there, and probably more knowledgeable than many of the adults. But he had never eaten candy floss, toffee apples, or doughnuts, and he had never abandoned himself to unrestrained laughter or awe. The Voice talked consistently, trying to calm Cain as new sights and sounds opened up around him. He had been on trips out of Afresh many times, but they were always well planned to avoid too much exposure at any one time. The circus blew all that away. As they guided him into the Big Top and found a seat, Cain began to feel overwhelmed. The Voice whispered in his ear. The Face held his hand. The crowd roared and laughed, a living, flexing mass of people dressed in every color imaginable, writhing and rolling with the show. A sickly sweet smell hung in the air, sticking to his clothes, finding its way through even when Cain covered his nose with his shirt.

The siren struck and he collapsed in on himself, shrinking in the seat as the Voice and Face frantically tried to pull him back.

They carried him outside, and when he clasped

his hands to his ears to exclude the roar of a thousand people he would never know, they did not try to talk him out of it. His two helpers placed him gently in the back of the car and clicked the door shut behind him. He opened his eyes at last and breathed in, content with the smell of old leather, the sight of the driver's seat in front of him, and the sound of the engine still ticking as it cooled from their vain journey here.

There were other times, progressively more successful. The Voice and Face learned a lot from that trip to the circus, and Cain was happy to go along with their new, more tempered plan to introduce the world to him. Even then the siren sometimes crashed in unexpectedly, shattering Cain where he stood and sending him back into the silent darkness, which he was beginning to believe was the only existence he could ever truly know.

With every step that Cain took, failure stalked him. Once or twice he turned around to see whether there were shadows where there should be none, listened for whispers behind garden walls and hedges, such was the sense of being observed. The Voice and the Face would not be pleased with this, he knew. He had to call sometime today to tell them how he was, and what could he honestly say? *The flat is fine, perfect, but I'm still afraid of everything.* He could not say that. He *would* not. And yet it was the truth.

He had spent six years at Afresh waiting for the day when he was old enough to leave and live on his own, put his broken childhood behind him. He would never completely forget, and Afresh never pushed him into forgetfulness. But he would learn to live with what had happened and, perhaps given time, understand it. His father had loved him, they told him, but he had not known what love meant.

Cain walked faster. He looked up when he heard some children shouting and screaming in the park he had sat outside the night before. He paused at the fence, watching them at play on the few swings, slides, and climbing frames that had survived vandalism at the hands of local youths. They shouted in glee, and he mentally urged them to shout some more. They wore bright clothing, pinks and blues and colorful character T-shirts, and he scanned around for more sustenance for his eyes.

Put me down! he thought. *Put me down now, you fuck!* But the siren was silent, its instigator hiding well back behind memory and nightmare. His father's image affected him at that moment as much as a faded photograph.

"Louder!" he shouted. "Play louder!" But his voice caused the children to pause, and their parents turned and regarded him with undisguised hostility. Cain smiled, trying to convey benevolence, but his expression angered them more. He hurried away, disturbed by their reaction.

He sought more. He had taken the coward's choice back at the crossroads, but he could still defy his father here. He would buy flavorful food and strong beer, a Mozart CD and some scented candles for his flat. Today he would sense life all around him. It would take time, he knew that. He could not rush headlong into the circus of life. He had to introduce himself gradually, an act at a time. The high-wire balance of meeting new people, the lion-taming efforts of fending off his old fears.

And that was when he saw the clown.

She was sitting on the pavement outside the takeaway Cain had used the previous evening. He could tell it was a woman even under the clown's outfit; her breasts were heavy, the curve of her hips obvious. The takeaway was closed now, but the clown ate yellow, greasy rice from a foil container, and Cain had to wonder whether she had bought it or found it. She was a happy clown, with a smile drawn from ear to ear, eyes tall and wide, bright pink hat with a real red rose protruding from its tip. Her suit was baggy and extravagant, even though spilled grains of rice had spotted it with oil. That only added to the effect. It was a riot of color and texture, and Cain could not help smiling when he saw the beauty and wonder in that.

I can see why kids love them so much, he thought. But at the same time, a very adult fear rose from somewhere deep inside, a fear of anonymity and disguise, of *inhumanness,* and he remembered reading somewhere that *everyone* is afraid of clowns.

"Nice day!" the clown said, jumping up and spilling rice across the ground. She danced over to Cain, long shoes slapping on the pavement, arms waving high and low. "Lovely day for catching a sunbeam—shall I get you one? Oh, I see you already have one!" She reached for Cain, tickled his ear, and pulled her hand back trailing a long piece of yellow crepe paper. "Put them in your ear and they'll burn your brain," the clown said. "Singe it. Scorch it. Melt it, and then someone will smell the burning and come along and eat it!"

Cain was speechless. His heart thumped, everything told him to back away and leave, but at the same time he found the display compulsive. Such sensory overload from one person, and Cain knew the siren was nowhere inside him, no threat at all. *Maybe I was meant to come this way*, he thought. *Maybe this is good for me.*

The clown turned and bent down in front of him, pulling her baggy trousers tight and wiggling her rump. Then she stood again, performed a perfect forward roll straight through the spilled rice, turned to face him and stuck out her tongue, blowing a shower of glitter into the air.

Cain looked around to see if anyone else was watching. There were a few shadows in the window of the grocer's, but he could not see their faces. Some cars passed along the road, but none of them stopped. For now he had this moment to himself.

What would my father think of this? Cain thought, and he laughed out loud. Right then, the sense of being his own person was very strong.

"Fuckity-fuck, my tits wobble in this getup," the clown said, slipping hand over feet in an impressive display of acrobatics.

"Pardon?"

"You heard!" She paused, panting, and Cain saw beads of sweat smearing her complex makeup.

"That's not much of a show for children," he said.

She shrugged her padded shoulders. "I adjust my

show depending on who's watching. Don't you?"

"I'm not a clown."

"Not what I meant at all." She sat down again, kicking the rice container aside, and leaned back against the window of the takeaway. "I'm fucking exhausted. You have no idea how much energy a little stunt like that takes. Fuck!"

Cain was dumbfounded. He heard a door open and two old women came out of the grocer's shop two doors down, glanced at the clown, and walked the other way, twittering like birds. A car came to a standstill at the curbside and disgorged three teenagers. Cain saw the father leaning across the front seats to get a look at the clown. The man caught Cain's gaze, glanced away quickly, floored the accelerator, and pulled off. The three boys smiled, pointed, and started jeering. But then the clown stood and walked their way, and they turned and ran.

She looked back at Cain. "Everyone's afraid of clowns." Her true smile twisted the painted one into a grotesque grimace, as if she had been struck across the face with an ax.

"Who are you?" he asked, because he could think of nothing else to say.

"Oh, I'm so sorry," the clown said, wiping her hand on her outfit and offering it for him to shake. "I'm Magenta from Flat Three."

Cain looked blank, trying to absorb what she had said.

"Flat Three, downstairs from you," the clown said, frowning, smiling again, shaking her hands and spraying Cain with water from false fingertips. She laughed.

"How do you know me?" he said.

"You've been wandering in and out ever since you arrived yesterday," she said. "I make it my business to know who's living in the same building as me. That's only sensible. It's only *safe*. I wouldn't want to share a building with a mass murderer, now, would I?"

"I suppose not," Cain said. Had she been standing behind her door all along? he thought. Watching through the peephole as he passed by, sizing him up, her feet turned at right angles so that her ridiculous shoes did not scratch the door and give her away?

"Well, are you?"

"Pardon?"

"A mass murderer?"

Her appearance had thrown him completely, and now she was playing word games. Surprised and confused though he was, Cain had spent years of his life talking to himself, often not knowing what he was going to say next. Sometimes, it was almost like talking to someone else. He could do word games too.

"Not yet," he said. "I'm still studying the theory."

"Ah!" she said, her fake smile startling some pigeons aloft. "A comedian! Excellent. I like a man with a sense of humor."

His gaze was drawn to her chest again, as if her comment had made her womanhood more visible beneath the baggy clothing.

"Humor is one thing that building lacks. There's George, I suppose . . . but I laugh at him, not with him. Peter has a sense of humor, but he doesn't actually live there."

"No, he lives in Heaven," Cain said. Magenta froze. Even her suit was still beneath her outstretched arms. For a second, she was a statue.

"Have you been in there?" she asked, and her question carried so much import, the weight of his answer obviously of great concern to this strange clown.

"No," Cain said. She seemed to relax a little, but the playfulness had gone. Even her suit seemed deflated, more scruffy and stained than before. "Have you?" he asked.

"Coffee? There's a little café around the corner—they do a great latte, and peach cake to die for." Magenta turned and started walking away without waiting for an answer. Cain followed. As he walked he thought about whether or not he wanted coffee and cake, his eyes were drawn to her shapely behind, and he realized with a strange stab of guilt that right here and now he was no longer afraid of the siren. With everything that had happened over the past couple of minutes—the colors, the shapes, Magenta's strange talk—it would have struck him by now if it was going to.

Where it had gone, he did not know. But the last thing he was about to do was question it. This was his first full day alone. He was still terrified, but already he was seeing some good signs. This clown woman calmed him in some way he had yet to understand. Perhaps because, other than Peter, she was the first person he had *really* spoken to.

"Or maybe I just want to fuck her," he muttered, and she spun around and glared at him as if she had heard. But a car was passing and he had barely whispered, and so no, she could not have heard, never.

His vague guilt at turning away from the challenge of the bustling city was lifting. And his confidence had already taken a boost from this strange encounter. He no longer felt scared, and that was something new.

A car screamed by and tooted its horn, and Cain shrank back against the wall of the café. He cursed himself for the reaction and his eyes watered from sheer anger. The siren remained silent, but it was still taunting him from deep inside, deeper than he would probably ever be able to dig. On his own, at least.

He looked through the café window and saw Magenta at the counter. And he decided that, yes, right now he really wanted coffee and cake.

Cain's father had told him that Pure Sight was the ability to perceive truth. It was not actual sight, but rather knowledge, experience, and certainty. As a concept few considered or knew of it, and of those who did even fewer found themselves anywhere close to possessing it. It saw through—and stripped away—all facets of humanity that tended to bring us close to "civilized." Civilization, his father said, was an unfortunate by-product of the power of reason. *Do you think we're really here to live together peacefully, spend all our time considering everyone else first?* he asked. *A pride of lions will attack another pride if they intrude on their territory.* He never explained his statements, as if eager for Cain to make out their meanings for himself.

Cain was his father's project. His father wanted him to achieve Pure Sight. He talked about it incessantly, trying to pump its wonder into his son, but Cain was only in his teens when his father died. He was confused, disoriented, badly damaged by the deprived state he had been kept in for all those years. As such, Pure Sight was as remote to him now as the concept of fatherly affection.

Still, since his father died and Cain was taken away from that house, he often wondered just how diligently his subconscious still sought Pure Sight of its own accord.

Cain carried his latte and slice of peach cake to the window seat next to Magenta. She had snatched a handful of paper serviettes from the counter, and now she wiped at her makeup, smearing vibrant colors across her face into a single bland mess. She wiped and wiped, spitting into the paper towels, her hand moving faster.

"Careful," Cain said, "you'll wear away your skin."

"There's always new skin," she said, closing her eyes as she rubbed at her forehead.

"So where have you been?" he asked.

"Huh?"

"To play the clown?"

"Oh, nowhere. Here. One show's over, the next could begin at any time."

"Street performer, then."

"I'm an impersonator, Cain. Always working." She grinned, and he saw her real smile for the first time, the clown's face having been rubbed into oblivion. It was challenging and attractive, confident and brash. It dared him to talk back.

"So who are you without the makeup? Still Magenta?"

"I'm always Magenta." She dropped the paper towels, sighed, leaned to the side so that she could see her reflection in the window. She looked for a full thirty seconds, as if it was the first time she had really seen herself. "That'll have to do for now." She took a long sip of her coffee.

Cain drank, looked around, but his gaze was always drawn back to Magenta. Her eyes pulled him in, green, gorgeous, intelligent, sparkling with wit. And she was strong, he could see that. She intimidated him. He glanced at her breasts and away again. She smiled.

"So how do you like your flat?"

"It's fantastic!" he said, pleased for the distraction. "Much better than I expected from . . ."

"From the outside? Yeah, everyone says that. It's a shit hole from the outside, but I think Peter does that on purpose. Keeps away the undesirables."

Cain shrugged. "It's the inside that matters."

"You think so?" Magenta asked, staring with an intensity that made Cain shift in his seat. "You think the facade is unimportant? Surely it's part of the whole effect?"

Word games again, Cain thought, but he only shrugged again. He wanted to chat to this woman—his neighbor—not enter into some deep philosophical debate.

"Well," she said, but her sentence fizzled out in the smoky café air.

They sat together and drank coffee, ate cake, stared from the window at the few people walking by, and only when the silence started to become awkward did Magenta ask Cain where he came from.

He had no wish to answer. If she knew his background, it would surely scare her off. She was pretty unique, of that he was sure, but she was a woman with a job, an income, and a flat of her own. Cain was, as the kids in the street had greeted him, another fuckin' nutter.

"I've just come here for a change," he said.

Magenta smiled and nodded. "Another fucking nutter, then."

Cain sat back and blinked at her, shocked as much by her brashness as what she had said. *The siren,* he thought, *it'll bear in and take me down soon, so much input here, so much to see and hear and smell and understand about this strange woman.* But the siren remained silent, and when Magenta laughed it was a pleasant sound, and he knew that she was not really mocking him.

"I'm sorry," she said, still giggling, "that's really fucking awful of me. I'm so sorry. It's just that Peter makes a living hiring out his flats to people who may not be able to get accommodation elsewhere. He's much more . . . open-minded." She raised her eyebrows and sat up straight. "How polite is that? I'm even complimenting myself, considering what I've done."

"What?" Cain asked, but she ignored him again.

"So please accept my apology, Cain. Don't want us to start off on the wrong foot. It goes for an entertaining time living in Endless Crescent—and *there's* a name! You don't seem all that unusual to me, to be honest. Nice guy. Something about your eyes, though . . ."

"I'm sorry if you don't like the way I look at you," he said, not really meaning it.

"No, not that, not at all. I mean, there's something powerful in there, deep, and deep down." She leaned across the table, knocking over her cup but ignoring the rush of coffee into her lap. She moved so close to Cain that he could smell her, strangely muted traces of coffee and the tang of something more elusive. "It's as if you know so much more," she whispered, and for the first time Cain thought he was hearing her true voice.

"I read a lot of books," he said.

Magenta snorted, sat back down, wiped at the spilled coffee. "Right, that'll be it, then."

They fell silent for a couple of minutes, Cain picking at his cake, Magenta scratching at the remnants of makeup and smiling at him. "Not much of a conversationalist, are you?"

"I haven't had much experience of it," he said.

"Was it so bad, the place you came from?"

Cain wondered which place she could mean—his father's house of torture and deprivation, or the Afresh home with the Voice and the Face doing their best to make him better—but then he realized that she knew neither.

"Only as bad as my memories make it," he said.

"Oh, very profound."

"Memory's changeable, don't you think? You ever had a dream that you thought was a memory, or a memory that may have been a dream?"

Magenta stopped picking makeup from the corner of her eye and nodded. "Oh yes."

"What's happened to me is like that."

"And what *did* happen to you?"

"You're very forthright," he said. She smiled, but did not withdraw her question. "Well, I've told you as much as I want to," Cain said. "As much as I've told anyone since . . . Well. And here we are, only just met."

"I'm glad you're living in Flat Five!" Magenta said, and she sat back and picked at her cake, embarrassed.

"So when is your next impersonation job?"

"It's not a job, it's my way. And I have no idea. The urge has yet to take me."

"You still have makeup on your face." Cain was suddenly tempted to reach over and touch Magenta's skin, wipe away the paint and feel how hot she burned beneath. But that would be far too familiar. The siren had once blasted him every time he touched something. It lasted for a week.

"I'll wash it off later. Cain, it's been a pleasure, and now I have to go. I'll get this." Magenta stood and threw a five-pound note on the table.

"Hang on!" Cain had no idea why he was asking her to wait, or whether he even had anything to say. She raised her eyebrows, inviting him to continue. "You're right," he said at last. "Everyone's scared of clowns."

She nodded and left, and he wondered just how much of himself he had revealed in that parting shot.

* * *

He remained in the café for a few minutes, finishing his cake and taking a few guilty bites from the slab Magenta had left on her plate. He hummed to himself, that familiar tune he knew but had never been able to name, and looked around as if expecting to find someone staring at him from another table.

After paying with Magenta's money, Cain bought a Mozart CD from a small music shop several doors away. He took his time walking home, still humming that tune, hoping against hope that Mozart would put a name to it but knowing that, as usual, it would remain a mystery.

He had memories of a time when his father tried to operate on him.

Cain is directed into a small room in the basement of the house, a place he has never been or seen before. It has a strange new feel to it, as if it has been added to the house or opened up only recently. Perhaps his father has just discovered this room. Its bright surfaces glare under the high-wattage lighting, the walls polished and gleaming, ceiling white and reflective, the few pieces of functional furniture all chrome and plastic sheets. If the room has not actually been built as an operating theater, then it must have taken little effort to turn it into one.

The furniture consists of an operating table—with channels for blood and fluids along either side and straps and buckles for tying the subject down—and a simple trolley covered with a surgeon's paraphernalia. Cain sees scalpels and saws, probes and clamps, gauze and stitching. He also sees more esoteric equipment, such as several acorns sharpened to a point, a large feather apparently dipped in molten metal, and a selection of pickled eggs of various species. He has no idea what purpose any of these could serve, but they are mingled with other equipment as if a natural part of any operation. He goes to ask his father, but the old man is washing himself vigorously at a sink in the corner. Not only his hands but his face, neck and shoulders, his arms and chest, scrubbing with a chunk of rough soap, scrubbing so hard that the flesh of his saggy stomach and hips wobbles with each movement. His skin is red-raw where he has washed, and Cain is sure that the surface will split at any moment.

Eventually, his father turns around, pink and glowing from the wash, hands held up, fingers splayed, and smiles down at his son.

It's all for the best, he says. *Sometimes a process has to be accelerated. You have to be helped along. How can you gain Pure Sight when your eyes pollute your mind?*

He sends Cain into the next room to strip and prepare for the operation. (Cain—eleven years old then, maybe twelve—can remember that room in detail, even though in reality he is quite certain that none of this has ever taken place.) There is a gown laid out on a bench, paper underwear, a paper hat with a ridiculous painted smiley face, as if to grin away the terror. There is also a toilet in the corner of the room, unscreened and without a seat. He needs to go before the operation—the thought of fouling himself under anesthetic is awful—but he cannot bring himself to sit down and try. There is no privacy here. There is also no one else in the house to see, but with that thought comes a low, variable humming noise from elsewhere in the room. There is a definite tune to this, and although Cain is sure he has heard its like before, it is unfamiliar. He looks around and there is no one with him, only shadows where light should fall.

He strips and the humming alters its tone, as if changed by grinning lips.

The gown is rough and itchy. The underwear is worse. Cain folds his clothes on the chair, then opens the door to go back into the operating theater. The sourceless humming stops with a snigger, or perhaps it is the door hinge squeaking. From upstairs he hears the heating creaking on, the boiler firing up; the realization that they were still at home comes as something of a surprise, and yet, perversely, a comfort as well.

Cain's father smiles as he loads a syringe with a foul green concoction, something glowing and steaming that will put Cain to sleep, small things bumping frantically in the glass tube as if eager to dull his consciousness.

It's all for the best, his father says, and his eyes have taken on the same sickly green tinge.

Cain lies down on the operating table and falls asleep.

In his dream he imagines a cool, scarp scalpel descending toward his eye, and when he wakes up he is always somewhere else.

* * *

He was unsure whether this was the memory of an old dream, skewed into a version of reality by time, or something more removed. There were no scars, no acorns pressed into his eyes, no feathered cuts across his throat. There was no evidence that this had ever happened at all.

Memory was a fickle thing, exercised as it was in a place where true imagination was the only place to wander.

Cain paused outside Flat Three, smiling self-consciously at the door in case Magenta was already home and watching him. He moved closer to listen. No sounds from inside, no music, no signs of life. Perhaps that urge to impersonate had taken her again on the way home. He wondered whether she had always been a clown, but it seemed quite certain that she had not. He looked at his fingers and saw colorful makeup smeared there, but then he remembered that he had not touched her after all, and the paint was gone.

He had seen nothing when he looked into her eyes—nothing more than he should have—and he was glad. He did not like knowing more. It made him believe that he was more like his father than he could bear.

He stood there for some time, thinking about Magenta, wondering who she was. An impersonator, but for whom had she been impersonating? Was she a true street artist, practicing her art for the love of it and nothing more? He had not seen a collection dish as she sat outside the takeaway. And a dozen local shops were probably not the best place to do something like this for profit.

She had been eating when he arrived; she had only actually performed for him.

"No," he muttered against the wood of her door. "I would."

Cain spun around. A man stood on the staircase leading from the ground floor, one foot on the first-floor landing, a bag in each hand. He had a long gray ponytail and a face as wrinkled as old leather. Cain felt vaguely guilty at being discovered leaning against Magenta's door, and he would have apologized if the man had not spoken first.

"I mean, I'm sure you would too. Sexy girl. Mostly. Difficult to tell sometimes, of course."

"I don't think I know you," Cain said, uttering the obvious, buying time to recover from the shock. His heart was beating the same way it did when the siren sounded, and he felt chided by this stranger.

"You don't, yet." Saying no more, the stranger set the bags down on the landing, unlocked the door to Flat Four, picked up his bags, glanced once more at Cain, and went inside. The door slammed shut, locks were thrown, chains rattled, and seemingly before the last key had turned Cain heard the first muted hoot of a pan pipe.

"Nice to meet you too," he said, but his anger lasted only seconds. It was melted away by the music. There was no real tune, but there is no order to the roaring of waves on rocks or the whisper of leaves in a breeze, and yet they comfort and ease. The music came to a sudden stop, cut off by a dull thump, and Cain hurried up the stairs to Flat Five. He glanced at the scored door next to his while he fumbled with his keys. Vlad had been found with his stomach eaten, Peter had said. Cain wondered whether whatever had done it had been looking for someone else.

Inside his flat he felt at ease once again. Alone. At Afresh he had sometimes preferred his own company, even though he hardly knew himself. He would sit for hours listening to music or reading, and then a sudden awareness of his own presence would shock him as much as finding someone else in the room. The Voice told him that it was a result of spending so much time cut off from outside influence, and that such an upbringing had inevitably created a solipsistic side to his thoughts. Free of his father at last, discovering the truth of the world with his senses as well as his mind, it was only natural that he sometimes thought of himself as a stranger.

He made a cold drink, put on the Mozart CD, and relaxed back on the sofa. Classical music always lifted and lowered him, swirled around and through him, and with his eyes closed he was easily lost to its influence, controlled and owned by every minor element of the whole. Closing his eyes also brought the siren closer; with less to hold it off it crept back, promising pain were he to overstep boundaries. But there *were* no boundaries anymore. He had to convince himself of that. He used the remote control to turn up the music, taunting the siren and cringing inside at the same time, waiting for the thunderous pain that would surely come again someday.

A tear rolled from his closed eye. He left it to run down his cheek, relishing the sensation.

The CD finished after an hour. He had listened in vain for any trace of that tune he hummed and which had been hummed to him, but there was nothing there. He would find it someday . . . and yet he was not certain he *wished* to find it. Because it was not simply a tune that he had brought out of his time with his father. And though that other element—that presence—had not appeared to him since being taken from the house in the chest, it terrified him still.

It was only midafternoon, but already he was tired. The sun cut in across the back garden and into his bedroom, and he opened the curtains before stripping and lying on his huge double bed. With Mozart now silent, Cain's mind was left to drift in other directions, and he fell asleep thinking of that dancing clown Magenta.

He woke up later that evening fully refreshed and relieved that his rest had been dreamless. But as the sun went down and the noises began, he wished that he were still asleep.

Initially it was quiet, with only the purr of occasional traffic and the distant voices of playing children marring the peace. It was twilight, the half-moon high in the dark blue sky, thin cloud cover smudging its light across the heavens. A few lonely birds sang their last before night came to carry them into sleep. Cain lay on his bed, chilled now that the sun was no longer resting across his body, but too relaxed to move. He had an erection and he held it, imagining it wrapped by Magenta's hand instead of his own. But in his mind's eye she smiled that strange, mocking smile, and he opened his eyes and sat up before asking whom she was impersonating, and for whom. His lust dwindled as he dressed.

And then the noises began. A loud thump—it came from downstairs, he felt it vibrate through his feet—followed by an expectant silence. Cain held his breath and stood still, waiting for more. As if waiting with him, the next crash came as he finally relaxed and breathed out. He felt this one harder than the first, traveling up through the balls of his feet and into his skull like the suggestion of chaos.

His telephone rang, and he realized that he had forgotten to call Afresh.

There was one final crash as he reached for the bedside telephone, and then a long, high scream that raised the hairs on his arms, tightened his balls, and made him wish for the siren to scream in and camouflage the cry.

He grabbed the receiver, barely registering that this was the first time he had ever answered his own telephone. The scream had faded away, and the building held its breath.

"Hello?"

It was the Voice, berating him for not calling, asking how things were, how was he, was he adjusting well, were the other residents welcoming, was the landlord helpful?

"Everything's fine," Cain said, thinking of that scream rising and rising until it seemed to pass out of his audible range. Perhaps it continued still, higher and higher, and he pressed the receiver to his ear to deny the scream any subliminal power.

Was he sure? the Voice asked. He sounded tired, worried, how about—

"Really, everything's fine," Cain said, trying his best to inject some certainty into his voice. "Just woke from an afternoon nap, that's all. Forgot to call you. Tiring day, everything's new." He kept his sentences short, listening for more noises from downstairs. Should he be going to help? Calling the police? An ambulance?

The Voice asked if he was *sure*.

"I promise. Look, I'll call you tomorrow. Oh, I met some of the other residents today."

The Voice rose, interest giving it a higher lilt, as it asked what they were like.

Cain could not reply. He was in a panic of indecision. He was on the phone now to the man who had helped him for the past six years, and he did not know how to ask what he should do. *I just heard a scream,* he needed to say, *like someone being killed. What should I do? And today I met the clown who lives downstairs.*

A laugh. It came from somewhere different, but still in the house. It was made androgynous by being filtered through walls and floors, but it was unmistakably the sound of merriment. And then another echoed the first, and Cain finally knew he had to respond.

"I'll call you tomorrow," he said, and hung up.

Somewhere in the building doors opened and closed. Children no longer shouted in the garden farther along the street; their parents must have called them in from the dangerous dark, taken them in to safety. The house fell quiet again, but it was a loaded silence, filled with expectation. Cain imagined the other residents standing at their windows as he was now, staring out into the deepening dark, wondering what they would see. The thought of that story came again, and he looked out into the garden in search of a murder.

Another door slammed, sending a shiver through the house. It held the sound of finality, and he knew that someone had left the building. He saw a shape staggering away from the house. It was just light enough for him to see that the shape was George. He seemed bent over as he ran, as if clutching something to his stomach, and his long hair hung down around his face in shiny wet clumps. He moved from the patio into an area of shrubs, paused, looked around, and hurried across the lawn until he was standing beneath a tree. George seemed to be favoring the shadows. Barely a shadow himself now, he headed off again, stumbled and fell, and even through the closed windows Cain heard the screech of pain. George rolled on the grass for a few seconds like a dog scratching its back, then stood and staggered to the rear of the garden. Cain lost him in the shadows, but as he opened the sliding doors he heard undergrowth being whipped and crushed, and cold moonlight revealed the heads of tall bushes thrashing at the night. George cried out again, and Cain almost shouted after him. But that image of others watching this happen was still there, and he chose silence. He stepped out onto the small balcony, glanced up at the roof ridge, down at the closed window on the first floor below. He seemed alone, but something felt staged about this whole thing. He had exposed himself by stepping out onto the balcony, but he already felt the center of attention.

Cain looked to the end of the garden again, and moonlight showed him the timber gate open and a shadow sneak out. George was gone, carrying away whatever pained him.

Cain would follow. He would not stand passively by, not like those people in the story. The idea hit him quick and hard, insistent as hunger, and the thought surprised him. He did not know George, and their brief meeting the night before had done little to endear him to the man. But the way he had been staggering across the garden, those screeches of pain . . . what if he *had* been attacked? He was holding his stomach as if he had been shot or stabbed, and then Vlad sprang to mind, the erstwhile occupant of Cain's flat, found dead miles from here in Rich Common with his stomach eaten. *There's nothing scratching at my door,* he thought. *Nothing seeking me tonight. It's George.*

Cain did not know exactly what drove him to shrug on his jacket and leave the flat. It was not purely concern for George, a man he did not know. A sense of humanity perhaps? But his father had done his best to leech that from him, and Cain still found it difficult to empathize with other people. If anything, it was curiosity. And perhaps a sense that because he *could* leave his flat—do what he wished, on a night filled with dangers unknown—then he *should*.

He closed his door and hurried downstairs, feeling eyes on him all the way.

The third door he tried at the back of the house led to the garden. The first had revealed the basement stairs, and the second hid a cupboard containing electric and gas meters, cleaning products, and an empty first-aid box. Each time he opened and closed a door he listened out for more laugher, but there was no more.

It was much cooler outside than he had expected. Night had fallen fully now, and the half-full moon shone through the wispy cloud cover and made shadows of everything. Its light seemed to deaden noise. A car went by, perhaps streets away, and the sibilant voice of a television came from somewhere to his left, but they were little more than whispers.

Cain had always enjoyed the night. He had spent so much of his childhood in the dark, hidden away, the gift of vision withheld. When his father was experimenting, darkness always sharpened Cain's other senses. He would smell cooking from elsewhere in the house, hear the sounds of timber settling around him as the building bled heat to the cool dark, taste rain on the air, even deep in the basement. Darkness was his friend. He had read that fear of the dark was usually fear of what might be in it. Cain had always been much more afraid of what he could see.

Fearless, he walked into the garden of Number 13. George's pain had been evident, but it had been from an injury that had happened back in the house, not out here. Glancing behind and above, he saw his own dark window and, to the side, the unlit window of Flat Four. If Whistler was watching, he gave no sign. Perhaps he was standing there touching his pipes, wondering when would be the best time to let his tunes float free.

Cain moved down the garden, trying to follow the staggered route he had seen George taking. Beneath the tree Cain paused and knelt down, running his fingers through the grass, trying to know more than he should. He closed his eyes and imagined himself back in that room in his father's house, alone but for the occasional humming, totally withdrawn, seeing and hearing and sensing nothing other than his own body and mind. He breathed deeply and slowly, trying not to smell, determined not to taste evening on the air. He willed the shadow to talk, but it remained stubbornly silent, sneering at the back of his mind, hidden away and promising nothing new. A guilty comfort settled over him. He hated that room, and yet it was where he felt safest, most at home, those feelings belying the years of effort at Afresh and the wishes of his conscious mind to leave that place far behind. Freeing his thoughts, Cain found peace in the worst time of his life. His fingertips brushed the cool grass, and the siren exploded in his mind.

He howled and fell onto his side, vomiting, hands clamped to his ears, but already the phantom sound was a memory. It left only pain behind. Cain panted, tried to lift himself from the ground and away from the smells of damp earth and puke, the feel of grass against his cheek. But the siren was gone. He was alone and afraid, back in the now.

Cain felt guilty and dirty, as if he had been caught masturbating. He often knew things he should not, and he hated that; it was left over from his father, the house, and the Pure Sight he knew so little about. But on the rare occasions when he tried to bring on that knowledge himself, he always felt like shit afterward.

This time, he knew nothing.

He stood and hurried through the garden to the back gate. It was open, and beyond was revealed a narrow access lane. Hedges and garages on either side shielded the lane from much of the moonlight, and most of it remained shadowed and unknown. It must have been a few minutes since George had passed this way, and Cain was about to despair about ever finding him when he heard the clatter of something falling against a garage door. Seconds later came a long, low moan of someone in pain, and he knew that George had not moved far.

Cain started along the lane. He was still shivering from the impact of the siren. He knew it was all memory, a Pavlovian reaction that he would probably never fully escape, but still his eardrums rang and his heart hammered with the memory. He tried to spit the taste of sick from his mouth, so redolent of the basement in his father's house. The sickness was a relatively new reaction to the siren. The Voice said it proved that Cain now knew that it was only memory, and not some curse that would haunt him all his life. Cain believed that it proved fuck all, other than the fact that his father had damaged him forever.

And besides, what was memory if not a curse?

He turned a corner and moonlight swarmed down, coloring the open space before him liquid silver. The area was faced on three sides with garages, many of their doors daubed with graffiti that may have looked at home in a modern art gallery. At least this was vandalism with pride. One of the garages was open, revealing darkness and the hint of a metallic shape lurking inside, the smells of leaked oil rich and potent. In front of the garages, in the center of the open area, lay a burned-out car. Its blackened frame seemed to reject moonlight, casting itself into a shadow, and Cain had a sudden unpleasant memory of his company in the basement, that humming thing that had taken up more space than it should. He edged around the car, not liking it one bit. By being burned and having its purpose destroyed, perhaps it had moved slightly out of the world.

There was a frantic sound of violence from the open garage. Something squealed in the darkness, a loud, sudden screech of pain. It could have been George, or perhaps it was only a rat being caught by a cat. Cain paused, trapped by moonlight. There came a crash of something being knocked over, a grunt of pain or ecstasy, and a burst tin of paint rolled into view, leaving a black streak behind as if wounded.

Cain darted to the garage next to the open one, keeping as quiet as he could. He almost called out to see if it was George, but something muffled his shout and he waited there for a while, listening to what was going on inside.

Something was eating; something else was being eaten. The sounds made by both were oddly complimentary and interchangeable. The victim screeched and whined and coughed, noises that were so reminiscent of pleasure and pain as to be unidentifiable. The thing doing the eating was making loud wet smacks, joyful grunts deep in its throat, and heavy swallowing sounds as it took down another chunk. He could have been listening to a porn film, or a horror movie about cannibals.

There was a rapid gasp, like the rush of air from a punctured lung, and one final, warbling cry that increased in volume before being cut off with a crunch.

Cain cringed, trying not to add his own scream to the night air.

He knew he should go, but he had to see more. Every book he had read told him that he should flee; it was only madmen and victims that did not run away from such sounds. Yet there was no reason to believe that George was in there. It was a cat eating a rat, or maybe a fox eating an old, injured cat. He had come this far, and he was caught. The sounds were horrible, but at least now it was only eating he could hear, not the final dying scream of the thing being eaten. That had already faded into the night.

He closed his eyes first, shutting out the moonlight to accustom them to darkness. Then he leaned around, turning so that he could look into the garage.

There was a small car in there, a soft-top, and its canvas roof had been shredded. Something sat in the front seat, slumped sideways, its face buried in the dead thing in the passenger seat. The tang of blood and insides filled the enclosed space, and when Cain tried to breathe through his mouth he could taste it on his tongue. He had never liked steak rare, and this was rarer.

The thing growled and lifted its head. It shook. Cain felt a fine spray hit his cheek and he stumbled back, wiping the blood from his face. A dog! Whatever it had in there looked quite large, certainly a meal's worth for a dog of that size. A cat, perhaps? He had always thought it a myth that dogs chased cats to catch and eat them, but all good myths had a basis in fact somewhere along the line.

The dog stank, a wet, cloying smell like dirty wet fur and the odor of neglect. He wondered what had been happening in that garage for the few seconds before he had emerged from the lane. It had been silent. Was the victim already caught by then, lying trapped beneath the dog's heavy paws, resigned to its fate but not yet being eaten alive? It was a disturbing image and he tried not to elaborate, but being unaware of every detail gave his imagination free rein.

His pursuit of George seemed far less important now, as if discovering that gruesome scene had always been the aim of this jaunt. Cain hurried back into the lane, pleased to be immersed in darkness once again, finding comfort in the weight of shadows. He realized that he would probably have no idea which gate led back into the garden. He had a sudden sense of disorientation, and for a moment he was sure this was not the same lane. It did not smell right, though that could have been influenced by the blood splashed on his cheek. It did not *feel* right. But there was something very different about the dark now. Not more threatening, but more mysterious. As if in agreement with Cain's thoughts, a bank of cloud drifted across the moon, hiding away anything profound.

Cain went unerringly to the garden gate, making sure he left it unbolted for when George returned. Because Cain was certain now that he *would* return. The night's events were beginning to take on a very staged feel, as if everything were happening for him. The thumping from downstairs, the laughter that was too loud, the scream, the square of garages with the skeletal car and single open garage door. Even the clouds had timed themselves to perfection as they blanked out the moonlight. He did not fear the dark, but right then, after what he had seen and knowing what perhaps roamed the back alleys, he would have welcomed the light.

Once through the back door and inside the house, he did not feel as safe as he would have hoped. It was only as he closed his own door behind him and turned on the lights that the danger began to recede. If the night was staged, it had the feel of a forgettable book, pulp fiction written without depth or feeling. By the time he went to his bathroom to wash the blood from his face, it had already gone, melted away by his sweat perhaps, or maybe never even there at all.

Suddenly tired, Cain went to bed without undressing and fell immediately to sleep.

And as suited that night, his sleep was filled with dreams masquerading as memories, or memories as dreams.

For four weeks his father has denied him anything other than the most basic food and drink. Sustenance had always been important, according to his father. But four weeks ago Cain was told it was time for the room again. The siren was ready, his father reminded Cain for a few days beforehand, ready to punish and guide. It was not until the first day ended that Cain realized what this new experiment would entail.

He sits up on his bed and looks around, expecting to see the window out onto the garden, the en suite bathroom door ajar, and perhaps he will hear the heavy silence still promising secret things throughout the house. He looks at his hands, his arms, and sees that he is a young boy again. That young boy is insecure with this knowledge—even more confused with the certainty that the older Cain should not be here; should, in fact, be in a flat in Endless Crescent—but Cain knows his younger self so well, and he smiles and offers comfort. He will be back there again, he knows. And though his younger self has no comprehension of "there," he seems to take heed.

There is only this bare, blank room, remarkable because it is unremarkable and he has not been here for a long time. It is clean, but looks grubby with its total lack of finish. The walls are bare gray blocks. The ceiling is skimmed plasterboard. The floor is polished concrete, with nothing to break its monotony other than his own faint footprints sweated into its surface. His dreaming self has prints much larger than that now, and the knowledge of his survival should help him cope and get through this. But sometimes it is only the moment that matters, especially when the moment is so filled with pain, confusion, and hunger.

Only one wall is broken, and that is with the door. The door itself has a slot at floor level, a flap that is lifted and locked from the outside. The young Cain knows what this is for, but the adult Cain is confused. His confusion is resolved when the flap lifts and a tray slides through.

The tray holds several covered dishes, and five beakers filled with drinks of various colors. His stomach rumbles, saliva fills his mouth, and as Cain remembers the curry he ate the day before, the siren blasts out of nowhere and drives him onto his back. He screams and thrashes on the cold concrete, and when the brief explosion ends, his mouth is dry again.

There are no smells from the food. He crawls to the tray and looks down at his hands. For a powerful instant he feels like an alien here, a cruel invader that has to be sent back to whatever nebulous adult future he has imagined, along with the extravagant friends and outrageous places with which he has surrounded himself. But the feeling is brief, and Cain bends to the tray confident that this is the past, not the now.

Taking the tray back to the bed, he feels eyes upon him. He looks at the door, but there is no sign of any spy hole. That has always been the case. Somehow his father always knows what he is doing in here. And he cannot only *see* his son, he can taste what he tastes, smell what he smells, because the siren is always there ready to assault Cain with pain and shame. He has never seen the siren, never understood where it comes from or what it is, but he guesses it must be the walls of the room itself. Still that sense of being watched, and he looks around the room, under the bed, seeing nothing.

Somebody starts humming. It is a tune he recognizes but cannot place. In his child's body he feels a very adult sensation, shivering as someone or something touches his soul with unknowable intent. Perhaps he is humming himself, but try as he might, he cannot change tune or tone. It is being hummed to him, not by him, and the tune is endless.

The tray contains one dish of something utterly colorless, odorless, and bland. It could be an unseasoned potato dish, or something with mashed rice, but he can make out no other constituent parts. *Gruel,* he thinks, and the word seems appropriate. Another dish contains a handful of fluffy rice and several large spoonfuls of chili, along with a glob of sour cream. There is a curry dish, a pasta bake with chorizo and mushrooms, and salmon in white sauce with green beans.

His mouth waters, he catches a whiff of the chili, and the instant that smell translates to taste the siren throws him to the floor. He knocks the tray and desperately reaches out to stop it tumbling from the bed, screaming at the same time. The siren stops, leaving pain behind as a hot throb in his head, and a brief flush of anger is put down by something dark lurking in his memory.

"Don't fuck him off," a voice says, "otherwise there'll be worse to come."

"What?" Cain looks around the room, seeing no one. But there is a presence there, a shadow where light should fall, and though it seems to bear no weight it holds import.

"I said don't fuck him off. And don't talk to me. He doesn't know I'm here."

Cain is confused and terrified. He is unsure which emotion is attributable to which Cain—the young one in the room, the old one dreaming in his bed—but they seem to suit both. He examines the drink in the beakers—water in one, coffee, strawberry milk shake, red wine—and stares at the tray, trying not to ask questions or look around at the shadow.

"In case you're wondering, he can't hear me," the shadow says. "His obsession deafens him. It blinds him too, and that's why he can't see that the light's being eaten. Can you see, Cain? Young Cain, old Cain, can you see the light?"

Cain glances up at the bare bulb hanging from the ceiling, squints, and from the corner of his eye he sees a shadow slinking along one side of the room.

"Eat, if I were you," the shadow says. "But careful what you choose. You know why the old fuck has you in here right now. Humor him, and leave the tasting for me."

81

Cain eats the gruel and drinks the water, avoiding the food and drink with any real taste or substance. When he finishes, he places the tray by the door and steps back, watching his father's wrinkled hands come through to take it away. There is no communication—no praise from a father to his young son, no words of comfort or encouragement—and though Cain is desperate to speak, the shadow sits at his back. He is certain it is laughing at him.

The humming begins again and Cain lies back in his bed, careful not to let the blanket touch his lips. As he retreats into sleep, meeting himself in there and knowing grander things, the siren waits for him to dream of taste.

"Pure Sight is so far away from where you are," the shadow says as Cain drifts away from that room. "The old fuck knows that, too. He's just doing this to torture you, Cain. He's doing it to hurt you. Because he knows he can never, ever have it for himself."

Cain came awake disoriented, frightened, and so alone. He did not know whether he was the young Cain or the older one, he had no idea where he was, and his friend the darkness served only to hide the truth, smothering him, entering his eyes and ears as if he were submerged in dark water. He opened his mouth to cry out, but the darkness slipped in there also, cool and slick, and he could think only of that shadow in the room in his father's basement. It was here with him now. Wherever he was, it was here to drown him and take him for itself. Bodiless, it wanted his flesh and bone, his home.

He finally sat up and cried out, expelling any idea of being smothered, purging that feeling and locating himself in a matter of seconds. He was in his new flat on Endless Crescent, and he had been dreaming of his time with his father. He needed food. He needed drink, something tasty to drive away the sourness in his mouth. He needed more than anything to defy the siren and lose the shadow.

Cain ran around his flat, turning on every light and closing curtains against the dark. He wanted no point of access for the shadows. Then he raided the fridge, sat at his dining table, and started eating. The first morsel of strong cheese took an eternity to reach his mouth—like sticking pins into one's own eyes, inviting intentional agony is not a part of any sane person—but when it touched the tip of his tongue and the siren stayed away, he chewed and smiled into the light. More cheese, ham, a selection of chocolates he'd bought the day before, and then he opened a bottle of Australian red and reveled in its rich, full taste.

As he ate and drank, he started walking around the flat. The walls were all the same creamy color. The paintings in the hallway were stark black and white. Perhaps, he thought, he needed a hint of color. Just a hint.

The dream hung on like an odor, but its effect had lessened. He could recall being frightened and alone, but simply recalling it would never bring that sensation back. Fear, like pain, was difficult to remember. He chewed against the dream. His father's hands, wrinkled like those of an old man. That shadow, talking and humming and denying its own existence, because surely his father would have seen it? He knew what his own lonely son was tasting locked away in that room, so surely he would have heard that voice and seen the shadow where there should have been none?

In the living room, Cain sat on the large chest he had brought here with him . . . and he realized that it had moved.

Peter had shoved it into the corner when he moved in two days ago. Like Cain's dreams, it was something that always had to be there but which he would prefer to ignore. And perhaps like the glut of his memories tonight, its contents were weighing it down. He had not opened the chest for years, since before it had been transferred with him to Afresh. The Face and Voice often spoke to him about it, suggesting that by confronting the fears from his past he would be able to tackle them. But he had told them that some things, whether good or bad, are simply best forgotten. They had not pushed him on the matter, but he knew they wanted a look inside, always.

After his father had died, in those long days when Cain was almost alone in the house, he had conspired to lock the shadow in the chest. By then he was more afraid of it than his father, the dreams, even the siren. It terrified him because it knew him so well.

Maybe he had moved it last night. He rapped on the wood, daring the shadow to respond. Silence.

He could remember little of those days alone in the house, his only company the slowly rotting body of his father splayed out on the living room floor. That and the shadow, which haunted his memories as it had stalked that house. He knew that he had sat next to his father for hours on end, constantly expecting the old man to smile and rise, reveal the escapade as yet another experiment performed on his son. He had tried sensory deprivation, emotional withdrawal; perhaps now he was using psychological torture to bring forth the Pure Sight he swore Cain must possess. But the man had remained dead, his form slowly blackening and losing definition, and Cain had eventually been driven away by the smell.

He remembered a fight, something inside himself, a struggle against logic and reason that left little more than a deep, dark absence in his mind. He knew the fight had been real, because the void was real. He could sense its lack of weight. It was a deep void, wide, and sometimes he thought it was so large that it was larger than himself. But that was impossible.

After the fight, something like peace, and the timber chest locked shut with something of that void inside.

And after that his time at Afresh, where people he had never met tried to help him make sense of his life. They said they could help find him a future. To do so, they seemed to spend all their time talking about his past. Maybe they were one and the same, and time itself was the great deceiver.

Cain stood from the chest and moved back into

the hallway, looking again at the black-and-white pictures of treescapes and stormy skies. The tang of cheese in his mouth suddenly made him retch, the aftertaste of the rich fruity wine adding to the effect. He concentrated to keep his stomach contents down, the bland landscapes calming him somewhat, but when he returned to the dining room and smelled the remnants of the mature stilton, he fell to his knees and vomited across the floor. The food and wine came up in great gouts, dripping from his nose. His stomach clenched and spasmed. It felt as though a great hand were closing around him, squeezing and purging him of taste. He puked again. His hands splashed in the mess, but he did not care. Smacking his mouth, he sounded like that mad dog eating something in the dark garage, and he was sick again, just bile this time, colored arterial-red by the wine.

Eventually, the retching calmed and he sat back against the wall, feet drawn up to avoid the puddle of sick. It stank, but the smell seemed to belong somewhere else. He wished he could lose his senses of smell and taste, turn blind and deaf, ridding himself of the curses of perception that his father had been so keen to reveal and destroy. But then the Voice came at him from the dark outside the windows, always waiting there to talk sense.

Whatever he thought he was doing, your father was only hurting you. There'll always be his love there for you to rest on, but remember, Cain, he was hurting you. There was no sense to what he was doing, no reason. He kept you there. He kept you alone.

"I'll always be alone," Cain whispered, and the dark grinned back.

He sat there until morning, watching his vomit dry into grooves cut into the timber floor by dead Vlad's wheelchair.

When his father died, Cain thought he finally knew what loneliness was. But there was always the shadow.

Chapter Four
Strangers

Cain opened the curtains and watched the sun rise. It emerged above a row of houses, a red smudge that manifested slowly from the polluted air, finally shaking itself free and heading skyward. Red sky in the morning, sailor's warning. The sunrise was startlingly beautiful in a way that he had never been able—or allowed—to express, but the siren remained silent.

In the cool light of day, he began to wonder what he had seen and heard the previous night. Banging, somebody screaming, and then laughter, as if he were being conspired against and tricked. George stumbling through the garden, holding his stomach as if stabbed . . . or perhaps only holding in his own mirth. And the dog in that garage, chewing and snapping and slurping its way into something else's still-warm flesh. It had all felt so staged. So false. So controlled. He had sensed eyes watching over his shoulder all the time, mocking him. The world laughed in his face as he saw import in everything, sensed significance in the wave of a leaf or shift of a shadow. Last night had been so unreal, like a movie played out in his mind. A movie in which he had played the leading part. He sat on the sofa and shivered, hugging himself close because there was no one else to do it, clasping his own shoulders hard, pressing in his fingernails to make sure he was still awake.

He felt so alone.

Birds sang outside his window, unseen but keen to be heard. Their song was insistently cheerful, even though their chicks may be lying dead beneath their nests or torn apart by a cat. They seemed to be singing for anyone but him.

Cars passed by, ferrying people to work or school or some other important place, leaving him in his flat.

A leaf scraped against the living room window, carried on the breeze, an early death anticipating autumn still several months away. It danced there for a while, tickling the glass as if requesting entry. Cain stood quickly, but the leaf, finding his image wanting, drifted away to some secret demise.

He felt so alone.

There were no noises from within the house, and he wondered whether everyone else had gone out. Either that or they were sitting still and silent in their flats, listening for him. Perhaps they were all together somewhere, wondering how he was going to react to last night's events. That was something he was still unsure of himself.

In the dining room, his vomit had dried on the

floor. He took a few minutes to clean it up, gagging on the stench but managing to not puke again. As he mopped he imagined that he was disposing of last night's experiences, scooping them up and tying the bag so that they could not escape again. Like his dream they lingered on, but also like his dream they were consigned to the parts of his mind where memories and nightmares became inseparable. He knew where he had been and what he had seen—his muddy boot-prints had staggered all over the flat—but he had to find a way to control his fear and confusion.

As a nightmare, last night took on a different shade.

He made himself a strong coffee and then called the Voice.

Hi, Cain, he said, *I was worried about you last night. You hung up so quickly.*

"Why didn't you call back?" Cain would not have been at home anyway, but he felt suddenly scared at the sense of abandonment.

You're your own man now. You have your own life, and a future. I didn't want to intrude.

"You wouldn't have been intruding," Cain said, but he remembered rushing downstairs to follow the injured shape of George, and he wondered just how he could portray any of this to the Voice.

So how are things?

"Fine. They're fine."

Any dreams?

"Plenty, but then you know that."

Bad?

Cain took a noisy sip of coffee for the Voice to

hear, giving himself a few seconds in which to think. "Different," he said at last. "It involved someone else from the flats. Bloke called George. He's already introduced himself, he came to . . ."

Wake me when I was screaming in my sleep, Cain thought. That was not something he wanted to tell the Voice.

At least you're dreaming about someone else.

"Yes, and it was nothing to do with the house, or my father."

Good. Cain, I'm proud of you. You've achieved so much in so little time. You realize that, don't you?

Cain looked around the flat, still smelling the results of last night's nightmare. Outside, the whole world continued without him. "Yes, I suppose so."

I could talk here for ages, quiz you, ask what you're thinking and what you're doing . . . but I'm happy to leave all that to you. This is your chance now.

"I'm on my own," Cain said, his voice flat and emotionless.

That's right. But though I won't question you any more, I want you to know that we're here if you need us. Day or night, any reason, absolutely anything. *You understand?*

"Absolutely," Cain said. "And I'm grateful. You need to know that."

I know you are. Take care, Cain.

"Thanks. I'll speak to you again soon." Cain hung up. *Grateful . . . grateful for being on my own.* He wondered whether that would have fit in well with his father's ambitions for Pure Sight.

* * *

Just before midday, he heard the front door two floors below slam shut. He dashed to his living room, looked out, and watched Whistler leave the front garden with Magenta. At least, he thought it was Magenta. She seemed slightly taller today, broader at the shoulder and narrower at the waist. But she was dressed in black jeans and a tight black top, very different attire from the clown costume, and it would have been easy to be mistaken. Perhaps today she was impersonating someone else.

Cain thought of tapping on the glass and waving, but he did not. He and Magenta seemed to hit it off yesterday, and he was keen to see her again. Yet it was her subtly altered appearance that prevented him from catching their attention, not Whistler's presence. She was a slightly different person, and he needed no excuse to feel like a stranger.

Peter had failed to keep his promise to show Cain around the rest of the house and tell him about the other residents. After some prevarication, Cain decided to visit Peter's dilapidated home across the street to ask him a few questions. He needed to know how to use the equipment in the laundry room—the clothes he had worn last night (*nightmare, it was a nightmare*) were dirtied from leaning against walls and kneeling on the grass, and still speckled with his vomit—and he also needed to ask about the scratched door next to his on the landing. There was no flat in there, he was sure— he had seen or heard no sign of anyone living there—but something had wanted in. An attic perhaps, a storage space squeezed in beside his own flat? He needed to ask Peter these things, and more. And he also wanted some company. The landlord had not put him completely at ease, but if it was a choice between him and Sister Josephine or George, there was no choice at all.

George. If they met again, Cain would have no idea what to say, or even how to look at him. He wondered whether George was home, if his stomach wound was still bleeding, or whether he had simply laughed himself hoarse.

Cain went downstairs. It was a hot, sunny day. He stood in the front garden for a while, listening to the sudden silence from beneath the spiky shrubbery, eager to walk through the gate but compelled to stay. There was something about this garden, a skewing of senses that he could neither explain nor even be certain of. He heard a baby crying from afar, but it could easily have come from behind him, somewhere deep inside the house. A car passed by on the road, sleek and silver, but its growl seemed a second out of sync, as if the sound took too long to pass through the garden hedge.

A woman pedestrian glanced in at where Cain stood watching, nodded uncomfortably, and Cain suddenly knew more than he should. He hated it when it happened like this, but it also gave him a guilty thrill. And even if he had tried, he knew that he would have been unable to avoid the consequence.

The woman was uncomfortable from the sex she'd had last night, a rough, frantic fuck with a man she had known as a friend for a long time. Her discomfort was both physical and psychological. Her perception of their friendship had changed drastically, plunging it into terminal decline. And yet she had been as keen as he. Cain saw deeper, past the woman's surface concerns to that coal-black knot of guilt that concerned her the most. What he had done to her, what she had let him do, belied the image of the man she had held to be true for many years. It disgusted and excited her in equal measures, and although she felt repelled by the night's perversions, she would welcome him into her bed again at a moment's notice. It would destroy what they had, as surely as hatred slaughters true love. But there was something challenging there now, something rich and risky. Before, the friendship had become simply convenient.

Cain reeled, taking a step back, shocked by the clarity of these alien thoughts. In the split second it had taken for the woman to nod at him, he knew everything, a confused stew of images and senses that made up a whole, coherent story. He could smell the faint whiff of their sex, feel the roughness of the man's hands and the grinding of the woman's teeth, and though none of the visions were clear in themselves, their combination was startling.

More startling was the woman's reaction. She looked away, face reddening, step quickening. She knew that he knew. Cain felt no surprise in her mind. Could guilt blind that easily? Or was this simply the way of things out here in the world? Perhaps out here strangers really *were* simply books to be read.

Cain ran from the garden and across the road, forgetting to look out for traffic. Heaven stood before him in all its shabbiness, so out of place in this street and yet so at home, as if it had been here first.

He turned and looked for the woman, but she had vanished. His sketch of her thoughts had faded quickly, like a dream already forgotten at daybreak, but a sour taste remained in his mouth. He spat, tasted sex, spat again.

"Drink?" Peter asked. "You look thirsty." He was standing in front of the run-down house, proffering a bottle of water. Cain had not heard the corrugated iron door being prized open, but he supposed he had been away on his own for a while.

"Thanks." He took the bottle and drank, relishing the ice-cold water washing taste from his mouth and throat.

"Single mum," Peter said.

"Pardon?"

"That woman you were looking at. Single mother, lives in a flat ten doors down from you. Nice girl. Very fuckable."

"Well, I wasn't really thinking about that," Cain said, an inexplicable blush burning his cheeks.

"Yes, okay, Cain. Anyway, I assume you were coming over for a social visit?"

"Just wanted to ask a few questions, really."

"Sure, no problem. So are you settling in all right? The others not giving you too much of a hard time?" He smiled broadly. Cain wondered whether he would always think of himself as subject to someone else's mockery.

95

"They're fine. I've met them all apart from Sister Josephine."

"And what do you think?"

"Well . . . Magenta is very nice."

"She is, isn't she? Was she working when you met her?"

Cain was not entirely sure. "Yes," he said. "She's very talented."

"You have no idea." Peter's smile remained as broad as ever, and it touched his eyes. Here was a man finding humor in his situation, and whatever the cause of that mirth, Cain could not help feeling self-conscious.

"So you live here?" he asked.

"Heaven? Yep. Nice pad, don't you think?"

"Well . . ."

"Ha! Don't let appearances deceive you, Cain. It's just a facade. Inside, everything is different. Glorious, intriguing, wonderful . . . different."

Cain waited for an invitation to enter, but none was forthcoming.

"So!" Peter said. "Laundry room! I never did finish the tour, did I? Very sorry about that. I'm a busy landlord." He strode past Cain and across the road, turning and waiting for Cain to follow. "Let's not be too long about it," he said, glancing up at the sky. "It's a lovely day, filled with potential. I hate to let potential fade away." He opened the garden gate and walked to the front door.

Cain heard the shrubbery rustling as Peter passed by, as if the things living under there were cowering away, or rushing to get a look at the man's legs. Either way, the landlord had caused a reaction.

* * *

"Sister!" Peter gushed. "You look ravishing today."

"I'll pass by, if you please. I have business to attend."

"More people to save?"

"Always."

Sister Josephine glanced at Cain as she pressed past him in the lobby. Her habit flowed like oil, so black that Cain could almost smell the color on it. Her Mona Lisa smile was welcoming but formal. And her eyes were a stunning green, so piercing, so cool and intelligent, that Cain gasped out loud.

"Hello, Cain," she said.

"H-hello."

And then she was gone, pulling the front door shut behind her.

Cain turned to Peter and raised his eyebrows, not knowing what to say.

"She has that effect on everyone," Peter said.

"She's a *nun?*"

"Either that or a stripogram. I've never seen her out of the habit. Though I'd like to, eh?"

"She's beautiful" was all Cain could say, and even through Peter's lecherous laugh he could not manage an impure thought about the nun. Later maybe, when he was over his shock. But right now, Cain could swear that he'd had something bordering on a religious experience. Her smile, so exquisite. Her eyes, so deep.

"Strange one, that," Peter said. He turned and headed past Sister Josephine's front door. "But as I told you, they're all a bit strange in here. Right then, laundry room!"

He opened the door leading to the basement, stood back from it as if contemplating something, and then glanced at Cain. "You sure?"

"Sure of what?"

"Sure you want to see the laundry room?"

Cain nodded. "I have laundry to do. And I wouldn't want to misuse anything down there. Why, is there a problem?"

Peter shook his head, the normally confident smile slipping into something more nervous. It looked painted on, like a clown's. "Nah, not really. I'm just not that keen on being underground."

"Don't like the dark?" Cain asked.

"The dark's fine. As I said, I just don't like being underground. It's the same as being buried."

"Except that there aren't steps up out of a grave."

Peter nodded, but he did not meet Cain's eyes. "Well, all right then, but we'll just pop down and up again. The stuff's easy to use, just basic washers and dryers." He started down the timber staircase, still talking, words tumbling over each other as nervousness took over. "The washer's more of a commercial design, bigger, more hard wearing, so don't be afraid to use it as much as you want. Electricity's included in the rent that you're having paid for you by Afresh, so no coin slots or tokens needed, or anything silly like that."

He flicked a switch, and a bright light flooded up out of the basement, blinding Cain for a few seconds before his eyes adjusted.

"Oh, the light's a bit harsh," Peter said apologetically. "That's down to me."

Cain paused halfway down the stairs, watching

Peter where he stood uncertainly at the bottom. The landlord looked around the basement, his eyes never resting, head jerking this way and that like a bird wary of predators.

"It stinks down here," Peter whispered, and Cain was not sure whether the comment was meant for him to hear or not. He took in a breath, smelling only drying washing and the faint tang of electrical equipment, and something altogether more earthy.

The basement was surprisingly large. The staircase stood in one corner, and the room extended so far out that Cain was sure it was larger than the house's footprint. Perhaps it went under the front garden, providing scant bedding for the plants that grew there. It contained several washers and dryers lined along the walls, a couple of ironing boards, and some airing racks adorned with clothing. He wondered whose laundry this was, and smiled as he tried to attach items with their owners. An old woollen jumper, that would be Whistler. Combat trousers, Whistler again, or perhaps George. Several vest tops and narrow jeans, probably Magenta. Her rack also contained a few undergarments, functional rather than provocative, and Cain felt a surge of heat to his groin. Strange that she would leave her panties down here for anyone to see, touch, or take. Very strange.

"There's a spare rack over there for you," Peter said, pointing across the basement.

Cain nodded, not looking. He was staring at one of the other full racks, trying to convince himself he was not seeing what he was seeing. He wanted to ask Peter, but the memory of that secretive laughter came at him from last night, group laughter, planning games and laying clues for him to follow.

"Don't worry about the chairs. Sometimes the Sister holds a sort of communion down here, people off the street, that sort of thing."

Cain barely heard. It had to be George's rack. It held a T-shirt, holed and still stained with blood. One hole in the chest, and others that were more like tears or gashes. And those wide terra-cotta stains, faded with several obvious washing attempts, but still there.

Peter glanced at Cain, followed his gaze. "People do tend to leave their washing out down here," he said, very slowly, "but they honor each other's privacy. I'd fuck Magenta at a moment's notice, for instance, but I wouldn't dream of touching her underwear." He stood in front of George's rack, obscuring it from Cain's view, and raised his hand toward Magenta's drying clothing. His fingers did not quite touch it, though they flexed and stretched. "I wouldn't dream of smelling it, either. Because there's respect down here. And it wouldn't smell of her anyway . . . not when she's been working."

"She's an impersonator," Cain said, confused now, unsure of Peter's shift from discomfort to issuing subtle threat.

Peter only smiled and nodded, glancing once more at the underwear he would never touch or smell, and then he pushed past Cain and rested his foot on the bottom step. "As I said, I don't like it down here, so I'm going back up. Any more questions?" And though his mouth made these words, his eyes spoke volumes: *There are no more questions.*

Cain made a point of turning away from Peter and looking around, trying not to see the clothing hanging there like secrets out to dry. He saw the chairs that Peter had mentioned—a circle of mixed dining chairs, settees, stools—and though he thought it odd having a gathering place down here, he did not dwell on it. It was dusty and damp and smelled of washing, but as Peter had said—and as Cain himself was coming to find—the residents here were a strange bunch. If Sister Josephine wanted to come down here and preach, that was her prerogative.

"And now that you've met everyone, I don't need to tell you anything about them," Peter said, climbing the staircase.

Cain had a brief idea that the landlord would shut the door and lock him down here, and though the dark never scared him, the thought gave him a second of panic. *Like being buried,* Peter had said. Cain hurried up the stairs, and Peter closed the door behind him. He smiled at Cain again, his confidence returned after their brief, strange sojourn downstairs.

"So now that's over with, if you'll excuse me I have a few things to do."

"Of course," Cain said, wanting to ask so much more. The door next to his, scratched as if something had tried to get in? George and his nighttime excursions? Magenta? But though the questions begged asking, Cain had begun to suspect that Peter was just as strange and involved as the others. He may live over the street in Heaven, but he was far from innocent.

* * *

Cain spent the rest of that day in his flat. He found some pots of paint under the sink. They were all old and mostly dried out, but a couple were salvageable, and he set these aside. The colors were brash and bright, nothing like the subdued cream that the whole flat was painted with now. Perhaps beneath the surface were shades and tints he could only guess at; those he had found in the kitchen, and others. This could be many flats in one, suiting various people, happening only now to suit him. The black-and-white paintings, the neutral-colored furniture, all was as he would prefer . . . and yet there was that idea growing in his mind, the thought that he could experiment on himself if he so desired. His father was long gone, and that torturous siren was still there only in his head. His brief forays into rich food and drink had come with a price, perhaps, but it was *his* body, *his* future and life, the Voice had told him that all the time. He was in control.

Cain took a knife, removed a picture from the hall wall, and scratched at the paint. It peeled away and fell to the floor like shed skin. There seemed to be several layers of the cream color, and Cain despaired of finding anything different, but then he saw the reason for the many coatings. The color beneath was a rich blood-red, heavy and dark. He removed a patch of paint the size of his hand and stepped back to admire the exposed color. He tried to imagine the whole hallway painted like this, but he could not. It was not fear of the siren or the indoctrination of neutrality by his father. It was simply that he was not capable of realizing such extravagance.

He scraped at the red, and beneath that was a light green. More scraping, and he uncovered a layer of terra-cotta, warm and orange. It reminded him of the bloodstains on George's T-shirt. The next scraping took him through to the plaster, but even that pinkness was more colorful than the bland cream. The peeled paint lay on the floor like a shattered rainbow.

Cain rehung the picture and stared at it for quite some time. It was a landscape of dead trees. Yes, there was something about dead trees. These were in black, white, and gray. Back in the kitchen, he scooped some of the usable paint onto a plate— there was red, blue, and some thick, stodgy yellow—and went back to the hallway. He would bring the dead trees to life.

The Face would have called it rebellion, but to Cain it felt like coming to life again.

In the end, he barely touched the painting. Once removed from the frame it felt like vandalism, and a few brief kisses of paint to its printed surface convinced Cain that he was doing wrong. He blew on the paint to aid its drying, reframed the picture, and hung it again. But even with only a slight touch the picture was transformed. The hint of color drew the eye, negating the bland grays with its surreptitious spread. His father would have hated it. Cain was pleased.

Several times that afternoon he walked into the hallway and simply stood and stared. There was so much color beyond the window of his flat, so much sensory input to sample, so many ways to steal himself away from the life his father had tried to create for him. Pure Sight was seeing clearly, and Cain realized now that his father had never understood even the basics of that. *Pure Sight is truth*, the old man had said, *it's seeing past the lies*. But for Cain, seeing past the lies was everything he had been trying to do since his father's death. His father was the greatest liar, the worst kind of thief, denying him the basic rights that any child should have. The right to run and play in the woods; the right to revel in wild imagination instead of staid histories; the right to explore food, music, the feel of damp grass on his feet and the sun on his face.

It took him until evening to realize why this small print, with its new hint of color, should draw him so much. It was because it was something he had created himself, expressing his desire to move on by his own undeveloped creativity. And that felt very good.

That evening he chose to sing instead of listen to music, and cook instead of eat a frozen dinner. He felt as far away from his father's influence as he had ever been.

After one more look at the transformed painting, he went to bed happy, almost content. The taste of dinner lingered on his tongue. He had pushed the chest back into the corner of the living room, and it felt light, as though containing nothing but air. He was not confident enough to open it—not yet—but his fear of it had receded to a memory, rather than something fresh and heavy.

He left the curtains open and felt the moonlight where it touched his bare skin.

Cain is in the basement room again, his older sleeping mind in the young version of himself, and he does not remember this at all. The room is dark, silent, bereft of odors, and he is sitting on the floor with his arms raised on either side. He is terrified with the knowledge of what is happening and what must have already happened. If he touches the floor, the siren will berate the contact. If he rests his hands on his knees, that blast of sound will hit him again. Tears threaten, but he tries to hold them back, his older dreaming mind finding it just as difficult as the young Cain. He pants with the effort of keeping his arms raised, but there is no feel of clothing against his chest or stomach. He moves slightly, and feels his sweat-slick skin sticking to the floor. He is naked in the dark, terrified, and he hates and loves his father at the same time. He does not know which version of himself feels which.

Cain coughs with the effort of holding back tears, the breath wafts against his hand, and the siren blasts into his skull. He cries out and clasps his hands to his ears, and the siren blasts again, again, single short explosions less than a second long, each one feeling like hours. Even with his hands over his ears the sound injures him, seeming to enter his body through his skin and flesh to pound at his heart, his ribs, his bones. The more he touches and feels, the more the siren erupts.

Something shakes him. He does not feel its

touch, cannot discern where it is holding on, but he is being pushed roughly back and forth. He lets go of his ears and raises his hands, and the siren ceases. The shaking, however, continues. And now there is a presence in the dark before him. It has no real weight, but still it fills space, and as the voice whispers in his ear Cain knows the shadow has touched him at last.

"I can get you away from the old fuck for a while. It won't be much of a rest, but it'll be a relief. Come with me."

Cain shakes his head, unable to believe that the shadow is real. His father would know of it, and its touch on his skin—though he cannot actually feel where it is making contact—would surely have ignited the siren again.

"Don't be an idiot! I know you know me. You accepted me months ago—years ago, depending on who I'm talking to—so don't shake your head at me. You want this?"

Cain shakes his head again. The violent shuddering stops, but then something forces his arm down and his hand slaps against his penis.

Cain hears the shadow's laughter a split second before the siren drowns it out.

The tears are flowing now, and he leans forward so that they drip straight onto the floor.

"Crybaby," the shadow says. "You going to let the crazy fuck beat you? Get up. Get up! *Wake* up!"

Still, the shaking. And now Cain is on his back, protected from the floor by some sort of material, and though he can feel it against his skin, the siren stays silent.

"You're not real," Cain whispers.

"And what's real?" the shadow whispers in his ear, shaking him again with a final violent nudge. "Your mad father's Pure Sight? Pah!" And then it bites him.

Cain snapped awake sprawled on the floor next to his bed, sheets and blankets twisted around his legs. He thrashed his arms, kicked his legs at whatever was biting him, rolled over in an attempt to break free, but succeeded only in entangling himself even more.

"Leave me!" he shouted, but there was no response.

Moonlight bathed the scene. Cain shoved against the floor with his feet, pushing himself back against the wall, and looked around the room. There were shadows, but none of them moved or spoke, none of them seemed deep. It may still be there, though. Watching and smiling. But it was no longer *biting*.

Slowly he calmed, his heart relaxing back toward normal, the sweat on his skin drying into the cool air. His arm hurt where the shadow had bitten him in his dream. He stood, the sheets still tangled around him, and reached for the bedside lamp. Squinting against the sudden light, he looked at his arm, turning it this way and that, but there was no mark there at all.

You'll always have nightmares, the Voice had told him, *it's the way your mind deals with what's happened to you. They're not pleasant, but they serve a purpose. They purge you. Imagine keeping all those memories, that fear and rage, bottled up inside?*

"Nightmare," Cain muttered.

He heard humming from the living room. It was that tune, the one he could never place, the same tune the shadow had hummed to him years before trapped in his father's house. He shook his head. He bit his lip and pinched his thigh. But he was already awake. The humming was muted and distant, and Cain knew why. It was coming from the chest. That shadow he had locked away, the impossibility from his childhood, was humming him a nighttime serenade.

"Shut up!" Cain whispered. He did not want to shout in case he woke his neighbors, and he almost laughed at how ridiculous that was. They were playing with him, toying with his mind, and he was afraid of waking them up.

The humming continued. The unidentified tune was a theme to his life.

"Shut *up!*" he said again, dropping the bedclothes, pulling on his jeans and shirt before walking to the door. He switched on the hallway light and glanced at the picture he had changed, taking strength from his action. The humming seemed to falter for a few seconds.

"Afraid?" Cain asked. "Afraid I have a mind of my own?"

The only answer was a low, deep chuckle from inside the chest. It sounded like a growl.

"You're not real," Cain said. "You never were."

"How's the arm?" the voice said. "Hope it didn't hurt too much, but I had to wake you up. Had to, because you have to see."

"I'm not listening to you."

"It's not Sister Josephine that uses the basement, it's all of them."

That circle of chairs, Cain thought.

"That's right."

He moved to the living room door, turned on the light, and stared at the chest. Watching it changed nothing. The humming started again, the chest remained still, and Cain should have burnt it or dumped it or cut it into pieces.

"I'm killing you," he said. "That hurt you, the painting I touched, didn't it? It offended you that I can find my own mind."

The humming paused, and then a huge laugh erupted from the chest. It was so loud that wood squealed as it vibrated and the chest thumped on the floor.

"I *want* you to find your mind! What, you think I'm your fucking mad *father*?"

I know you're not, Cain thought, but there was no certainty there at all. He had no idea of anything. He glanced back over his shoulder, and from this distance the painting looked exactly as it had before he'd touched it. He may as well have not bothered.

"You think I'm that mad *fuck?* Go to the basement and see. See what you're missing because of him. Just *see!*"

"I'll live without you," Cain whispered, his words slow and so filled with feeling. His body was on fire, nerve endings sparkling beneath his skin, his balls tingling. He was plugged into something he did not know he had, and though he had never been brave, he felt pride at confronting this thing. It was a shadow that could never be, the manifestation of his father's madness and his own confused love and hate of that man, and now it was trying to steer him. He never believed that he would be its master, but now, listening to a phantom voice from the chest that contained it, Cain truly believed that he was going to be all right.

"Of course you will," the shadow said. "I don't wish for anything different. I'm *for* you, Cain, not against you."

"Go away," Cain said.

"Then go to the basement." The voice fell silent, the humming stopped, and Cain knew without touching it that the chest was empty. He moved into the living room and lifted it by one of the metal handles. It felt even lighter than the wood and metal that made it up. And Cain felt strong.

He knew he was foolish to go, but it felt as though he had told himself.

Creeping down the staircase from the second floor felt like being back in his father's house. Complete stillness and silence surrounded him, yet the potential for violence accompanied his every step, a breath held and waiting to bellow. He was afraid of the siren, but there were still other dangers much less known. He had chosen not to use the staircase lighting, in case it alerted anyone to his midnight jaunt. There could have been anything on the next stair ready to trip him. Four steps down someone could have been standing there, hands outstretched, nails sharpened, ready to rip at his eyes and claw out his throat. Strange that the face Cain saw in this image belonged to George.

But the darkness did not frighten him. He was used to the darkness. And knowing more than he should, he was able to mentally see his route down to the basement unimpeded and empty.

Still he kept quiet, not wishing to wake anyone. He passed Magenta's door and imagined her inside, asleep and dreaming of everyone she had ever been. Whistler's door presented him with nothing, so Cain headed down to the ground floor, hand slipping along the rail to guide his steps.

As he paused outside Sister Josephine's door, he thought he heard muttering from inside. Maybe she was praying. Or perhaps she had something that hummed to her as well. Cain looked around, startled, wondering whether his own shadow had followed him down. But everything was still and shadows sat where they were supposed to be, waiting for dawn to drive them down.

Artificial light from the street bled through obscure glazing in the front door, providing a subtle illumination to the lobby. Cain was able to step right up to the nun's door without touching it. He put his ear to the wood and held his breath. He could still hear the mumbling, but Flat One was as silent as an innocent's sleep. He moved along to George's flat, and that was when he realized where the sound was coming from.

He should have known from the instant he first heard it. The shadow had told him where to go after all, and now he knew why. The basement was alive, lit from within, light bleeding beneath the door and marring the floor like an immovable stain. The voices came from within.

Cain could just discern individual voices. Not the words—they were distorted by the bulk of the house—but one or two of the owners he knew. Peter, scared of being underground, chattered and laughed. Somebody else echoed the laughter and said a few deep, gravelly words. Whistler. A woman's voice came next, and Cain could not make out whether it belonged to Magenta, Sister Josephine, or neither of them.

He almost went back upstairs. If he did not investigate any further, then he would discover nothing he did not want to. These people knew each other, they had lived here for longer than he knew, and now they had a stranger in their midst. Why shouldn't they gather for a talk, perhaps a drink? Who was he to intrude?

But in the basement, at three in the morning? There were a million better places to meet. It smelled down there, and it was probably cold and damp, and a sudden burst of laughter convinced Cain that he had to see. It reminded him of the merriment he had heard as George stumbled away through the garden, bleeding or giggling to himself. It *excluded* him, and he hated the mockery inherent in that sound.

He had no idea how he could change that, but still he reached for the door handle.

The instant his hand touched the door, the basement fell silent. *And now the siren,* Cain thought, his fingertips caressing cool metal, the taste of fear rich in his mouth. But the sound that came from beyond the door was something else entirely. It was a flowing, whispering whip like a sheet being flicked from one end, and then a thud as something landed on the staircase just beyond the door.

Cain withdrew his hand, but it was too late.

The door was tugged open, light flooded out, and he squinted against the silhouette that stood there. It seemed to absorb the light and project it directly at him, as if to blind, and as he closed his eyes the smell of honey came at him in a wave, warm and sweet as if heated by hot skin.

"Oh, you're such a dreamer," Sister Josephine said.

Cain stepped back in shock, bumping into the opposite wall. *Dreamer*, she had called him, and he must still be dreaming now. Even with the light shining from behind her, her green eyes gleamed bright.

The nun was naked apart from her wimple. Her greased skin glittered, catching the basement light and diffracting it through whatever she had spread across her body. A hundred rainbow smears sheened her skin. In one hand she held a clay pot. Smiling at Cain, she raised it, dipped in her other hand, withdrew it loaded with a thick golden cream. She spread this across her breasts. They shifted beneath her hand, swaying heavily back into place, gleaming. The rest of her body from her heels to her forehead was similarly adorned, shining with impossible light.

"Sneaking around in your sleep, Cain? You've caught me putting on my magic cream."

"It's all a dream, Cain!" someone shouted from the basement, and it was Peter. Whoever else was down there laughed along with him.

Sister Josephine smiled at Cain, never once dropping her eyes as she scooped out more cream and pasted it slowly between her legs, parting her knees slightly to give better access. Her expression was frank and challenging. The scent of honey was strong and it reminded Cain of sex, its tang familiar and yet so unknown when allied to this beautiful woman standing before him.

"Bet you want to give her a hand!" Peter called, and again the laughter from the basement excluded Cain, shoving him back from any hope of acceptance.

"Don't listen to him," Sister Josephine said quietly, bringing her hand across her stomach, her chest, up to her throat and face. "He only mocks you because he can never be you. He doesn't know the Way."

"I'm not dreaming," Cain said. "I've just woken up." A bee buzzed across his vision, lazy in the dark, and disappeared behind Sister Josephine's shoulder.

"Really?" the nun said. She dropped the pot and it fell slowly to the floor, far too slowly, landing upright with hardly a sound. "Hmm," she said, raising her arms, stretching like a cat in front of a fire, "I'm all magicked up." She stepped forward and reached out for Cain, the smell stronger, her body warming the strange cream and permeating the air with its odor.

The urge to reach out and touch her was unbearable. Cain had had sex, but always with women at Afresh, and none of them had looked anything like this. Sister Josephine's green eyes bore into him, and he felt as though they were perusing his soul.

"You can't touch me," the nun said, "because you're still asleep."

She put her hands beneath his armpits and lifted him up. He kept his hands held out from his body, afraid to touch her, feel her warmth, sense her with his fingertips, in case the siren came in and shattered his mind. She seemed to expend no effort in carrying him, and as she walked along the hallway to the stairs, he became certain that she was gliding.

"Don't forget, you're dreaming!" a voice called from the basement, and this one could have been Magenta. Whistler's pipes cooed a few notes. Everyone laughed again, and someone growled, and then they all fell silent as the naked nun took him upstairs.

"You're not walking," Cain said, unable to tear his gaze away from her dazzling eyes. Her breasts brushed against his chest as they moved, their groins touched briefly. Yet he could see only her eyes.

"I told you, I'm all magicked up. What a dreamer, Cain. What a wonderful dreamer you are. You know the Way already, for sure, you just need showing. I'd show you. I would."

"Then show me," he said, not understanding or caring.

"You're asleep."

They were back in his flat, even though he could not remember coming through the door. He heard the buzz of insects, though none were visible. The lights were on. They were still floating inches above the floor. They passed by the picture he had changed, and it shone gold as fresh honey.

Sister Josephine laid him in his bed and took off his clothes. There was no hope in him, no idea that she would join him, because there was so much more to her than sex. *Divine,* he thought, and it sounded right. Even when she pulled off his briefs and set his erection free, he was not embarrassed, and she barely glanced at it before standing and floating back toward the hall.

"I'm dreaming," he said.

Sister Josephine nodded, and something like relief seemed to cloud her eyes. She flicked her hand at the air. A smear of cream left her fingertips, and Cain felt it patter across his body.

"Sweet dreams," she said, and as she left the flat it grew dark once more.

Cain spent an hour after waking thinking about his disturbed sleep. The hidden memory of his father's house to begin with, the torture when he touched, the ongoing experiment to deny him all the sensations of living. And then his strange trip down to the basement, the glowing, magicked-up image that was Sister Josephine, and his desperate need to touch her. Those green eyes of hers had stuck with him, cool memories of glacial intent.

The chest remained silent in the living room, as it always had and always would. It only ever moved in his mind.

And was he *losing* his mind?

When he eventually sat up and saw the smear of cream along his leg, he had almost convinced himself that it had all been a dream.

* * *

At Afresh, the Voice and Face had tried to make a life for Cain. He knew them as the Voice and Face because that is what they had always been to him. To begin with, he had known their real names, but they had not tried to make him use them for very long. Their emphasis had been on enabling him to find his own way, aiding and guiding, but never steering him. If his own preference was to dispense with their names, then that was a part of his progression.

The Face was the first person Cain saw after being taken out of his dead father's house, smiling at him, calming him, soothing him with a look that was part pity, part fascination. It was the honesty of that fascination that stayed with Cain. The Voice was the first Voice he heard, standing behind the Face and beyond Cain's field of vision; he had spoken many casual truths that Afresh had then taken years to prove to Cain. As the smell, the sound, and the feel of his father's house faded behind him, and the wide blue sky looked like a place of freedom for the first time instead of the ceiling of an endless prison, Cain asked the Face and Voice if they would be his friends. They both began to cry, and Cain—young, naive, sheltered, and damaged—saw his own sadness and wretchedness mirrored in them.

He had been sixteen when his father died and he was taken from the house. He had been out of the house many times before, but always in his father's company, and never farther than the local village. Even here there were sights, sounds, and sensations that his father said would pollute his mind,

contaminate the purity that would lead him to Pure
Sight. More often than not, he had remained in the
car with the windows closed and white noise playing through the stereo. People looked inside sometimes, wondering at this pale boy sitting in a locked
car at the height of summer, but Cain's expression
invariably moved them along. Once, some kids
started tapping at the windows like curious birds,
pulling faces, wanting to be friends but not quite
knowing how to deal with the peculiarities of
Cain's situation; they could hear the white noise,
and they could see the sweat staining Cain's
clothes. Their eyes were curious and searching, but
Cain could give nothing back. One of them smiled,
and Cain turned away; he knew *how* to smile, but
not yet *why*. The kids' faces were browned by freedom, their eyes alight and alive, and their elbows
and knees were scarred and scabbed with self-
inflicted adventure. Cain's only wound was the
continually fresh sore of the siren. His father burst
from the shop and started raging at the children,
and Cain closed his eyes to shut out the sight. He
kept them shut, comforted by the dark and the
white noise, until they were home.

Each trip from the house had exacerbated Cain's
sense of loneliness, of not being real. He was his father's son, but not his own person. He pinched
himself and bit the inside of his cheek, alone and in
his father's company, to see whether it felt and
tasted different both times. It did not. But that did
not convince Cain that he was anything other than
his father's subject.

The Voice and Face spent long hours, longer

days, trying to convince Cain that his father had loved him. They pointed to all the good things he had done: the access to a huge library, the years he spent teaching Cain the sciences. And later, when they thought that Cain was ready to read them, they let him have his father's journals. They were filled with scientific ramblings and extensive, wandering talk of Pure Sight, much of it so obscure that even Cain could make no sense of it. The Voice commented that it was almost as if Pure Sight were a place, not a supposed state of mind, and his father had spent years trying to persuade Cain to travel there. If so, it was a place not of this world, somewhere with no rules or laws, no controlling factors or forces other than truth, the *real* truth, the truth of things exposed and made clear by one's own purity.

Cain read the first few pages, understanding little, and then he burned the journals in the gardens at Afresh. The Voice and Face came running, but Cain said, "I'm only burning what damaged me." And much as they seemed distraught, they left him alone.

He had regretted that burning for a long time. It destroyed much of what had hurt him—the evidence of it at least, and his father's mad reasoning behind why he had treated his son so—but sometimes, especially as he grew older, Cain wondered just how much of himself had been incinerated in those flames. His history lived in his father's words. He had watched as the books blackened and spat the ash of their past at the sky, and in dreams it was his own flesh peeling off and rising on columns of

Tim Lebbon

heat. And though physically it was painless, the
emotional hurt was immense and irreparable.

Cain sometimes woke up crying from his dreams,
and when the Voice asked what was wrong, he said
he was mourning his dead father.

Chapter Five
Player

Cain showered, dressed, drank coffee and ate toast for breakfast, and all the while he was barely there. He may as well have been back in his father's house, with the minimal attention he paid to the taste and smell of the morning. He was at the basement door with the naked nun, listening to the laughter as she flew him upstairs to bed like some naughty boy caught spying on adult things. He was out chasing an injured or laughing George, losing himself in the lanes and alleys between streets, listening to something eating in the dark. He was visiting Peter in Heaven, and although he had never been inside he knew that the dilapidated shell of that house was misleading, and therein lay hidden truths. His father had wanted him to have Pure Sight, and he had it now, because everything was a deception. Knowing that was surely emphasizing his own purity. The others were deceiving him, playing games with the new residents because they had nothing better to do. Perhaps they knew each other so well that an outsider was always subject to the same treatment and ridicule. He remembered the hearty laughter coming from the basement, and whether he had really been down there or not, the overt mockery in that was more than evident.

Even from Magenta. She was the only one he had met and thought he could get along with. He had heard her own laughter mixed in—at least, he was quite certain it had been hers—and that cut surprisingly deep.

They were excluding him. He had spent so much of his life alone—the Face and the Voice were the only two people he had ever considered as friends—and now, given the chance to create his life anew, make his own friends, he was more alone than ever. That saddened him, but he was not surprised. He knew that he was far from normal, whatever they told him at Afresh, and yet he still had no real idea of what normal meant. He had extensive knowledge of some subjects, gleaned from all his reading, but very little in that most important area of all: life. His father had seen to that.

Cain could find no discernible emotion within him in connection with his father; no love or hate, no curiosity or disinterest. It was almost as if he had become one of those obscure scientists in the books he gave Cain to read, so obsessed with their own purpose that they lose sight of themselves and those around them.

Cain never wanted to be like that. He wanted to find out what normal was, and become it. Fuck Pure Sight. And fuck anyone who tried to persuade him otherwise. His father had made him unique, he hadn't been born that way, and now he so wanted to shed the skin of his old life that it almost hurt.

Finishing his breakfast, he looked from the window, down into the garden where he had followed George. He could see the tree beneath which George's shadow had paused, and where he himself had knelt to see whether there were any signs on the ground. That was where the siren had hit him. From up here it seemed impossible that this garden was the same place. That was patently absurd, but then so were naked flying nuns. He closed his eyes and Sister Josephine was there, her piercing green eyes finding him easily, heavy breasts glistening with magic cream. Cain stood, angry at the stirring in his trousers, angry that she could do that to him. He felt the whole building laugh at his arousal.

He would go for a walk, buy some food and drink, find a park and spend the day there reading. And while he was reading, he would be thinking of what was happening here. Should he tell the Face, the Voice? If he did, would they take him away? For all that had happened, he still relished and valued his newfound freedom. He had been saved at Afresh. But the thought of returning was almost as painful as the idea of going back to his father's house.

So he would sit and read and think, and somehow he would grasp hold of these flailing threads of his new life and tie them up.

* * *

The taxi dropped him at the corner of the largest park in the city. The gates were cast iron, extravagant and old. The trees growing along the park's perimeter were huge, a variety of species obviously planted at least a hundred years ago to provide a natural barrier. There were railings set into the top of a natural stone wall, their spiked points dulled with successive coats of green paint. An old gatehouse stood to one side of the gate, its windows and door bricked up years before, holding only stale air inside. It gave the entrance to the park a sense of safety and tranquillity. And Cain would be anonymous in there. Alone as ever, but to everyone else in the park he would be just another face. They would not know his story, his background or his reasons for being there. For all they knew he could be normal.

There was a row of shops across from the park, and he bought sandwiches, potato chips, chocolate, and a bottle of flavored water. The shopkeeper barely glanced up as he paid, and Cain wondered at the myriad stories that woman must miss in the eyes of her customers. She would never know his own tale, but for once, instead of making him feel even more alone, this made him feel special.

As he passed into the park, time slowed down. He could still hear the vehicular bustle of the city, but it seemed so much more distant, as if the trees around the perimeter sucked in chaos and breathed out serenity. It reminded him of the feeling he had experienced upon first entering the garden of 13 Endless Crescent, but this was more benevolent, and not as loaded with mystery. This was simply nature wending its way through time, and mankind benefiting from its journey.

He chose a path at random and followed it into the heart of the park. The place was very well kept, planted areas neat and trimmed, the grass cut and watered, and there were benches at frequent intervals. Many of them bore memorial plaques for people who had loved to visit here. There were others in the park, but not many; school and work must keep the place quiet during the day. He passed a woman pushing her baby in a stroller, and they exchanged polite smiles. The baby gurgled something at him and Cain turned away, embarrassed. A dog ran up and sniffed around his feet, and a man called it away, apologizing, throwing a ball and sending his hound plunging into a bank of undergrowth. It growled, there were a few seconds of panicked rustling, and a squirrel darted from the bushes and ran up a nearby tree. The dog bounded after it, the ball forgotten.

Cain walked on, enjoying the heat of the day and the peaceful world around him. People found peace in different ways. A young woman skated by on roller skates, her curves accentuated by her tight clothing, knees and elbows padded. She ignored Cain as he moved aside to let her pass. A woman lay on the grass, reading. A man walked among a rose garden, sniffing blooms. Farther into the park, several women sat with their carriages in a circle while their toddlers ran about, fell over, laughed and cried. Cain did not know any of these people, and they did not know him. They were all alone here, and what stories did they have to tell?

The man sniffing the blooms, was he a painter of lost souls?

The woman reading her book, could she imagine unreality into being?

The roller skater, did she have a blade on her belt, even now sticky with the blood of a recent kill?

Cain doubted it, but he did not know. He knew no one. Everyone here—all these people having fun, relaxing, exercising, reading, pontificating, being busy living—could be as strange as the people in his house. Some could be even stranger. Every story is particular, and if "normal" is merely an average life, there are infinite extremes either side of that to be filled.

Cain had been thrown in with a group of people he had never met, and for once, living life on his own for the first time, he had to learn about them himself. Back at Afresh, any new resident was walked around the grounds and introduced, an act thought by the administrators to be an essential part to fitting in. But Cain was starting to realize that fitting in meant discovering things for yourself. Everyone perceived things differently, even the truth.

He had come here to rest, and he tried to cast such thoughts aside.

He walked on. The path twisted and turned and he lost himself in the park, purposely losing track of the junctions he passed over and the turns he took. He passed by pergolas, benches, and small ponds, and eventually emerged from a wooded area onto a gentle grassed slope, broken here and there by single trees or flower beds. At that moment there was no one else in sight, so he walked twenty paces out onto the slope and sat down in the sun. There was shade beneath the trees, but he would move there later.

The view was stunning. At the bottom of the long slope was the main lake, obscured here and there by tall trees. A flock of ducks drew lines across its surface, and there were a few rowing boats out, their occupants mainly just sitting back and enjoying the slight movement as their heartbeats rocked the boats.

Cain ate his food, drank some water, started to read. He was reading *The Glamour* again, and as ever he found it easy relating to the characters' experience with invisibility. Cain felt that he could enter a room and remain unseen by anyone there. The sound of birds in the trees around him gave a curiously apt sound track to the novel, singing as if they were alone, without any humans ready to make out the secrets in their songs. He smiled at this, pleased that he could nurture such thoughts. His father had not made him that way.

An hour passed, he finished the drink, and he had read twenty pages of the novel. And when he realized that for the last fifteen minutes he had been reading the same page over and over, he tried to tell himself that the peace of the park was distracting.

Too many birds, singing and whistling their way through the day. Little kids playing and crying somewhere, their mothers cooing unintelligible succor to them. The occasional swish of leaves as a breath of air danced through the trees. The park was talking to him, calling for him to relax. He closed the book and lay back, content to listen.

Cain heard the sound of music carried on the breeze. He jumped up and looked out for Whistler. It was surely not his neighbor, probably a car stereo blasting from one of the roads outside. But his instant reaction brought home the truth. He was not here to relax, he was here to decide what to do.

He picked up his litter and his book, bagged everything, and walked down toward the lake.

They had been playing him. It was ironic that the efforts they were expending to fool and confuse him made him feel more alone than ever. His pursuit of George had felt arranged, though he had no proof of that. Last night, however, was clearly a play from start to finish. And the only way to become involved in a play and influence its outcome was to become a player.

It was as easy as that. Cain's mind was made up before he even realized it, and by the time he reached the lake and started walking around it, he was making plans. He would not let his dreams control him, and he would not let the others in the house control his dreams. He would declare a new start to his life—here, now, in this park, at this precise instant—and determine to shed once and for all the stifling memories of his past. The dreams may still come, but he would better them. Magenta and Whistler and the others may toy with him for their own amusement, but from now on he would play his own part, not merely sit it out as a passive victim of their games. From that would come acceptance, and perhaps even more of an understanding of how the world worked. To make his own life, he had to understand others. He would not let them frighten him away. Perhaps they *were* all odd, but they certainly did not have the monopoly on weirdness.

Pleased with himself, Cain bought an ice cream from a van and sat beside the lake. He heard music again, drifting across the water as if risen from its depths, and this time it was not the borrowed echo of a car stereo. He recognized the style of this, the sound, the rounded vibrations and exhalations of pan pipes. And as he looked across to the far side of the lake, he dropped the ice cream in his lap.

Even at this distance, Cain knew that the figure was Whistler. Tall, gray hair tied in a ponytail, his long black coat flapping out behind him even though the breeze was only slight, he walked across the grass slope where Cain had been sitting ten minutes earlier. And he was not alone. Like some modern-day Pied Piper, he led a strange procession after him: a woman pushing her baby in a buggy, a cat slinking from tree to tree for cover, a squirrel loping across the grass, several birds flying, hopping, flying again. All of them followed at a distance as if afraid to draw too close. Whistler seemed unaware or unconcerned; he simply played his pipes, strolled along, looking at the ground before him as if the rest of the park held no interest.

"No!" Cain said. He stood, his first inclination to run around the lake. *"No!"* He would catch up with Whistler and quiz him, or follow along with the others to see where they were being led. "It's my own life. Leave me *be!*" He turned, brushing ice cream from his crotch, and started running around the lake.

Whistler had obviously followed him to the park and waited to make his presence known, expecting Cain to fall for the dupe and follow him. And now was the time Cain could make his own play. For whatever purpose, they were toying with him, his decision to flip expectations was about to be put to the test.

With Whistler here, Cain would be able to break into his flat. Perhaps then he would see what the tall man was all about.

As he ran from the park a shadow passed over him, fleeing rapidly across the grass and disappearing into a clump of trees. A waft of warm honey came to him and faded just as quickly. He looked up, but saw only a flicker as something disappeared above the trees.

Too big to be a bird, he thought. But he shook his head and ran on. They were not going to trap him like that. His mind was made up.

The street was deserted and the house seemed quiet. The garden welcomed him with its customary covert rustlings, but he would not be drawn by them today. The front door was locked, so he used his key, slipped inside, and closed it again behind him. The lobby was still. A clock ticked somewhere out of sight, the doors to the basement and back garden were firmly shut, and he heard no signs of life from upstairs. If Magenta was in her flat above him she was motionless, perhaps waiting for him to move first.

He hurried upstairs and stood outside Whistler's door. For a second he had a sudden flush of doubt. What if the man in the park had not been Whistler? But Cain was *certain*. It was too much of a coincidence for it to have *not* been Whistler. He would not let false doubts derail him now. He listened at the door, holding his breath, waiting there for a full minute. There were no sounds at all from inside; no music, no cautious footsteps.

Cain tried the handle, but the door was locked. He held the handle down, nudged at the door with his shoulder, and heard the frame creak. It did not sound very strong, but breaking in was not the right thing to do. Whistler had done nothing to him—none of them had, not really—and there was no justification for smashing his way into the man's flat, invading his privacy, doing something that Cain would hate having done to himself.

Those doubts again, assaulting his confidence.

Still, Cain turned the handle again, worked it back and forth, then listened at the door. No response from inside.

If only he *could* get in . . .

Cain had seen lots of films and read lots of books at Afresh, finding early on that his preference was for the fantastic. He had lived impossibilities, and now he wanted to read of them as well. Many of his preconceptions of how life was on the outside came from his viewing and reading. Any single source would have been damaging; basing his understanding of life on, say, *Something Wicked This*

Way Comes would not be the best way to adjust. But as a cumulative whole they not only presented him with a whole world, but made it as wide and varied as possible. And in that world, people sometimes did foolish things. Like leaving spare keys on the tops of door frames.

Cain felt above Whistler's door, and his fingers touched metal. He and the pan pipe player had obviously read some of the same books.

Already he felt guilt, cold as the key in his palm. It stared up at him accusingly, daring him to use it, urging him not to. After all the bad that had been done to him, Cain had no wish to unload it on other people. Yet simply looking around the flat could not be harmful, could it?

He felt alone in the house, and not only because it was deserted. Some people claimed that they would rather be hated than ignored, but for Cain anonymity would be preferable. At least that way he could still live his own life. Loneliness was something he was more than used to; being actively picked on was not.

If entering Whistler's flat gave him the upper hand in any way, then it could not be a bad thing.

It's your life now, the Voice had said. Cain was terrified by that, but he agreed. And he had to protect himself.

For some reason, slipping the key into the lock brought on a fear of the siren. Perhaps the thrill he was feeling at acting for himself was something his father would have abhorred. Pure Sight, the old man would have said, relies on purity of mind and soul. Cain was happy to sully himself.

The door swung open and the siren remained absent. Glancing around the landing, checking that no one had witnessed his crime, Cain moved inside Whistler's flat and shut the door behind him.

Wherever he had been, he had always belonged there. His father's house had been maintained to keep Cain within its walls, for whatever nefarious reasons. Afresh was not only a home, it was a secure unit, dedicated to treating Cain and holding him within its grasp. Here, in a stranger's flat, he had stepped outside the realms of his own existence and entered someone else's world.

Everything was different, and for a minute he was overwhelmed by the rush of sensory input, remembering the siren again, the agony in his head and the anger in his heart. There was a heavy smell of herbs permeating the flat, warm and fresh and complex. The carpet was pink, the walls a luxurious green, the paint so textured that it looked like felt lining the hallway. Pictures hung at dozens of random locations on the walls, all seemingly chosen at random; landscapes, impressionist art, portraits, technical detailing, abstracts, flowers, animals, nudes, sex images, pictures verging on pornography, religious iconography, and more. Walking along the hall felt like taking a dozen journeys, and in the end Cain closed his eyes, breathing heavily and wishing he were back in his flat. There at least familiarity would keep him calm.

Whistler's living room was such a startling contrast that the plain white walls, carpet, and monotone furniture hit Cain just as hard. It felt so empty, so soulless that he almost backed straight out, preferring the intensity of the hallway over such a sensation of nothing. But then he noticed the glass-fronted bookcase in the corner filled with red-spined tomes, and he went to investigate. The doors were unlocked, and Cain opened one leaf to read the book titles. He was not sure what to expect; he had barely spoken to Whistler, and hearing his music so briefly could communicate nothing of the man's intellect. But judging by the explosion of style in the hallway, he guessed that the books would cover a multitude of subjects, both factual and fictional. What he had not expected was that each one had been written by Whistler himself.

There were more than a hundred books in the bookcase, all of them titled *My Philosophy*. They were numbered 1 to 113 and shelved in exact numerical order. Each book was identical save for the number, and they all looked new and untouched. Perhaps they were empty and awaiting inspiration. Or perhaps that emptiness itself was Whistler's statement.

Cain rested his fingertips on Volume 23, felt the soft coolness of real leather, closed his eyes, and enjoyed the sensation. He did not know what he should not, and he was glad. The siren remained silent, and he was grateful for that also. The idea of his father's face hovered into view in his mind's eye—he had never been able to remember the old man's true features, not exactly—but Cain was not afraid. He tried to make his father smile, but it was not a memory he was certain of, so the expression broke up and fled into the dark.

He opened his eyes, shook his head, and closed

the bookcase door. He could not intrude this much. He had his own life to make, and part of the foundation for that was a determination to be a good person. Not like his father. If Cain ever had children, he wanted them to look at him and *believe* that he was good.

He glanced into the kitchen. There were vegetables hanging from hooks, colorful crockery from a dozen exotic locations, framed photographs on the walls showing animals in varying stages of slaughter, from alive and breathing, to butchered and chopped. A pig's head sat on the draining board, a trail of black blood still leaking slowly into the sink. Cain stared at its eyes, but their glitter remained still, their insides dull. That he had expected more disturbed him greatly, and he turned and hurried back through the living room and into the hallway.

Cain had learned that Whistler was as different to him as he was to Sister Josephine. They were *all* different, and perhaps *everyone* was this different. Not just those in this building, but the others in the street, the district, the city, the country. His reading had conveyed so much, but as the Face had told him, there was no substitute for real life. Maybe every book he read could not even begin to touch on the wonders of existence. Perhaps the world was much larger and more diverse than he could possibly imagine. His imagination had, after all, been held prisoner until he was a teenager.

"Fuck you, Dad," he said quietly, meaning it, and his anger boiled up in a way he had never experienced before. He should not be scared of Whistler, but his father had hobbled his development so much that all he could feel was suspicion and fear. He should not be worried about the way Sister Josephine had manipulated him, but he had no idea who she was, where she came from, or what she meant. If it were not for his father, at least he would have some idea, some experience or knowledge that could perhaps help him to understand the nun, at least a little. She was no more to him than a character in the books he had been reading since his teens; almost beyond belief. He could still not see her as a *person*. "Fuck you, and the Pure Sight you so wanted to give me. So where is it? Does it help me now? Can it make me see my way?" *Old fool,* he thought. But already he had said too much.

Sometimes Cain's mind played tricks on him and he thought he was actually back at the house.

His father is still alive, Cain is in the room, his mind is ruled by the siren, and his life at Afresh and now beyond is a dream given to him by his father. *Dream yourself to Pure Sight,* the old man says. And in this strange dream of freedom Cain meets people he can never know, and they show him things that can never be. His father watches him, ready for the moment when his son's Pure Sight will at last be revealed.

Chapter Six
Follower

He was about to leave the flat when he saw an extra door in the hallway. Cain had one bedroom, Whistler seemed to have two, and the door to the second was closed, bearing a sign reading, "The Followers."

There's only bad in there, Cain thought. But he was not sure whether it was something he should not know, or perhaps simply fear.

The door was not locked. If the room contained secrets it should have been, but that was no justification for Cain to open the door. He did so anyway, stepping back in surprise at the smell that wafted out. It was the stink of age: must and mold, dust and old, old ideas. It seemed to subdue the colors in the hallway, as if an obfuscating gas had escaped from the Followers' room. Maybe it was Whistler's dressing room? He was not a modern dresser for sure, and the aroma of age and mothballs seemed to fit this image. But that idea seemed *not* to fit.

This smell was more important that that; it held more weight than thoughts of which trousers or jacket to wear. It could have been the stench of an ancient tomb, broken open for the first time in centuries and laden with the timeless musings of the lonesome dead. Smells like that would surely carry a curse.

The bad smell should have discouraged Cain from going any further. And on its own, it would have. But Cain had other senses, and though he heard nothing, he saw a thin slice of what was in the room. And though he tasted nothing but dust, he felt the power of that place drawing him in. It did not feel dangerous—it was too impersonal for that, too remote—but it *did* feel daring. Through the slightly open door he saw a line of shelves, and he gasped at what they contained. Animals, all of them stuffed, mounted on plinths or backboards. He nudged the door a little wider and revealed more of the same. There were several squirrels in a woodland tableau, though Cain had never heard of squirrels grouping together like this before. Two badgers sniffed at the muzzles of dogs—a Labrador, and another breed confused by bad taxidermy—instead of snarling at them. Birds posed in midair, courtesy of stiff wires and blocks of wood.

If these are the Followers, who were they following? Cain thought. He remembered what he had seen in the park, and shook his head. That was just too weird.

The room was divided by at least two high bookcases, staggered to form partitions that created a route through turning left, right, left again. There must have been a window at the other end, but as yet it was hidden from view. The smell was still there, and now that he knew where it came from—dusty pelts, dried skins—it was even more repellent. He wanted to go, leave this sickness behind, and he actually took a step back. But a tail protruded around the first corner in the room, bushy and red. Cain had only ever seen a fox in books.

He rounded the corner and the fox was eating a chicken, the frozen grasp of its jaws matched in detail by the crepe-paper gush of blood from the chicken's ruptured neck. Here at least was a realistic depiction. And yet on a shelf above the fox a rat toyed with a legless cat, the rodent's paw stretched out as if dealing a never-ending coup de grâce.

The most disquieting thing about the displays was not the lack of movement but the utter silence. Everywhere he looked there were animals running, fighting, cowering, sleeping, or fucking—two field mice had been truly mounted after stuffing—and yet the room was totally quiet. It was so unnatural that Cain made noise on purpose, pulling his feet across the carpet, coughing, making sure that he was not alone in here with the stillness. He drove the silence out. And when he realized that he had started humming the unidentified tune from his dreams, he turned to leave.

He expected a shadow to be waiting behind him, but there was only the fox and chicken.

What all this meant, he could not begin to understand. An innocent hobby of taxidermy, perhaps, but it felt so much more than that. There was no care over how the animals were represented, for a start. These were not considered studies of the creatures in their natural habitats, but creations for Whistler's own entertainment. Why else would the badgers be sniffing at the friendly dogs, the rat fighting the cat?

And—

There was something else. Turning around, looking at everything from a new angle, Cain realized at last. Every animal had its head cocked, as if listening to distant music too high-pitched to be audible to any human observer. The fox, chicken in its mouth, held the same pose, as if in life the chicken had been forgotten. The field mice were paused in their rutting. Squirrels had abandoned their search for nuts. It did not matter how accurately or not they were posed, each animal was listening for something. And though they were all dead, dusty, and rank, Cain truly believed that they could all hear.

He bent down and stared into the fox's eyes, but they were dulled with concentration.

Cain knew he should leave. He was terrified of what he had found. He'd had the clever idea that by coming here he would be taking positive action, but now he was only more confused. However hard he tried to convince himself that Whistler was as normal as a million other people, he knew that he was wrong. Cain was blinkered and damaged, and perhaps governed more by his past than he had yet admitted to himself, but he was not stupid. Whistler was not normal, and now Cain had invaded his flat, seen his secrets, disturbed his space to such an extent that the man would surely know.

The smell was out of the room, the pig's eyes had seen him in the kitchen, his shadow had passed across the pictures in the hall. Cain had left his mark simply by being here, and he had no idea what form Whistler's revenge would take.

But there was that one last turn in the room, tempting him with secrets. Hidden away by one tall unit, Cain had only to take three steps to round the end of the bookcase and see the rest of the display. It was impossible, but it seemed even quieter than the parts he had already seen. Perhaps because it had not yet been polluted with his breath or his heartbeat.

So quiet . . . almost as if something waited for him around there.

He hummed that unknown tune again, waiting for the shadow to reveal itself, but he had no audience other than the dead animals, forever listening. He wondered if they heard him and knew the tune.

Indecision almost made Cain shiver; he needed to go one way to get out of here, and the other to see what was left. His mind tore him both ways. He rested his hand on the end of the bookcase, so that a simple lean would enable him to see around the corner. There was a window behind there; he could see the splash of natural light, he was so *close*.

He should go, flee Whistler's flat now, get back to his own place and phone the Voice for a talk, comfort, some reassurance—

He had to see, even though he knew that to turn this corner would take him another step toward somewhere dark—

Humming the tune, Cain leaned around the corner.

He had no idea of what to expect, but the smiling face disarmed him completely. His heart thumped hard, double speed, and a cool twist of shock reached up into his throat and prevented him from drawing breath.

Magenta . . .

The woman sat in a rocking chair, hands clasping the handles, her brunette hair brushed straight and flowing over her shoulders, feet placed together on the floor, red-painted toenails visible in her open-toed sandals, neat trousers, expensive blouse, jewelry catching the daylight filtering through the curtained window and throwing it back at Cain. And her face, expertly made-up and beatific, smiled at him from her place of rest.

She had Magenta's eyes . . . and yet the rest of her was different. The face was rounder, not long and pinched. Her hands were small and dainty, whereas Magenta's were large, long-fingered, used to hard work. Her nose was smaller, her mouth wider. And the smile on her face—constant as she sat with her head cocked to one side, listening— was empty and dull. A smile that Magenta would never give, whoever she was impersonating, because there was so much more to her than that.

And yet those eyes, powerful and piercing, even with no moisture to give them depth.

"Magenta?" he whispered, instantly feeling foolish. The woman was stuffed after all.

Her eye flickered, and Cain fell back against the shelves. An ocelot's beak stabbed him behind the ear, a rat's teeth grazed his palm, but he could not take his eyes from the woman in the chair. *Rocking chair,* he thought. *If she were alive, her heartbeat would set it moving.* But there was no movement . . . other than those eyes.

He stared into them, trying to see into their depths. They were dry. Perhaps the movement had been caused by a bird flying past the window, subtly altering the light coming through?

Or perhaps she was alive.

She stared, and Cain stared back. He could hardly breathe. The tension was unbearable, a thick silence that one of them had to break soon, building and building toward some terrible pressure. He held his breath and heard his heart, but there was nothing else. She would laugh soon, unable to carry on the charade any longer. The trick had been played, and however complex the chain of events that had led Cain here, they had succeeded in pulling him in. Perhaps now they would leave him alone.

Cain took a sudden step toward the woman, hoping it would startle her into moving. The rocking chair remained still, and her eyes were now staring at his chest. He was so terrified that he burst out laughing.

He would touch her, see if she was warm . . . but that was something he could never do. No matter how long he stood here, the finality of that touch would keep him away.

If she's not alive, then Whistler murdered her! Cain thought, the true horror of what he was seeing hitting home for the first time. He had barely had time to think about how she had died.

There was a crash from somewhere else in the building, and Cain recognized it as the front door slamming. He waited for a reaction from the woman—

(*Magenta, it* can't *be Magenta, can it?*)

—but still she stared, head cocked as if listening to Cain's internal ramblings, the fear, the doubt, the dawning realization of the terror behind the scene he had discovered.

Someone was running up the stairs.

Cain turned and threaded his way back between the loaded bookcases, and as he exited the room filled with the Followers, he swore he heard a parting chuckle from inside.

The footsteps had stopped, though he was not sure where. He moved quickly along the colorful hallway, knotted up inside with fear, expecting the siren to sing at any moment. Glancing through the peephole in Whistler's door, he saw that the landing outside was deserted. He opened the front door and prepared to flee.

Peter leaped into view from the right, eyes wide, sweating, perhaps through exertion, perhaps not.

Cain stumbled back and fell onto his backside in Whistler's hallway.

"Quickly!" Peter said. "Here!" He held out his hand, and Cain reached up automatically. The landlord helped him to stand and then pulled him from Whistler's flat. "We have to leave *now!*" he said. "He's coming home!"

Not long before his father died, Cain and he began having real conversations. Thinking about it afterward, Cain had put it down more to the fact that his father was lonely than because Cain himself was growing up. The old man never claimed to miss his wife, but sometimes he stared into space for such long periods of time, his eyes so distant, that he must surely have been thinking of someone long gone. And perhaps he also had the inkling that Cain was somehow approaching whatever epiphany he had planned for him.

"What is Pure Sight?" Cain asked one day.

His father glanced at him, surprised, and went back to peeling apples. They were in the kitchen, a sterile, stainless-steel-lined cell with little color on the walls, and no pandering to decoration. Peel fell to the worktop and formed impromptu twisted sculptures, and Cain wondered whether he could make anything of them. The meanderings of the mind, perhaps. The aimless twisting of lonely thoughts. He felt as alone as his father appeared, though he would never tell him that.

"All this time and you have to ask?" His father rarely looked at him when he spoke, as if afraid of what he would see in his son's eyes.

"All this time and you've never told me."

"Of course I have. I've told you it's the perception of truth, lying at the heart of what makes us real. It transcends civilization, religion, faith in anything but reality. It's the purest thing there is, and to have it is to be blessed." He went on peeling, and for a while the steady *scrape, scrape* was the only sound.

Cain frowned, twirled one of the strings of apple peel around his finger, creating different shapes of loneliness. "You've told me what it's meant to be, but not what *you* think it is."

"I think it is what it's meant to be, and that's what I've told you."

"Not everything is what it's meant to be. The books say we're meant to be with God, but you tell me He isn't there. So how can you be sure of Pure Sight? What is it to you, Dad?" Cain rarely used the familiar, usually managing to communicate with his father without calling him anything. Although cut off from the world, he was more than aware that there was something precious missing between the two of them. He had read of love in history books, and for him it was that distant.

"What is it to me?" His father glanced at Cain and then sighed, setting a half-peeled apple down on the worktop.

Cain sat still for a minute or two, eyes downcast, glancing at his father every now and then to see whether the old man was going to respond. *Angry now,* Cain thought, *and sad too. Sad that it's taken me so long to ask, perhaps. And heartbroken that he has no way to answer.* Even then, at thirteen, he knew things he should not.

"It's nothing to me," his father said, "because I have never known it. And I never will. Age has corrupted me beyond that ultimate knowledge. I'm tainted by time. I've seen too many things, both beautiful and terrible. I've tasted blood and spice, and heard birds singing and people screaming. I've smelled insides turned out and the first spring blooms, and felt summer rain and the acid sting of defeat. I've tried, son. I've tried as hard as I can. But it's way past me now."

"You don't have Pure Sight?" Cain said, aghast,

because every second of his life he had believed his father was trying to pass something down to him, not create it anew.

His father looked at him as he spoke this time, staring into his son's eyes, trying to impart meaning that Cain was too young to appreciate. When he remembered that occasion years later, Cain liked to think it was guilt. Perhaps even the need for forgiveness. "You're still young enough," his father said, "and I've done my best for you."

"But . . ." Cain had no idea of what to say.

"It's back to the room tomorrow," his father said, suddenly stern and distant again. "There's something else we have to do."

Cain never again witnessed the old man so vulnerable. That one time contained the totality of Cain's memory of his father's hidden love. Everything after that was pain and sadness.

As Peter pulled Cain up toward the second floor, the house's front door opened and slammed again. Peter turned, his finger held to his lips to beg silence, and climbed the last three stairs as if walking on glass. Cain followed, fear and confusion persuading him to imitate the landlord. They stood on the small landing outside Cain's room and listened to Whistler find his keys, unlock his flat and enter. He shut the door, and Cain expected him to burst out again within seconds, shouting and raving and seeking the intruder that had broken into his home. But though they stood still for at least two minutes, there were no more noises from Whistler. No shouting, no pan pipes, nothing.

"Keys," Peter whispered, so quietly that he may have only breathed. Cain handed over his keys; Peter unlocked the door and entered his flat. They walked through to the living room, careful not to make any noise in case Whistler heard them, and sat down at the table.

"He's got a dead woman in his flat!" Cain whispered.

Peter shook his head, scratched behind his ear, stood and looked across the street at his dilapidated home.

"I *saw* her! Stuffed, along with a load of animals, all kept in one room. Stinking. *Horrible!*"

Peter did not turn, nor seem to react. From what Cain could see of his face, he now seemed calm and contemplative. Gone was the wide-eyed panic from outside Whistler's door.

"Are you toying with me again? Are you going to *say* anything?"

Peter turned at last, quickly, as if he had just come to an important decision. "I have plenty to say. But not here. Not now. If you're not doing anything later perhaps we can go for a drink, have a chat, and—"

"Stop being so fucking casual about this!" Cain said. He wanted to shout, but Whistler's presence just a few feet below was still strong. "We need to call the police! I'm not going for a drink, I'm getting on the phone right now—"

"Please, Cain," Peter said. He sat down again and reached out, grasped one of Cain's hands in his own, held tight. His palms were cool with old sweat. "There's so much more to this than you know. You've barely seen the shadow of the truth."

"You sound like my father." Cain snatched his hand away and stood, pleased at the alarm on Peter's face. "Whatever you have to tell me, nothing detracts from the fact that Whistler has a dead woman in his flat."

"Really?"

"Yes. I saw her."

"Have you seen a dead woman before?"

Dead man, my father, but I was with him for days. I knew for sure. I saw how nature deals with dead things. The black; the rot.

"No."

"Then perhaps she wasn't dead."

"I'm certain she was," Cain said, but then a sound echoed in his memory, the chuckle he may have heard as he was rushing from the room.

"Things aren't always as they seem," Peter said. He clicked his fingers, and as Cain glanced down he could have sworn that Peter's thumb detached, bounced on the table, and rejoined his hand.

"What was *that*?"

"A cheap trick. A sad deception. I don't have it in me to do it for real."

Cain shook his head and stood from the table, staring out at the street, wondering what Whistler was doing below them even now. Checking telltales left across door openings? Sniffing the air, sensing intrusion like a dog?

"So what are 'The Followers'?"

"Whistler's faction. Supporters. Whatever."

"Rats and badgers and, and, and fucking *mice*?"

Peter stared at him as if regarding a petulant child, one that had no knowledge of anything beyond its own introverted existence, its imagination fatally disabled by some fault in its upbringing. And Cain, angry and scared, felt like that child.

At last Peter stood and went to the kitchen, opened the fridge, and took out a bottle of milk. *How can I tell him?* he was thinking, and Cain knew the landlord's mind, yet another thing he should not know. Peter's thoughts were a stew of concerns, from guilt—its subject not apparent—to anger and frustration. And sadness. That was in there too, the same kind of self-indulgent melancholy that had informed Cain's father's voice those final times he and Cain had really conversed. *How can I tell him so much when I don't even know him? He's a stranger to me, and—*

"Sometimes it's easier to deal with strangers," Cain said.

Peter spun around and stared at him, startled, his eyes wide and afraid. "You have it," he whispered. And then he shook his head and went to leave.

"Have what?"

"Something I can never have! Your father strove his whole life to raise it in you, and—"

"You knew my father?"

Peter stood at the living room door, glancing out into the hallway and apparently noticing the altered pictures. He smiled, the expression melting away the fear that had been apparent there before. "He really did go to the extremes, didn't he?"

"I don't understand any of this." Cain felt cold

and alone, and so much like the child Cain that he almost started to cry.

"Come out with me this evening. I'll tell you more. Rest assured, I'm not here to hurt you."

"And what about the others? Are they here to hurt me?"

"They don't know what hurt is," Peter said. "Come across to Heaven at eight. We'll talk." And after one final ambiguous smile, he left Cain's flat without another word.

They don't know what hurt is. That was no answer. And now, with Cain's life turning to riddles the more he tried to make it his own, Cain wondered how much his father had known of hurt.

Cain was desperate to leave the flat, flee the house, but it was that thirty-second journey out of his door and down two flights of stairs that kept him in. He looked down into the street and saw none of Number 13's inhabitants, but that meant that they could be anywhere. Whistler was in, he knew that, although Cain had heard no sounds from below since he had come home. Whatever that tall stranger was doing, Cain did not want to know; he was afraid that much of it involved him. Perhaps he was in his Followers' room right now, rearranging dust that Cain's breath had shifted, seeing the truth of the intrusion reflected in the animals' dead eyes. And the woman? How would she reveal Cain's invasion of her privacy? Perhaps Whistler would play her a tune on his pipes and she would rise, awaken from the deepest sleep of death to impart secrets through leather-dry lips.

He stood and paced his flat, purposely making a noise so that Whistler knew he was in. He switched on the radio and turned it up, enjoying the noise, though loud music was always more of an annoyance than a pleasure for him, itching rather than soothing his eardrums.

The others could be anywhere. What did *they* have to hide in their flats? George, the man he had followed to the place where a dog ate something alive in the dark. Sister Josephine, the nun who had perhaps smeared her naked self with magic cream and flown Cain upstairs to his bed, or perhaps not. There had been a smear on his leg when he woke, but maybe it was evidence of his own aroused state, and his nightmare-befuddled mind had turned it into a seed of lies. And Magenta the impersonator, whose eyes he thought he had seen somewhere else. If she *had* been impersonating that dead, stuffed woman, then her performance was exemplary.

Only a quick trip down those stairs, past the faceless front doors, through the front garden that felt farther away from the street than it should . . .

Peter had known his father. Cain had no doubt of that, simply from the way the landlord had spoken of the old man. *He really did go to the extremes, didn't he?* He could never have made something like that up, and he could not be talking of anyone else. Perhaps their meeting that evening would shed some light on the old man.

Yet this worried Cain. His limited understanding of his father came from his own perspective, no

GET UP TO 4 FREE BOOKS!

You can have the best fiction delivered to your door for less than what you'd pay in a bookstore or online—only $4.25 a book! Sign up for our book clubs today, and we'll send you **FREE* BOOKS** just for trying it out...**with no obligation to buy, ever!**

LEISURE HORROR BOOK CLUB

With more award-winning horror authors than any other publisher, it's easy to see why CNN.com says "Leisure Books has been leading the way in paperback horror novels." Your shipments will include authors such as RICHARD LAYMON, DOUGLAS CLEGG, JACK KETCHUM, MARY ANN MITCHELL, and many more.

LEISURE THRILLER BOOK CLUB

If you love fast-paced page-turners, you won't want to miss any of the books in Leisure's thriller line. Filled with gripping tension and edge-of-your-seat excitement, these titles feature everything from psychological suspense to legal thrillers to police procedurals and more!

As a book club member you also receive the following special benefits:

- **30% OFF all orders through our website & telecenter!**
- **Exclusive access to special discounts!**
- **Convenient home delivery and 10 days to return any books you don't want to keep.**

There is no minimum number of books to buy, and you may cancel membership at any time. See back to sign up!

YES! ☐

Sign me up for the Leisure Horror Book Club and send my TWO FREE BOOKS! If I choose to stay in the club, I will pay only $8.50* each month, a savings of $5.48!

YES! ☐

Sign me up for the Leisure Thriller Book Club and send my TWO FREE BOOKS! If I choose to stay in the club, I will pay only $8.50* each month, a savings of $5.48!

NAME: _____

ADDRESS: _____

_____

TELEPHONE: _____

E-MAIL: _____

☐ **I WANT TO PAY BY CREDIT CARD.**

☐ VISA   ☐ MasterCard   ☐ DISCOVER

ACCOUNT #: _____

EXPIRATION DATE: _____

SIGNATURE: _____

Send this card along with $2.00 shipping & handling for each club you wish to join, to:

Horror/Thriller Book Clubs
20 Academy Street
Norwalk, CT 06850-4032

Or fax (must include credit card information!) to: 610.995.9274.
You can also sign up online at www.dorchesterpub.com.

*Plus $2.00 for shipping. Offer open to residents of the U.S. and Canada only.
Canadian residents please call 1.800.481.9191 for pricing information.
If under 18, a parent or guardian must sign. Terms, prices and conditions subject to change. Subscription subject
to acceptance. Dorchester Publishing reserves the right to reject any order or cancel any subscription.

JOIN NOW!

one else's. He had never met anyone who knew the man, and the Voice and Face had only talked of him in their professional capacity. They had never seen him alive, never looked into his eyes and seen the dark seed of madness nestling there like a cancer. Talking to someone who had known his father threatened to give Cain a whole new angle on his existence, and he was not sure he truly wanted that. He had spent the years since his father's death trying to come to terms with what the old man had done to him, and why, and though there was much left unknown, Cain felt that he had reached some level of understanding and acceptance. When he met Peter that evening, his whole world could be turned on its head.

He should ring the Voice and reveal his fears, tell him what he thought was happening here. *They're all against me,* he would say. *I'm so alone.* But the Voice may well suggest a return to Afresh, whether he believed Cain's tales or not, and that was something Cain could not abide. The place had never been a prison, but now that he had tasted real freedom—however strange—it would crush him if he ever had to return.

He sat on the settee, leaned back, and closed his eyes. He had no intention of sleeping. Besides, something kept him alert. There was a gentle tapping coming from the chest in the living room, the place where the main representation of his past was locked away. Much as he tried to ignore it, Cain wanted to listen to whatever message it had to convey. He looked at the chest to see if it was moving. It had shifted a few inches out of the corner where he had left it . . . or perhaps he was mistaken. It seemed to have turned as well, but maybe the settee had shifted as he sat down, subtly altering the angle from which he viewed the room.

The chest had been silent for all his years at Afresh. Perhaps now whatever was inside tasted its own freedom at last.

Humming started somewhere, that tune again, and Cain accompanied it with a soft whistle. He stopped suddenly and the humming followed suit, and from far away he thought he heard pan pipes continuing on for a note or two before falling silent.

"There's the room next door," a voice said, and Cain recognized it as his own. Talking to himself? Why not? He closed his eyes again and sat back, and before he knew it the steady tapping and humming from the chest had nursed him into sleep.

He sees the shadow, even though it is pitch black. It's a strange sight, like seeing a beam of light at midday, and stranger still because a shadow is less than nothing. It is an obscuring of light, and in this place of utter darkness that is impossible. Yet the shadow sits beside him, a solid presence that shifts and changes as time passes by. And now and then it talks to him.

"Must be a day gone by now," it says.

"Yes, at least." Cain nods and nothing changes. He closes his eyes, but the darkness is no less intense, even though he senses an inner light struggling to be released. He wonders whether this is what his father is looking for, but he is too afraid to find out.

It is very quiet in the room, not because this is a test of silence, but because there is nothing to say. Cain would sing a song if he knew any. Childish tunes that may have formed in his mind were eradicated years ago by the siren, and now music is something that lives only in the regular drum of his heartbeat, the strum of blood rushing through his ears. He finds no pleasure in these sounds, because they are perceptible only when he is alone.

Sometimes the shadow hums. The tune is unfamiliar to the child Cain, but the dreaming adult Cain knows it of old. Knows it, but still cannot name it. He goes to hum along, but the shadow tenses beside him, aware of what he is about to do. Cain can feel the waves of disapproval emanating from it. He always thought that the shadow hummed the tune, but now it seems to come from everywhere. Perhaps such complete darkness gives the shadow free rein.

Cain lifts his hand in front of his face and flexes his fingers, but he can see nothing. Only the subtle displacement of air confirms that his hand is even there at all.

"Maybe two days," the shadow says. "How would you know? How could you tell?"

"I think just a day," the young Cain says, and the dreaming Cain is amazed and impressed at his own calmness. *I may have been here for days, but I sound so cool,* he thinks, but he is talking about himself, and the admiration falters. *Then why can't I really* remember *any of this?*

Sometimes his father slips some food into the room, and Cain finds it by sense. Not touch or smell: He simply knows where to look. Although the young, innocent Cain finds nothing remarkable in this, the dreaming Cain is shocked. *Could I do that now?* he thinks, certain that the answer would be no.

"I think even three days," the shadow says, "or maybe even a week Without the sun, you just can't tell. Pure Sight could tell you, if it fucking existed. Hah! Pure Sight? What a fool the old fuck is!"

Cain wants to admonish the shadow, but talking to something not there would only invite in madness.

"You'll remember this in the future," the shadow says. "Maybe when you need to, or maybe not. Perhaps just in a dream, though you might think it's little more than a nightmare. You'll remember this. Hello, you! Hello Cain! And you'll hear me talking."

"You're not there," Cain says, and a brief flash of light hurts his eyes. The siren explodes into the room and he slumps to the floor, screaming, his hands covering his ears. "Not fair!" he yells, but the shadow is whooping somewhere else, a victory yell.

Cain sits up again, both of his imprisoned minds reeling from the effects of the siren. It strikes at the very heart of him, and he has long suspected that it is so much more than a simple sound. He doesn't know exactly what it is—something in his head, touching a place that hurts the most—but he *is* certain that he does not wish to feel it again.

"Cain's got Pure Sight!" the shadow yells. "So

fucking pure he's seeing lights! Hah! The old fuck
must be mighty pleased with you now."

Cain tries to move away from the shadow, but it
is everywhere. Instead he tries to close his mind to
its presence. But like the siren, it seems to be something that bypasses his senses as well as using
them. He is aware of the shadow inside him, and
the more he thinks of it the more it grins, like the
potential of violence threatening him with a dark
bite.

"Leave me alone!" Cain whispers, and he sees
lights again, dancing and weaving in front of him,
before the siren screams out to shatter his mind
once more. It takes him longer to recover this time,
and when he does the shadow seems to have vanished. The pitch darkness is now just that, with
nothing else hiding behind its folds of void, and
Cain sits in the center of the room with his eyes
closed. The young Cain hopes to dream himself old
and out of here, and the older Cain knows that this
will never work. Somewhere outside, his father
paces the rooms and halls of the rambling country
home, knowing what he is doing to his one and
only son. That hurts Cain more than anything the
siren, or the shadow, can ever do.

"You think he gives a fuck?" the shadow's voice
whispers from somewhere farther away than the
walls, and it starts humming that unknown tune
again, as if its inscrutability is mockery itself.

There's the room next door, the shadow said, and
Cain snapped awake.

There was a brief thumping, a cackling, and as

he sat up on the sofa the chest smacked down on the floor. It had moved several inches from its last position. Cain stood and pushed it back into the corner, flush with two walls to make it more difficult for it to move. It was heavy and it scratched the floor as it moved. He glanced at the extravagant padlock, patterned with twists of fake gold and silver, but he had lost the key years ago. Even if that were not the case, he would never open it.

There's the room next door. The door next to Cain's, with the scratches down its length, had almost become invisible over the past couple of days. There had been more on his mind, and the story of Vlad and how he had been killed had taken a backseat. That was the past, while it was the present obsessing him. Now it was something he could investigate without having to venture downstairs past those staring doors. He glanced at his watch; six o'clock—two hours until he had to go and meet Peter, hear about his father from another's viewpoint for the first time ever. He had to do something to fill that time.

Grabbing a short knife from the kitchen—to help him break open the door, he assured himself, not as protection, not at all—he went to his front door and looked through the spy hole. The small landing was deserted, and standing quietly outside, holding his breath, he could hear no sign of anyone else in the house. Whistler may still be there in his flat, but if so he was utterly silent. Paying whatever weird respect he owed to his Followers, perhaps.

Cain turned to the door next to his own and examined it. It was actually slightly shorter and narrower than his own, not a true front door at all, more a glorified hatch. It must lead into whatever roof space was left around the edges of his attic flat. He traced the deep scratches with his fingers, wincing as a splinter slid beneath his skin. If something with claws had found it desirable to get inside, then perhaps he should not. But his curiosity was fired now, and if there *was* anything threatening in there, he had the knife.

He tried the handle, but the door was locked. There was no spare key above the frame this time, so he tried to prize the knife blade in past the handle to slip back the latch. He had read about doing this in a dozen crime books, never once believing that he would one day be doing it himself. In books, the perpetrator was inevitably looking for evidence of a murder, or his kidnapped wife. This was not quite so worthy, and Cain had no reason to believe that it would work. He heaved, the wood groaned and split, and with a metallic snick the handle suddenly flipped up and the door opened. *Breaking and entering twice in one day,* he thought, surprised. *The Face would be proud.*

As the door swung inward a smell wafted out, and Cain stepped back in a panic. *Death,* he thought, *I'll smell old death like in Whistler's flat, and perhaps they're all in on this together!* But though the smell was one of age, it was stale rather than rank, the odors of dust and time, dried paper and old clothes giving home to insects and mold. It was also the stench of a room that had not been used for a long time, and Cain wondered whether anyone had been in here since Vlad's death.

The police, surely? But somehow the thought of their intrusion seemed too mundane for such a place and such a death.

He felt on the wall inside the door, surprised to find a light switch. Before he flicked it he paused, closed his eyes, and considered what it was he may find. Whether or not Vlad had been his real name—and it seemed unlikely—the last occupant of his flat had been a strange sort, put in a wheelchair by a circus accident and living on the second floor of a house without a lift. Who knew what he had been up to? Nobody Cain had spoken to had seemed to like the old Russian very much.

Perhaps they had picked on him, just as they were picking on Cain.

He flicked the switch and opened his eyes.

It was a corridor more than a room, one wall sloped with the roof to form a triangular space just tall enough for Cain to stand in. Not that he *could* stand, such was the profusion of boxes, bags, and loose items stacked in there. That smell of age and must came at him again, as if given new life by the light, and he coughed as dust settled on his throat. When he finally realized what filled the attic, he knew he was breathing in dust from the skin of a dead man.

Circus paraphernalia. Vlad must have traveled far and wide during his life as a trapeze artist, and he had gathered all manner of items on his journeys. One box overflowed with colorful clown's clothing, as if the clown's spirit was eager to rise. Another held juggling sticks, some of their tips blackened with fire, others sharpened to a deadly point. Tied bags of clothes were piled at the junction of sloping wall and floor; they had been there for so long that they seemed to have sunk down and merged, almost blending into the structure. He wondered what he would find were he to delve deep into their depths, and whose names would be written in the clothing, and where those people were now.

The tall wall was unlined. The partition's timber studs showed through, bearing half a dozen old posters. They had all faded with time, and the one farthest away had sprouted an impressive array of fungi across its bottom half, but they all proclaimed the Great Vladosvic as the most talented trapeze artist the world had ever seen. Vlad was depicted performing various daring acts of acrobatics, all of them seemingly without a safety net. Cain wondered which backflip or triple spin had dashed him to the sawdust and broken his back.

When Cain clambered into the attic space, he had a brief, intense sensation of shifting farther than one single step. It was as if this room were in another city, not under the eaves next to his own flat. He stood still for a few moments, letting his stomach settle, gathering his balance, shaking his head. The feeling had gone. Perhaps he was just tired.

He began lifting the lids on boxes and ripping open polyethylene bags to peer inside. Some of the contents were enigmatic in the extreme: a lady's leotard, sequinned with fake diamonds and bearing an oily handprint across one breast; a whip, which he thought must have been for controlling animals, before he saw the wicked blades tied into each of

161

its nine tails; a false leg, socket grubby with use; and in one bag, a crystal ball. It swam with colors, and however still Cain remained, the ball's depths seemed to shift and swirl, as if excited by the sudden presence of light after so long. Perhaps the sudden temperature change caused by the open door was affecting the crystal. He lifted it from the small wooden pedestal that supported it, held it in both hands, and tried to shield it from the light. Nothing changed. Cain stared closer and colors swam without touching, like exotic fish in an endless mating dance.

And then shadows filled the ball, and Cain dropped it to the bare timber floor. It rolled between his feet and drifted sideways, disappearing into the pile of bags and boxes stacked against the sloping wall.

Cain turned, shaken, readying himself to move on, and saw something that seemed so out of place. Leaning against the vertical wall stood an old changing mirror. Half the lightbulbs were missing, the glass was cracked in several places, and it was smeared with something that looked like dried blood. The smear spelled out words that Cain did not wish to see: *I'm here because they think I'm just like them.*

He knelt before the mirror and stared. He reached out to touch the glass, a dark crack distorted his reflected hand into a wizened claw, and he recalled the story of Dorian Gray. Perhaps Vlad had sat here before this old mirror to find his prime again, and when something had happened—something that drove him in here to hide instead of merely reminisce—he had written a message to his younger self: *I'm here because they think I'm just like them.*

Perturbed, but hardly surprised, Cain moved on. If anywhere would have contained hidden truths, it was this room with the wounded door.

Another sprawl of faded writing faced him from one of the posters: *They won't leave me alone.* It too was written in blood, and some of its message had flaked to the floor as if forgotten with its writer's death. Cain knew who the words referred to, and already a picture was beginning to build. Vlad must have come here, rented Flat Five—even though he relied a lot on his wheelchair—and then found himself vilified by the others in the house. Set upon. Toyed with. *I'm here because they think I'm just like them,* he had written, and in that strange dream Sister Josephine had said to Cain, *You know the Way already, for sure, you just need showing.*

And what was the Way, if not Pure Sight?

Perhaps I'm just like Vlad, he thought.

There was another message painted on a circus admission price board. Cain had to lean down and blow away a layer of dust to reveal it fully, but when he sat back on his haunches he saw: *They tell me I'm not who I am.* That chilled Cain to the core. Not only had they abused Vlad, they had confused him as well, and what had happened to him in the end? Eaten, if Peter was to be believed. This crippled old trapeze artist had been found miles from here, minus his wheelchair, with his stomach eaten away. *Did he know himself when he died?* Cain thought. *Or had they tortured him that much?*

And as if to taunt him more, that was when Cain saw the wheelchair. It was folded neatly and tucked behind several split bags at the rear of the attic space. He could not reach it from where he squatted, and neither did he wish to. Even the light barely touched it. Chrome glowed, leather merged with the dark, and Cain was sure that dried blood-stains on the wheelchair would reveal their own obvious message.

Strange . . . they never even found his wheelchair, Peter had told him on his first day here.

He had to leave. This place had been a refuge, a sanctuary for the crippled old man, and the difficulty he must have faced getting in here made it feel even more special. By leaving the room as it was after his death, the landlord had revealed the true extent of the invasion into Vlad's life. The bloody writing spoke of that, splayed as it was across important references to his history, as if to obscure his past just as the others in the house had endeavored to offend his identity. And much as Cain suddenly felt empathy for that victimized man, he did not feel that he should be here. This was a private place, made more so by its user's death. Perhaps it would change in the future, but right now it should remain as it was, lonely and sad.

Scrawled on the floor at Cain's feet, previously unseen, six words: *They know I'm going to tell.*

Those claw marks on the door? Cain thought. *What put them here? And why?*

His answer stared him in the face as he turned to

leave. Above the door hung an old photograph of Vlad in all his glory, swinging from a trapeze with one hand and waving to the photographer with the other. He was young, fit, full of life, and his smile promised nothing of his grim, lonely demise.

Across the picture were the words *They're going to kill me tonight*.

Cain closed the door behind him, and for some reason it felt like a betrayal.

Pushing his fear aside, he ran downstairs and across the street to Heaven, vowing that there he would find answers.

Once at the house, Cain felt slightly more relaxed. He was an hour early at least, but if Peter was in Cain would demand that they have their talk now. If the landlord was not there . . . then Cain would wait. It was a sunny day, he was out in the open, and he had plenty of time. He would sit on the low wall outside Peter's run-down property and watch the world go by.

Glancing over his shoulder back at Number 13, Cain saw a flicker of flesh pass by Magenta's window. Below hers, Sister Josephine's window was dark, curtains drawn, and he wondered whether she was in there magicking herself up even now.

He could not wait out here, exposed and watched.

Cain bashed on the corrugated iron door of Heaven. From inside there came a scampering sound, like dozens of small animals running for cover, and then a frantic hissing and squealing. He stepped back slightly from the door, still within

Heaven's shadow, and waited. He felt incredibly exposed with Number 13 at his back. He glanced around, but Magenta's window was bare.

Heaven fell quiet. The squealing had died down, leaving a loaded silence in its wake. Cain thought he heard footsteps, but they could just as easily have come from the next street as Heaven. What the hell had possessed Peter to give his house such a name? Irony obviously, but he did not really seem like the kind of person to court controversy.

Cain knocked again, louder and longer. The noise shocked him and he drew back, remembering the siren and how it had hollowed him out with each assault. He looked around guiltily, but no one appeared to be watching. The street was quiet, considering the time of day. People should be returning home from work, kids should be out playing. No cars, no strollers. Maybe . . .

"Fuck it!" he scolded himself. Paranoia was getting the better of him. The Face would smile and shake her head, and tell Cain that everyone's lives revolved around one another. The only person fixated on Cain was Cain.

He reached out to strike the door again as it was pulled open, squealing across bare concrete.

"You're early," Peter said. "I'm not ready yet."

"I don't care, we need to talk. I need to know what's going on here. And you have to tell me about my father."

Peter looked angry, and that in turn angered Cain. What the hell did the landlord expect him to do? There was no explanation to the body in Whistler's room other than murder.

"Wait just a minute," Peter said. "I have to get something, then I'll be out. There's a pub I know— we can go there, sit in the garden."

"I want to know everything," Cain said.

"I'll tell you what I can." Peter pushed the door shut, and Cain heard him muttering something as he receded inside the house.

I'll tell you what I can, he'd said, which was very different from saying, *I'll tell you what I know.* Cain still did not trust the landlord, not one bit, even if he *had* come along and rescued him from being caught red-handed by Whistler. There was design in that, too. There was too much hidden, a dozen mysteries just breaking surface but keeping their bulks riding below the waves of understanding. Cain was confused, frightened, and alone. He knew he should call Afresh, but he was terrified that they would ask him to return. And besides, now that he could possibly discover more about his father, and why he had done what he did, the surrounding enigmas seemed like tributaries of the same river. For now he would go with the flow.

He moved out of Heaven's small front garden and stood on the pavement. As if pleased that he had no intention of fleeing, the street had come to life. Cars passed left and right, filled with squabbling children and tired parents. A woman walked along the opposite pavement, holding a little girl's hand and talking into a mobile phone at the same time. *Perhaps Whistler just grabbed her off the street,* Cain thought, but there was much more to what he had seen. Peter had said that, and Cain believed him. Not because he thought the landlord was trustworthy, but because of the look in the stuffed woman's eyes. She was not Magenta, he was sure of that now, but she had still seemed happy to be there.

And that chuckle, Cain thought. It must have been something tumbling from a shelf, or his ear popping, or maybe it was his unconscious utterance of fear as he heard the house's front door slam shut. But there was also the niggling idea that if he had stayed just a few moments longer, the woman would have broken down and started laughing at him. *Surprise!* she would have said. *Had you fooled! Oh, Cain, we're having* such *fun with you . . .*

Peter opened the front door behind him, slammed it shut, and joined him on the pavement. He was carrying a battered, oversized leather book, holding it to his side as if ashamed of whatever it contained.

"What's that?" Cain asked.

"It's a photo album," Peter said. "Now, come on, I don't want to do this in sight of the house."

That was the first time Cain had heard any hint of fear in Peter's voice. And he realized that Peter may be as much a pawn in whatever game was being played as he.

Intrigued, afraid, and yet filled with a vibrancy and excitement he had never felt before, Cain followed Peter along the road.

For a long time after he first arrived at Afresh, Cain believed that he was the only reality. He was real, the here and now, and everything else around him was the product of his mind. There was no proof that a chair could exist, because Cain could be imagining its solidity. There was no evidence that the Face was real, because Cain could have dreamed her up himself. *Would you be so cruel to yourself?* the Voice asked, referring to the terrible things Cain had been through. But Cain only shrugged, and said that with nothing to relate his life to, cruelty was an empty concept.

Chapter Seven
History

It was a suburban pub, given over mainly to average pub food and big-screen sports viewings. Its facade was mock-Tudor, smothered with ivy and pocked here and there with bay windows and several entrance doors. A specials menu stood by the main door, proclaiming the quality of their lasagna, beef curry, and scampi. Guest ale this week was Dog's Dinner. Inside was all dark wood and chrome, sports prints on the walls, sticky carpet by the bar. A few couples sat eating a postwork meal, mostly silent and pale. A family occupied one corner, the parents hassled and the children happily picking up chips from the floor, flicking peas at each other, and generally reveling in the adventure.

Peter ordered a bottle of red wine and some chips, and he nodded toward the back of the pub where a stained glass door led out into the garden. The beer garden was an impressive size, and surprisingly well maintained. Tables were dotted here and there at random, and one or two were nicely secluded, hidden from general view by large potted plants and well-cropped hedges. Peter headed for one of these, farthest from the pub and nestled between a high hedge and a wild rose garden. He placed the photograph album gently on the end of the table, as if keen to keep his distance, and poured some wine.

"It's not often I get out," Peter said.

"Likewise."

Peter smiled, and Cain thought it was the first genuine smile he had ever seen from the landlord. Perhaps being away from Endless Crescent made him more himself.

"So you were at Afresh from the time your father died, right up to now?"

Cain nodded. "It was all I knew as home. People cared for me there." He said no more; his use of the word *care* spoke volumes.

"Still, that's a long time ago. He's been dead, what, five years?"

"Six."

Peter nodded, sipped his wine, and looked around the garden. Cain followed his gaze and actually found himself enjoying the moment, pressured as it was by the potential of revelation. The wine was good, the weather was pleasant, the garden gave over a relaxed feel. Bees buzzed the bushes around them, and birds squabbled and squealed in the trees, arguing over dropped food. He glanced at the photograph album, leaned back on the seat and stretched his arms, looked at the album again.

"Let's talk about Whistler first," Peter said quietly.

"You know so much and I know nothing!" Cain said. "You have me at a disadvantage. I thought you were just the landlord, but now you tell me you knew my father, what he was doing, doing to *me!* And what I saw in Whistler's flat, everything that's been happening to me there, you seem to know it all. You're not just the landlord, are you? You're involved."

Peter nodded, sipped his wine, and sat back in his seat. "So tell me what's happened," he said. "Tell me what *you* think has happened."

"The others are casting me out," Cain said, remembering the lonely, unrelated messages in Vlad's attic. He could mention that he had been in there . . . but for now he decided to keep that to himself. Having a secret or two may be to his advantage.

"They've lived there together for a long time," Peter said. "You're a stranger, you've just moved in. It's bound to take them time to accept you."

"There's more to it, and you know it! They're *playing* with me. Magenta, the nun, George, Whistler, all of them have toyed with me to some degree. Sometimes it seems almost harmless, other times not."

"You sure you haven't imagined it all? Dreamed it?"

It's all a dream, Cain, Peter had shouted from the basement.

"You told me I had it," Cain said. "What did you mean by that? Don't avoid the issues here, Peter. You brought me here for a reason, you brought that album with you, so there's going to be more to this conversation than you trying to persuade me I'm mad."

"Oh, I know you're not mad," Peter said quietly. "I know that."

"So talk. *Please*."

Peter's eyes darkened and his manner seemed to change, from casual to defensive. He glanced around the garden, into the bushes and up at the sky, and Cain remembered the sensation of being flown up the stairs by the naked nun. *A dream*, he thought, but that smear on his leg had not been his own spunk, he had always known that. It was Sister Josephine's magic cream, left there when she had put him to bed.

That had been no dream.

"It's very difficult," Peter said.

"I'm not dull. My father may have kept me locked away from the world, but I read, and I've read so much more since. And Afresh wasn't a prison. I have little experience in life, but I know a lot about it. Peter, please, don't fuck with me. Everyone else is fucking with me, and they're laughing at me, and I can't stand it anymore."

"So go back to Afresh," Peter said, and that sardonic look shifted back across his face.

"Don't . . . fuck . . . with me." Even Cain was surprised at the menace he managed to project into his voice. *No more!* he thought, and he thought it hard, and he knew by Peter's expression that the landlord had heard those words in his own mind.

"You do have it," Peter gasped. "The Way." He finished his wine and leaned across the bench to look into Cain's eyes. "You know something of it, but you're unwilling to accept, or not able to. Do you see behind the veil of reality? You know things you shouldn't? You can tell things about people, sense their thoughts, know what they're thinking or what they're going to do next?" Peter's surprise had given way to excitement.

"Sometimes," Cain said, admitting it for the first time to anyone. All those years at Afresh, all the love and effort the Voice and the Face had given him, and he had never offered them a clue.

"It's a trace of the Way," Peter said. "Just a hint of what the others in the house all have, a splinter of their talent. They can do that, and so much more. They don't only hear what you're thinking, they can influence it. Had any bad dreams, Cain?"

Cain nodded. "Some. And some that maybe weren't dreams."

Peter lifted his hands as if demonstrating a point. "What's this 'Way' you talk of?"

"I think you know."

"Pure Sight," Cain said.

"That's what your father called it. Different people call it different things, but mostly when someone finds it, it's simply the Way. It's a route to all things, a way to knowledge, a path to clear thinking and honest understanding."

"They all have it in the house?"

"Yes."

"And you?"

Peter glanced away, and the sadness that swept across his face was shocking in its intensity. "I'm just someone to serve them," he said quietly. "Everyone with talents has hangers-on. I'm a

174

hanger-on. I know of the Way, always have, but I've never been able to achieve it. I have dregs of it, as you've already seen. Here." He picked up the wine bottle and flipped it into the air, uncorked. His hand darted out and the bottle landed upside down on his little finger, spinning there, no wine dribbling out at all. And then Peter's hand began to turn a deep, dark purple as it absorbed the wine.

"Shit." Cain leaned back, but Peter shook his head, brought the bottle down to the table.

"A trick, that's all," he said, holding out his hands in a reassuring gesture. They were both pale, untouched by wine, and the bottle itself was still virtually full. "I have just a fraction of what you have, the ability to influence. Did the bottle move, or did you only think of it? It doesn't matter."

Cain shook his head, stood from the table, and walked to the rosebushes. The flowers were red and fat, the aromas beguiling, but a few of the blooms had leaves spotted black with blight, and blackflies smothered unopened buds. Perhaps everything that was beautiful on the surface had faults waiting to appear. He had barely lived anything of life; he had yet to find this out.

"So, Whistler," Cain said. He kept his back turned to Peter, looking at the flowers, seeing past the surface beauty to the raw nature beneath.

"Whistler plays his pipes, and people hear truth in his music."

"I hear only music."

"Everyone's different," Peter said.

"What do you hear?"

Peter was silent, and Cain turned around to see

why. Tears streaked the landlord's face, dripping from his chin and spotting the wooden table with dark rosettes. Cain was shocked. Not by the tears, but by the look of abject misery on Peter's face. He stared off into the distance, mouth slightly open, and his right hand stroked his throat as if trying to knead the sadness away.

"I was one of his Followers, years ago," Peter whispered. "Whistler is the oldest resident of Number 13. He's so old . . . nobody really knows. He's been around; Dubai, Mexico City, Tripoli, Hamelin. And he's the reason I bought the place, the reason I do what I do." He shook his head and wiped his eyes, snorting, turning away as if he could still hide the tears.

"What made you follow him? What did you hear?" Cain felt sorry for the man, but there was too much happening here to call a halt now. Besides, he felt that Peter *wanted* to talk about this. He spoke quietly—as if trying to ensure what he said remained a secret—but there was no sign of him clamming up.

"I heard . . . such wonderful promise. It's as clear to me today as when it happened thirty years ago. I was sitting outside a café by the side of the river in York. I'd been wandering through the city all morning, wallowing in its history, exploring as many side streets and alleys as I could, seeking the honesty of the place. Back then, everywhere I went I sought the Way, as if it was an inscribed stone I'd find in a building's foundations, or a secret whisper that traveled the atmosphere, just waiting to be heard. Your father and I were still speaking then, but we were no help for each other, none at all. We wanted the same thing; we just went about it in vastly different ways. He searched inside, I looked everywhere else. We were both so wrong."

"My father . . ."

"Let me finish, Cain. It's all part of the same story. Understanding me will help you understand your father, and there's so little I can tell you about him. I hadn't spoken to him for years before you were born. I hardly know the man he became. Hear me out, and then I'll show you some pictures." Peter put his hand on the album and removed it instantly, as if the book were hot.

"Go on," Cain said, fascinated. He poured them both another glass of wine, and the singing of fluid on glass sounded like distant pan pipes.

"I'd been inside York Minster for two hours, walking its length and breadth, going up into the tower and out onto the roof, looking everywhere. I passed the same people several times. The look on their faces was a uniform blankness; they were impressed, but the emotion barely left their eyes. It was as if they had a magic-sink, something in their eyes that stole away wonders as soon as they saw them. I saw my own wonder and craving reflected in their sunglasses. They seemed not to notice.

"I read tomb inscriptions, searching between words and letters for hidden script, reading them upside down in case the letters were skewed. I closed my eyes and ran my fingers over the engravings, in case they said something altogether different that way. I so wanted to prize up a tombstone, open a mausoleum, because where better to hide secrets? Every stone tomb I walked over in that great place held the promise of revelation. I could almost feel and hear the darkness inside vibrating with potential. I would get in and crush open the powdery skulls of long-dead bishops, and in the dust of their brains would be the knowledge of the Way. It would be mine, simply by discovering it.

"But I could find nothing, and breaking into tombs was not my sort of thing. I was a passive searcher; looking behind shop facades, listening to illicit conversations, following a smell back to its source. I did a lot of that back then, looking for the Way as if it was a *secret*. It took me decades to realize that it's as obvious as we want it to be.

"So that lunchtime in York I sat outside a café by the river and watched the tourist boats drifting by. They were like floating rainbows, everyone wearing bright shirts and hats as if to display their extravagance to the world. I can't remember what I was wearing. Never been a follower of fashion. Being a follower means you're not thinking for yourself . . ." He trailed off, staring down at his hands where they were clasped together on the table.

"But you followed Whistler."

Peter nodded and went on. "I was there for an hour or more. I'd eaten lunch and was almost through a bottle of wine. And then everything seemed to go quiet. In such a place that's rare; there were hundreds of tourists milling around, swans and ducks and geese chattering on the river, cars and tour buses passing back and forth over the river bridge, people chatting in the café behind me, planes passing by high overhead. It was a noisy day, and that didn't bother me, because in such noise there's always the possibility of a single sound that might mean something. But as I was sitting there looking out over the river, there was a moment of silence. All conversationalists must have been taking a breath; the traffic was paused, waiting for lights to change; there were no planes above us; the birds were all eating, or taking off, or roosting somewhere different. Just for the briefest instant the world took pause. And that was when I heard him."

"The pipes?"

"Whistler's pan pipes. They were the most natural thing in the world, audible to anyone who cared to listen, and yet I knew instantly that the tune would lead me closer to the Way than anything I had ever known. They were subtle, quiet, and I knew they came from close by. Their sound was pure, unsullied by echoes, untainted from passing through the fume-laden air.

"I leaped up and looked around. The cacophony had kicked in again, but that didn't matter, I had heard it, heard the hint of what I had spent a lifetime searching for. And I knew that once I'd heard it, it would never lose itself to me again. I was not worried anymore." Peter took a long swig of wine, held his head back, and closed his eyes, as if relishing the sun on his face.

"So you found Whistler?"

"Eventually. It took some time. It took another year."

"How? Why? I don't understand."

Peter sighed and shook his head. "Neither do I.

Understanding isn't what's required; all he wants is acceptance. From that moment on, I was Whistler's follower. I listened for him wherever I went, always convinced that I would hear him again. I thought he was my route to the Way. I really, truly believed that, because it all felt so right." He paused, stood from the table, and strolled to the bushes Cain had been inspecting a few minutes earlier. "You see these roses? Beautiful. Each of them utterly flawless in its individuality."

"They've got blight," Cain said. "It'll kill them in the end."

"So negative," Peter said, smiling back at Cain. "But until they die, they're perfect in their simplicity. More perfect than anything Man has ever made."

"What happened when you found Whistler?"

"I knew instantly that I'd never know the Way." Cain thought that Peter may be crying again, but when he came back to the table his eyes were dry.

"So what is Whistler? What are his followers? What does he do to them?" He thought of that woman in the flat, completely still, stuffed or maybe not.

Peter smiled, and it was filled with real good humor. "This," he said, "is where it all gets a bit difficult. I think we need more wine. I'll get some, and when I come back I'll tell you more."

"Why?" Cain said. "Why are you telling me all this now?"

"Because I think you deserve to know. The Way is not a secret, and—"

"I don't give a *shit* about the Way, or Pure fucking Sight!" Cain said, raising his voice more than he had intended. A few people turned, eyes wide, and then just as quickly looked away again. "All it's done for me is to destroy my childhood and steal away my father. It's left me fucked, so fucked that I can't handle life. I have the chance to make things right for myself, and I spend my time running around frightened of my neighbors!"

"I don't care whether you give a shit or not," Peter said. "Because you have it, and one day it'll reveal itself fully for sure. I'll be back. Don't run off." He stood and walked back through the garden toward the pub.

Cain was left sitting at the table, staring at Peter's back. He was angry and frightened at the same time, and he even felt some measure of sorrow for Peter, this man who had been bound to Whistler for years. Whether that binding was intentional or not, it had grasped Peter fully. Maybe it was the promise of what he could not have that kept him following the piper. Or perhaps it was something deeper and darker. Cain would do his best to find out as soon as the landlord returned.

So for now Cain sat in the pub garden with a glass of wine, a bee buzzing his head, and several other patrons doing their best to not stare his way.

And the album. It perched on the end of the table like a present waiting to be opened. It could contain anything. Such potential sat between its worn covers that Cain thought it almost a shame to open it, defining that potential and thereby destroying all other possibilities. In Cain's reading of science books—both with his father and afterward—the theory of multiple universes had fascinated him. The idea that at any moment in time there were infinite variations to what he would or could do next was humbling. He hoped those other Cains made good choices, but really they were all him, *exactly* him, and that made him feel more alone than ever.

In each universe, the photograph album could contain anything. He reached out, opening the album and not opening it, throwing it away, burning it, rejecting it, and welcoming its contents into his heart. Right here and now, he drew his hand back and simply stared, trying to see through the covers to the heart of what it contained. He concentrated, but knew nothing. In another universe, he knew everything. He hummed the nameless tune—the music the shadow had hummed—and somewhere he recognized it and knew exactly what it meant. He wished he were in that universe.

But he could wish forever, and his own life and existence was here. Somewhere else he was much, much worse off than he was now. Somewhere else again, perhaps Vlad's fate had already befallen him.

Peter emerged from the pub carrying another bottle of wine. "You look thoughtful," he said.

"Busy resolving the meaning of life," Cain said, and he could not help returning Peter's smile.

"Whistler," Peter said, sitting down, recommencing the conversation before Cain had a chance. "Yeah, Whistler." He poured the wine, opened another bag of potato chips, and crunched his way through a mouthful, all the while looking over Cain's head at the clear blue sky.

"So?" Cain said at last.

"So you've seen the room in his flat filled with his followers."

"Yes, animals and a woman. Stuffed. Killed and stuffed."

"Not killed," Peter said.

Cain frowned, not understanding. "Animals don't commit suicide, Peter."

"Not suicide, either. They're not dead."

Cain raised his eyebrows and thought back to that afternoon, his experience in Whistler's flat, those musty creatures moldering away in the spare room. And the woman tucked away in the corner, so lifelike and yet so obviously dead.

"I'll explain," Peter said. "As best I can, at least. I've no right to do this, no right to betray Whistler's history and Way to you. But I think it will work for you, and therefore you deserve it. As I said, whether or not you want what your father called Pure Sight, I believe it wants you."

Cain said nothing, although those words stung him with memories of his father. *After so long?* he thought. *Can Peter be right after so long?*

"Whistler's followers hear something in his music that appeals to them. I heard the potential of the Way. It was as though he makes the one true music we should all hear and know. It promised me so much that I could not help but fall under its spell. Others hear the same thing, I suppose, but in their own different ways. And the animals . . . who can say what animals think or believe? Maybe it's just a nice tune; perhaps there are frequencies that get in their heads and affect them. But Cain, you've seen those creatures in his room, the way they're standing there, frozen, listening forever. It has as much meaning to them as to me."

"They were dead and stuffed," Cain said. "I smelled them."

"They're not dead," Peter said again, firmer this time. "They're Whistler's main followers. He plays to them nightly, and each morning I suspect they're in a slightly different pose. They're so enrapt with his music and what it conveys that they've forgotten to do anything else. Their life is his music. Their mind, their memory, their concentration, is obsessed with the one tune that did it for them. They smell, I suppose, because they're slowly mummifying. Not drinking, not eating . . . just existing somewhere in their heads, living their dreams."

"That's grotesque."

"You may think so, but I'll bet they're the happiest beings on the planet."

"What about you? Why aren't you in there? Why aren't you happy?"

"I never heard him well enough." Peter drank his wine and poured some more. His eyes were starting to glitter with drunkenness, but his voice was firm, his words clear. "The woman, she came to him a couple of years back. Really latched on quickly, never left his side for months, and then suddenly she began to drift away. Usually with the animals it's very quick, but with her there came an awkward time when Whistler had to leave her in the room, not quite gone. She tried to get out and follow him, but she'd lost the use of her limbs. She screamed for a while. In the end, he stayed in there with her for three days, playing nonstop until she became still. He continues to play to her, but not quite so often."

"Why?"

"I suppose he has other things to do."

"No, I mean *why*? Why does he do it? What's he gaining from all this?"

"Why do you breathe, Cain?" Peter asked, eyes wide as if surprised at the question. "Why do you drink, why do you eat?"

"To survive."

Peter held up his hands, explaining everything.

"They were arranged," Cain said, remembering the strange tableaus in Whistler's flat. "Set up in weird poses. Not right."

"He does that for his own reasons, and I have no idea what they are. Maybe it's something as simple as him playing games."

"I don't understand any of this. I don't know if I believe you. It's ridiculous. Absurd. And . . . I don't understand."

"Do you need to understand something for it to work? If we understood everything, imagine how boring life would be."

Cain did not reply. A butterfly drifted down and landed on the photograph album, and he watched it stretching its white wings, bathing in the sun. Whistler was as inexplicable as that butterfly.

"I'm sorry it's no easier," Peter said. "I've been with him for so long that I'm used to not understanding. He plays his tune and sometimes I get lost, but I always come back. Not like those animals, or that woman. Wherever they are . . . I'd give anything to be there."

"They found the Way?"

"Oh no!" Peter said, shaking his head. "Not at all. They've been lost on its path. They're swallowed in Whistler's Way, shadowed by his greatness, *part* of that shadow. Very few get to know the Way—or Pure Sight, as your father chose to call it—but often those who do affect a lot of people with their knowledge."

"So George, Magenta, and Sister Josephine have it?"

"In their own peculiar ways, yes," Peter said, but his face became guarded, his eyes downcast.

"So if it's such a personal epiphany, how come they all come together?"

Peter shrugged. "Likes attract. Protection in numbers. Tribal instinct."

"Tell me about them. Can the nun really fly? Who is the real Magenta? And George . . . what has he got to do with a wild animal?"

Peter's expression showed that there was more left to say, but he leaned back and crossed his arms. "I've told you too much already. I can't go on, not about them. They trust me."

"You're talking as if they're another species!"

Peter looked at Cain but did not reply.

"I need to know, Peter. You can't just string me along like this and then leave it. They're against me, all of them. Are they dangerous? Should I leave?"

"They're not against you, Cain, they *can't* be. They're way beyond taking sides. They're gifted with what they have and they use it, and sometimes people like me—and you—get caught up in that. In your case that's good, because it'll help bring out what your father nurtured in you. And yes, they can be dangerous. Can't everyone?"

"For fuck's sake—"

"What about your father?" the landlord asked, gently touching the photograph album. The butterfly fluttered away. "Don't you want to know about him? That's what you came for really, isn't it?"

Cain looked at the album, and suddenly he was terrified. There could be photographs of his father in there as Cain had never seen him. He may be about to learn so much more than he had ever known about that cruel, naive old man who had kept him incarcerated for years. And right then, with the wine singing in his veins and the evening sun fading on his skin, Cain was not sure he wanted to hear.

"I need to piss," he said. "I'll be back in a minute. And then maybe you can tell me about my father."

"Leonard and I go way back," Peter said, smiling up at Cain.

Cain went into the pub, and the unbelievable thought thumping through his head in time to his heartbeat was *I never knew his name, I never knew his name.* Leaning against the wall in the Gents toilet, he cried as he pissed.

When Cain returned to the beer garden, Peter and the photograph album had vanished.

Good, he thought, but that was immediately replaced with an intense disappointment and anger. Not only had Peter given him some small assurance that he was not imagining things with Whistler and the others, he had also offered a chance for Cain to discover things about his father from another perspective. It was a unique and unexpected opportunity, and now it was gone, at least for a while.

"Went off in a bit of a rush," a voice said. Cain turned to a table tucked away between some trellis, and a young woman sat there nursing a bottle of beer. She was quite obviously waiting for a friend to return from the pub and she seemed nervous. Her smile faltered, and she hid it by raising the bottle.

"Which way?" Cain asked.

The girl nodded at a gate exiting the garden. "He was looking up at the sky, and he went as if he saw something scary. Just jumped up, picked up that big book, ran. Knocked over your bottle of wine."

"Did you see anything?"

The girl shrugged. "Dunno. Big bird, that's all. Buzzard probably, they circle here sometimes looking for leftovers and stuff in the pub garden."

"Big bird," Cain echoed, thinking of the brief glimpse he had caught of the shape above the park earlier that day. "Thanks," he said.

"No problem."

As Cain turned to leave, the girl's boyfriend emerged from the pub, throwing a cautious glance his way. Cain smiled, but it did not work; the boy hurried across to the table and sat close to the girl. Cain turned away. Such affection. There had been sex at Afresh, but never closeness. It was something lacking in his life. He supposed he was destined to be alone, as isolated now as he had been in that room in his father's basement. And now that Peter had vanished, he felt as though he were being experimented upon all over again.

Cain left the pub, strolling at first, then walking faster. The sun was settling down behind the high buildings in the city, and the smell of hot smog was slowly fading into a cool echo of the day.

Peter could not be far ahead. He had that album, and in there were truths that Cain was terrified of facing yet felt he must. It may even contain pictures of his mother, the woman he had never, ever seen. His father had refused to talk about her, saying only that she died when Cain was born. But there must have been a time when there was love between her and the old man? Affection? Cain had no idea whether knowing that would change anything for him, but he had to find out.

He glanced up at the sky, but there was no sign of any large bird.

Cain was sure he could remember the way back to Endless Crescent. Peter had led the way earlier, and there had been several turns at the ends of streets and through narrow alleys. But the way he was going felt right, and for now he was confident with that.

He started walking a little faster. Peter was hurrying as well, Cain could sense that. *You have it,* Peter had said, and Cain tried to analyze how and why he knew that Peter was walking quickly. There was no logical answer. He simply knew the Way things were.

For the very first time in his life, Cain considered

the possibility that his father had succeeded. For years Cain had viewed Pure Sight as a madness. Even when he knew things that he really should not, he dismissed it as a peculiarity, an effect of his long incarceration, an exaggeration of his senses when they had been so forcibly starved by his father. Now, knowing all this, he wondered whether that torture really had opened up his inner perceptions, just as his father had intended.

I don't want it.

Peter stopped, looked up, searching for pursuit.

Not if it does to me what it's done to Whistler.

Peter was scared, and a bitter, inexplicable sense of betrayal simmered in his mind. He clasped the album to his chest as if it could protect him against blows, running now, dashing along an alley lush with overhanging foliage. He ducked and pushed his way through, head down, and Cain saw every movement, knew every thought.

"I don't *want* it!" Cain shouted, but he began to run as well, ignoring the curious stares from passersby.

He came to a junction he did not remember from before, turned right, then realized that left was the correct way. He did not question his reasoning, because he knew where it came from. He was reading Peter's route, sensing it in the air as if the landlord had left a trace of himself behind; a smell, a sound, the taste of his fear. *And now the siren will cut me down,* Cain thought, but he had begun to believe that he would never hear the siren again. He had passed that time. This was the first day of his new life. Chasing Peter felt like pursuing his own destiny, and much as he claimed he did not want it, Pure Sight beckoned from every street corner. Cain did not even consider halting the chase.

The sun had fallen into the city now, smearing its pink afterglow through dirty brown smog. Cain reached a point where the street split in two and took the left fork, leading down a gentle slope toward a small park. He caught sight of a shape disappearing around the corner of the park, and he was sure it was Peter. He ran harder, feet pounding the pavement, his heart thrumming with the unaccustomed exercise. The rhythm of his footsteps seemed familiar, and it took him a few seconds to realize that it matched the beat of the tune hummed by the shadow. Cain started humming himself, glancing into doorways and gardens, not expecting to see the shadow but searching for it anyway.

He turned right at the park. There was no sign of Peter, but the road ended here, and several paths and lanes led off at different angles. Cain chose a route without hesitation, the image of Peter going the same way clear in his mind. He breathed in the smell of the photograph album; time, and lost memories.

Something flitted overhead, drifting out of sight behind a house just as Cain looked up. *Big bird*, the girl had said. Cain sniffed. There was no hint of honey in the air. People just do not fly.

"Peter!" he shouted, not really expecting the landlord to stop. Why was Peter running? And why was Cain chasing him? He could see him again tomorrow if he so wished. Perhaps because

Cain had built himself up for an evening of revelation, and their discussion about Whistler had not been enough to satiate his hunger for knowledge. There was George and Magenta and Sister Josephine to consider, and of course, his father, old dead Leonard, whose name Cain had only just come to know.

The path curved slowly around to the left and became more overgrown. Fresh leaves scattered the ground, just visible in the fading light, and Cain smelled the sap of recently broken stems. The stench of dog shit came to him, and a second later he saw a glistening footprint in the center of a huge dog turd.

"Peter!" he called again.

Cain heard footsteps behind him. They ran in concert with his own. Stopping suddenly, he crouched down. The footsteps stopped as well, but it took one or two extra paces for their owner to react. Peter was ahead of him, and now someone was following on.

A *swish* marked the passage of something through the air just above him. He glimpsed only a shadow against the darkening sky, moving quickly across the narrow path, and it was impossible to distinguish its shape.

As if frustrated by the long pause, the footsteps behind him recommenced, slower this time and more cautious.

Cain ran. *A trap.* Peter had led him into a trap, a network of paths and alleys they had not used on their journey to the pub, dark places, narrow places, and now that he was totally lost the trap would spring and he would be caught within its as-yet-unseen jaws. What those jaws would do to him—hold or chew—he had no wish to find out.

"Stop!" The voice came from behind, and Cain had no intention to obey. He was scared and excited at the same time—scared that they were closing in on him at last, and excited because he did not truly believe that they would hurt him. Not after what Peter had said. They were weird, they were strange, perhaps they were not even wholly human. But they were not murderers.

Vlad?

Cain shook his head and ran on. There was no point calling ahead at Peter now. If the landlord was going to stop at his behest, he would have done so, and Cain had no wish to reveal himself to his pursuer more than he already had. He came to a junction in the path, one way leading back to a main road, the other plunging into a confusion of allotments and houses. He closed his eyes and breathed deeply, not concentrating at all, letting his mind wander until it pictured Peter taking the path toward the road. Cain smiled, pleased that he would soon be somewhere where there were other people.

The footsteps were gaining, a shape flitted by above him again, much closer than before, and this time he caught the scent of honey. Sister Josephine's magic cream. The main road felt like the safest place to be.

The path to the road was maybe two hundred paces long, overhanging with plants and obscured here and there by collapsed timber fences where undergrowth had weighed them down. As Cain began running, a shadow occluded the far end, blocking off his line of sight to the main street. The shadow moved quickly toward Cain, and the footsteps came from behind as well, closer and closer and never letting up.

He was trapped, caught in front and from behind.

Maybe this is it, Cain thought, but even then he did not truly fear for his life. *Vlad, there was dead Vlad, but he was something totally different. He did not know the Way.* The implied admission in that thought shocked him, scaring him more than the shape rushing at him along the path.

"Cain!" the shape shrieked, and it was Peter, his voice high-pitched with terror, pleading, and maybe warning as well.

"Peter? What—"

"Cain! Stop!" Cain spun around as his pursuer finally caught up with him. Magenta! But not the Magenta he had met before, nor had he ever imagined her like this. Her leather trousers and jacket gleamed where they caught street light, and her black T-shirt was stretched across breasts much smaller than he remembered. Even in the dusky light of the overgrown path he could see that she was taller than before, leaner, and her hair was now long and blond. Her face had changed, too, in some subtle way that he would have put down to weight loss had it not been only days since he had last seen her. The eyes were the same. Perhaps, windows to the souls that they were, she could never change her eyes. On her belt he saw the handles of knives, the tips of throwing stars, and the dull black butt of a pistol.

Magenta the impersonator faced him down, sweating slightly from the exertion.

"Cain, *please!*" Peter said. Cain turned to Peter, and over the running man's shoulders he saw something else at the end of the path. Something impossible. It was a dog, but the largest he had ever seen. Easily five feet tall at the shoulders. Big head, wide jaws, and eyes that glittered with fury. Even at that distance, Cain could make out the eyes.

It ran.

"Cain!" Peter threw the photograph album, and Cain plucked it from the air. The landlord's face was filled with dread and loss, terror and sadness, and Cain took one uneasy step toward him.

"No!" Magenta said, and she shoved Cain along the path leading into the allotments.

"I'm sorry, Cain!" Peter shouted. "I should have told you everything."

Cain stumbled for the first few paces and then found his footing. He glanced back just in time to see the huge dog leap on Peter's back.

"Peter! We have to—"

"No," Magenta said again. Her fingers bit into his shoulder and pushed him along, but Cain could not help but look.

Peter screamed. It was a long, high cry, and it surprised Cain so much because everything about today was secret. He had that unshakable feeling, the sense that all of this was taking place below the surface of understanding, somewhere darker than these alleys and much less known. He was certain that even if people heard the scream they would attribute it to children playing, or someone's TV turned up too loud. And when a gardener next came along this path, he would see—

The dog clasped its jaws around the back of Peter's neck and bit hard. It shook its head, raked at the fallen man's back with its claws, growling and salivating and crunching its teeth into gristle and bone. Cain thought he heard a whisper from the dying man: "George." But it may have been air escaping his shredded lungs, or the sound of clasping plants scraping along Cain's own clothing.

A second later, the path curved and they lost sight of Peter. But he was not out of mind.

And when that gardener came, he would see a splash of blood and imagine it to be evidence of a cat's nighttime kill.

No! Cain tried to drive his visions away. He wanted to ignore them, he hated the Way, despised Pure Sight, but right then he knew things he should not, and he could not control that. He knew the pain and terror in Peter's mind, the sensation of his spine and ribs being splintered from behind, the dog's claws raking flesh from his legs, its jaws grinding to gain a better purchase on the back of his neck. Cain cried out and closed his eyes, but he saw the bloodied mud in front of Peter's face and felt the last ragged breath leaving his body in a cry of pain and total, utter betrayal: *"George . . ."*

"Come on!" Magenta snapped. She slapped Cain's face. He dropped the album and bent to pick it up, and Magenta slapped him again. "Come *on!*" She led them through the allotments, across small streets that Cain had never seen, and all the while something was following them. It darted across the open sky, leaned out from behind chimneys, squatted down on rooftops, giggling, laughing as they passed by.

"Ignore her," Magenta said.

"Her?"

"I think you know by now. Stop doubting yourself."

"Sister Josephine." He looked up as they ran along the next street and there she was, sitting astride the ridge of a roof, smiling down at them. Her habit flowed about her, her wimple catching the sinking sun's light, and a second after Cain saw her she slipped from view behind the house and rose again into the sky, little more than a shadow.

"I'm seeing things," he said, "it's my imagination." But he knew that was not the case.

"Did you imagine the dog tearing Peter to sheds?"

"George?"

"George."

"You. Your weapons. You have a gun and knives—why didn't you use them? Who the hell are you today?"

Magenta slowed and glanced over her shoulder, and her eyes would have told the truth even had she not spoken. "Your savior."

They ran on. Sister Josephine no longer seemed to be following, although Cain still scanned rooftops for her telltale shadow. He also kept glancing behind, expecting to see the mad dog on their trail, running them down and doing to them what it had done to Peter. He was terrified. This was as real and bloody as his life had ever been, and his senses were in overload.

Now they are *murderers,* he thought. *George—or whatever George is—is a murderer.* What he had just witnessed cast a whole new light on the night he had followed George into the garden. But he had heard the others laughing at him, mocking him, and he wondered whether Magenta had been one of them. Magenta as she was then, at least.

Magenta led them left and right, through streets and alleys, gardens and parks. She ran like an athlete, her movements spare and assured, her body comfortable with the exertion. She was little more than a shadow herself, and he almost lost her a few times. But she was always waiting around the next corner. *She* never lost *him.* By the time they slowed to a fast walk, it was dark. The sky was clear, the moon was half full, and starlight bathed them.

"Are we going back to the house?" Cain asked, gasping for breath. It was the first time he had spoken in half an hour, and even then Magenta seemed disinclined to answer. But he persisted, grasped her shoulder and spun her around. She snorted, and he gasped; he felt such power in her knotted muscles, so much potential. And as her eyes bore into him, he withered beneath their gaze.

"Where else would you have me take you!"

"Magenta, I don't know what's happening here. I have no idea! I've just seen a man killed by a . . . a whatever. George? A dog? I'm so confused! Please, don't take it out on me. I need your help."

"Face up to your fucking life and you'll help

yourself." She looked over Cain's shoulder, making sure they had not been followed. Even though her eyes were wide and her breath came in harsh gasps, she seemed unafraid. That, at least, was a comfort. Cain looked again at her tooled-up belt and wondered whether he had any choice but to obey her. She was his savior, but he'd had little say in the matter.

"I've been trying to do that ever since I came here," Cain replied. "And you . . . *all* of you have been trying to drive me out."

Magenta raised her eyebrows and held her breath. "You really think that?"

"Yes!"

She stared at him as if examining a curiosity. Then she shook her head and turned away.

"Wait!"

"Come on," she said. "I'll take you back to my place. They won't do anything while you're there. Not that I believe George would ever touch you anyway, even when he's . . ." She trailed off, leaving so much unsaid.

"George just killed Peter, and you're going to go home? What about the police?"

"We're beyond all that," Magenta said quietly. She stopped again and turned, held Cain by the shoulders so that she could stare him straight in the eyes. He found it extremely disconcerting and yet he was mesmerized, held there by the budding understanding that she was as different to him as George, Whistler, and Sister Josephine. This Magenta exuded danger in rich, red waves.

"You've changed," he said.

"It's what I do. It's what happens to me along the Way. Now listen, Cain, and listen well. I like you. I liked you from the moment we met when I was clowning about, because . . . because I *have* to like you. However I try to drive my feelings, that's only natural. I don't like many people, but when Peter told me you were coming here, I knew we'd be crossing paths more than once. That's destiny. Peter's mistake was in telling you more than he should and revealing us to danger."

"Us? You're in with them. I knew it. I've heard you laughing at me with the rest of them. But why save me if you're with them?"

"I'm not 'with' them, Cain. There's something you still don't understand. Actually, there's plenty you don't understand, but one of the main things is this: Knowing the Way is a lonely thing, because it changes us beyond all recognition. All of us take it in a different way, and none of us are right or wrong, because we're so far removed from what you think of as civilization. That's why we don't need to call the police. Laws are for sheep." She spat that last word as if it stung her mouth.

"And sheep are normal people, is that right?"

Magenta glared at him, then away again.

"And that makes them less than you, because they don't have Pure Sight?"

"They're not less, they're just different. They are to mice as we are to them."

"How humble." Cain wanted to leave her then, flee this woman who thought she was way beyond the law, outside society. There had been a murder, and he should report it. But deep down he knew that what she had said made some terrible sense, the idea that all this was happening out of sight of normality, in a place where the extraordinary was ordinary. The nun flew, George changed into a wild dog, Whistler played his hypnotic tunes, and Magenta was someone different each day. The Way had taken them along strange paths, routes untrodden by all but a few. Cain imagined his own future opening up as wide as theirs, and just as far away from the beaten track of predictability.

"So what the hell do you know about my father?"

"Let's just get back," Magenta said. "You have a lot to learn about yourself."

Cain looked at the photograph album tucked under his arm. He had resisted the temptation to stop and open it ever since seeing Peter so savagely killed, as if looking would bring him the same fate. Now the chance to sit down and look through the album was close at hand.

Peter was dead. Poor Peter, whose mocking tone had covered the deep-set sadness he carried within. He had never found the Way, even though it appeared he had spent his life around those who knew it.

I don't want it, Cain thought, and images of his father jumbled through his mind: feeding Cain, berating him, torturing him. This photograph album may contain so much more, and truth could take away some of the pain of his past. Or perhaps it would only go to make that pain worse.

Cain followed Magenta through the night. He thought of the Face and Voice, and realized that he had not called them when he should have. Things had changed so much since his last call, he had no idea what he would say.

Hello, my father was right all along. I do have it. They tell *me I do.*

Cain shook his head and wished for a normal life.

"Normal is average, and you will *never* be that," Cain's father once said. "Mediocrity is an offense against the potential of our minds, a slur on the promise of our species. Why build a computer and use it to time an egg? Why create the wheel and use it to gather potatoes? People keep to the narrow roads already set down for them. They don't look beyond their lives. They don't shift the veil. You are going to be so, so special, Cain."

Cain was seven years old, and he had never climbed a tree.

Chapter Eight
Family

They reached Endless Crescent without further incident. When Cain and Peter had walked to the pub earlier that day, it had taken only twenty minutes. He and Magenta seemed to have been running for hours, and he believed she must have taken him right across the city and back again, moving via side streets and little-used roads in an effort to shake any pursuers. But why do that when what pursued them lived in this house?

Cain was utterly exhausted. Unused to such exercise, he had almost fallen behind, but Magenta's strong hand—and those deep eyes—encouraged him on. That, and the sense of danger she exuded, the weapons on her belt ready at a second's notice. If she was his savior for tonight, then the more dangerous she was the better.

Heaven sat behind them, Peter's tumbled-down home, and there were no lights in its windows tonight. Cain thought that perhaps he would try to get inside tomorrow, but he had no idea what the rest of this night would bring. Perhaps tomorrow's plans were best made when dawn touched the east.

"Home sweet home," he muttered, but Magenta did not respond. They walked through the front garden—still it watched, breathed, filled with secretive rustlings—and Magenta opened the front door.

"Do I have anything to fear?" Cain asked, suddenly certain that once he entered the house he would never leave again. "Once I'm in there, is something going to happen to me?"

Magenta turned on the doorstep and her eyes softened. "Cain, haven't you been listening to anything? You're as special as us, as unique. You just haven't admitted it to yourself."

"Peter thought he was special. That didn't prevent George from tearing out his spine."

"Peter never knew the Way, and he said too much. If he'd do it once, he'd do it again. He was the landlord, but even after so long it appears he would have betrayed us. We can't have that."

"You knew this was going to happen?"

"No, but I'm not surprised."

"So what do you do?" Cain asked. "What are your special superhero powers? What has the Way given you?"

"Freedom," she said, smiling at Cain as if he were a child. "Knowledge. Truth. It's given me a real life, not one dictated by preconceived notions of right and wrong, good and bad. I'm anyone I want to be, Cain. One day I'm white, next day Asian. One day I'm someone men would die for, next day they don't even see me. You have no idea of the power in that."

"I came here looking for my own life," he said miserably. "I never wanted to get involved with everyone else's." Wherever he looked he saw Peter on the ground, the dog raking at his back with its unnatural claws, and he could still taste the fear and dirt in the landlord's mouth.

"You'll find it," Magenta said. Her voice was so certain.

Magenta's flat appeared normal, and yet there was something about it that disturbed Cain greatly. To begin with, he could not quite pin down what that was, but it did not take long for him to see the sham.

The hallway was lined with bookcases, and each shelf was jammed with books stacked vertically and horizontally. He glanced along the spines, but there was not one title or author he recognized. None of the spines were cracked or creased; all of the books were unread. He remembered Whistler's strange volumes of *My Philosophy,* and he suddenly had no wish to open these.

The living area was sparsely furnished and decorated in soft green, the dining area empty apart from a tiny table and one lonely chair. The kitchen looked brand new, highly polished stainless-steel fittings set off against white units and a concrete slab floor. It was well kept, neat and tidy, completely unused. Cain went to the bathroom, and as he stood peeing he looked around at the highly polished fittings, the sparkling floor, the bath and shower cubicle that were all far too pristine to have simply been *cleaned*. These were *untouched*.

Magenta was in the living room when he came out, sitting in the middle of the floor, stretching. She nodded at the photo album he had put on the sofa when they came in. "I guess you'll be wanting to have a look at that now. Feel free to use my bedroom if you want some privacy."

"I'm not sure . . ." Cain said. "Some things are best left unknown."

"You really think so?" She stood up straight, raised her eyebrows, and shrugged.

"What are you doing?"

"Changing." She smiled at his startled expression. "Don't worry, I'm nothing like George. It comes and goes with my moods. It's just the Way for me. Causes some bastard aches and pains sometimes, so I stretch out as often as I can." She shrugged off her black jacket and unzipped the fly of her leather trousers, squirming them over her hips and dripping them to the floor.

"Maybe I will use your bedroom," Cain said, abashed. He picked up the album and tried not to look at Magenta, and the harder he tried the more he looked. She was smiling at him, but there was nothing sexual about it at all, nothing enticing.

"Sorry if this makes you uncomfortable," she said, "but I can feel something coming on. Wait and see, if you want. If it will open your eyes a little bit more, it can only do good."

I don't want Pure fucking Sight! he thought once again, but Magenta grabbed the hem of her tight

T-shirt and lifted it over her head in one motion, and he could not move. Her body was lithe and athletic, her breasts small, her hips narrow. She sighed and stretched, the muscles on her legs and stomach tensing and releasing as if happy to be free of unnatural hindrances.

"You're gorgeous," he said, unable to help himself. *I saw a man killed tonight, and now I'm telling a naked woman she's gorgeous.* But Peter's death seemed distant already, as if it had happened far away in place and time. If that was Cain thinking more along the Way, then he could live with that small part of it; it gave him comfort.

"Thanks," she said matter-of-factly. "Sometimes, I guess." She lifted one arm behind her head, stretched one leg out in front of her, squatted down, and groaned as joints clicked with the sound of pebbles on concrete. She turned her head to either side, similar crunches greeting each movement, and her face creased in pain.

"Sorry, Cain," she said.

"What for?"

"Well . . ." But she said no more. Her body flipped sideways onto the floor, and Magenta groaned again, squirming on the carpet. Something moved beneath the skin of her stomach, flexing it, pushing out as if eager for release. It rose higher, parting just below her ribs and pulsing up under her chest. Each breast seemed to grow in size, and her nipples changed from soft and pink to hard and dark. She whipped her head on the floor, blond hair trailing. Her fingers scratched at the carpet—

Cain saw a forest of plucked threads, evidence of many previous changes—and then Magenta's hair was suddenly brunette.

He stepped back. There was a new woman before him already.

"Shit," she moaned, twisting on the floor, her legs filling out, arms thickening, and something happened to her face. *"Shit!"*

Cain turned and ran for the hallway. He meant to flee the flat, but the thought of the ravenous George out there, and perhaps that flying, freakish nun, held him back at the last second. He went into Magenta's bedroom instead, the album clasped to his chest like a talisman, and he shut the door on her swearing and thrashing and her long groans of pain.

He sat on the double bed—it was made up, and the bedding smelled new and just out of the packet—and listened to the noise from the living room. Magenta's voice had deepened a little, and her words, though confused, seemed to be singing out some strange mantra. It was not a prayer as such, but there was a pattern there. Even though Cain could not decipher the meaning, it sent a chill into him, as if he were hearing his own death sentence in a foreign tongue.

Panicked, confused, and feeling more and more as if he were living a dream, Cain went to the window to see if he could escape that way. He looked out over the street at where Heaven sat bathed in moonlight. Nothing moved behind its windows. Its door was firmly shut, and the overgrown garden— ideal home for hedgehogs, foxes, and other night dwellers—was utterly still and deserted. He tried the window, but it was locked. Besides, it was a sheer fifteen-foot drop to the ground. And if he jumped, he would end up tangled in spiky undergrowth.

The album called to him, begging to be opened.

Magenta had fallen silent. Pressing his ear to the door, Cain could hear heavy breathing and the occasional groan accompanying the creak of floorboards. He guessed she was standing up, slowly, becoming accustomed to her new body.

New body? What the fuck was that all about?

The album was warm from where he had been carrying it. Warm as flesh. The covers were of soft, worn leather that could have easily been human skin. He sniffed the book, and it smelled of lost times.

The bedroom door opened and Magenta peered in. She was a brunette now, heavyset, high cheekbones, taller than she had been before. Her eyes were the same, though, and they communicated with Cain, telling him not to be afraid, everything was all right, he would understand soon enough.

He stared, unable to speak past his amazement. A sense of wrongness set him shivering, and he hugged the album for any comfort it could give.

"I'm exhausted," Magenta said, her voice husky and new, "but I'm not rude. You can sleep in here tonight. And tomorrow, if you're ready, I'll introduce you to George and the nun." She closed the door without waiting for a reply.

I should run. I should return to Afresh, tell the Face and Voice what was happening here. They'll take care of me, as I am obviously, patently mad.

And yet . . . and yet there was the photograph al-

209

bum, the one Peter had gone to such great pains to give to Cain before being slaughtered. And within its covers there may be answers to questions Cain had not yet conceived.

Slowly, squeezing his eyes almost shut, Cain let the first leaf fall open.

Cain's father had always refused to answer any questions about the past. "The past is gone, the future is fluid, it's the here and now that matters," Leonard would say, and that was always his response. Even as a child, Cain soon came to realize that this was a way of avoiding the truth. There was so much his father could have told him—about his mother, their life together, and Cain's own time as a baby and young child—but the old man chose to remain silent on the matter. However much Cain asked, the answer was always the same. And sometimes, like a grumpy dog woken from a midday sleep, his father snapped at him.

"Why are you so keen to hear about the past? Aren't you happy with the now? Don't you think I'm doing enough for you, helping you, doing my very best to give you the life you deserve?"

"Yes, Father," Cain would say, knowing that there was no other answer for him to give. And Leonard would grunt and nod, walk away, retreat to his study to conceive of some other cruel test to try and thrust his son toward Pure Sight.

Cain would spend the inevitable lonely hours following such an exchange wandering the house, which was always open to him, and searching through parts of his father's library, which was not.

It always came as a disappointment to find that the books his father studied were much the same as his own: texts on science, mathematics, astronomy, natural history, with nothing given to the exploration of imagination. Back then, Cain had no concept of fiction as an entertainment—it was, he thought, a dark and lonely madness inside him—but he knew of art and expression, and he was saddened that none of the books in the house stretched that way. He would spend hours searching through great tomes on the laws of gravity, hoping that there would be a page or two at least alluding to leaps of imagination. But in such books these leaps were referred to as theories, whereas Cain was searching for dreams.

Sometimes he thought he may find a secret slip of paper that his father had forgotten about, a letter from his mother, something to show that there was more to Leonard than he ever revealed to Cain. But the books were clean, pure, honest volumes with nothing hidden away, utterly closed to interpretation.

In many ways, Cain was blinkered to reality and the true worth of things, but he had always been aware that his father had a past that would perhaps explain much of the present. He had never started to question what was happening to him—what his father was doing—until he was eight years old. From that point on he sought not only Pure Sight, as overseen by his father, but also his own hidden truth, his own story. He started to silently question what his father was doing. And though the possibility of escape never crossed his mind, Cain had become more and more uncomfortable with the way his father was steering his life.

The siren never, ever knew of these thoughts. Somehow the boy kept them to himself, where they grew and grumbled, rooted in an unsettled part of his mind.

He always believed that these thoughts were the source of his shadow.

His imagination never had been very strong.

The first page in the album contained a letter. It was a missive of love, dated thirty years before and written from his mother to his father. Cain opened it from where it was folded in on itself and began to read. At first it did not affect him at all. The sentiments seemed trite, the wording clumsy, and the writing itself was spidery and unsure. But a few lines in he suddenly realized exactly what he was seeing, and it hit him hard. His mother had *touched* this letter. This was of his mother's *mind*. He sobbed out loud, uncontrollably, and dropped the book to the floor. It fell open to reveal several pictures, all of them variations on the same pose: his father sitting astride a horse, with a woman who could only be Cain's mother holding its reins. She looked so gorgeous, so alive, that he had no idea how she could have ever been a mystery to him. This was the first time he had ever seen a picture of her—even after his father's death, no trace of her existence had been found in the house—and he felt as though he had known her his whole life.

Tears blurred the image, and Cain wiped at his eyes. The book stared up at him as if innocent, though it was anything but that. It contained proof of all the lies his father had ever told him. There were images of him and Cain's mother happy together, smiling, looking forward with the future at their fingertips. Somewhere in their sparkling eyes was an idea of Cain, the child they would have in the future, and the limitless potential inherent in that new, small human. He wondered what his mother would have thought of him now. She had died giving birth to him, so Leonard had claimed, but right now Cain had no idea what to believe. His father had always told him that the future was fluid and changeable, but for Cain the past was equally so. Leonard had made it like that. The truth was elusive.

Perhaps in this photograph album Cain would find the skeleton upon which he could flesh out his own history.

He leaned down, still dripping tears, and picked up the book. He closed it so that he could start again at the beginning.

A sudden crashing sound came from outside. Cain started, heart skipping a beat. Something was being smashed on the floor, again and again. It was so violent that he felt the vibrations against his skin, as if the air within the flat shook with each impact. He ran to the door and opened it a crack. Peering across the hall and into the living room, he saw Magenta sitting cross-legged on the floor, hands on her knees, head dipped as if she were asleep. The banging came again, and it was not Magenta. She lifted her head, moved it slightly left and right, rested again.

Cain closed the door, terrified of whatever was causing the ruckus. It stopped and started, stopped again, and by moving around the bedroom he could place where it was coming from: directly above him, from the living room of his flat.

It sounded exactly like the wooden chest being lifted and dropped, again and again.

"Hello, shadow," Cain said. He was not surprised. He closed his eyes and opened them again, found himself in the same position and situation, bit his lip, finally convincing himself that he was not in any normal dream. Perhaps it was a fugue of madness, but then madness breeds it own reality.

The crashing stopped, as if whatever causing it had heard his voice. Cain smiled and looked up at the ceiling, wondering just how close he was to his past. "You don't want me to see this, do you?" he whispered. There was a high-pitched screech as the chest moved a few inches across the floor.

What am I imagining here? he thought. *What am I seeing, smelling, hearing? I must be asleep, but my senses work, and it's the strangest dream ever. And in dreams, can I find the truth?* He opened the album at the third page, looked at the photographs of his father as a young man. *There he is, but is this real? Was he really a soldier? Did he have a mustache like that, his hair cut short, his body fit and lean? Or is this only my mad idea of what I could find, were I only to look?*

Perhaps madness is the Way, after all.

"Voice?" Cain whispered. "Face? You wouldn't believe the shit I've got myself into here." The chest was silent, the shadow still once again.

Cain sat back down on the bed and started leafing through the book. He turned each page slowly, not wishing to rush the process of revelation.

Here was his father in the army, posing next to an armored vehicle of some kind. A laughing man stood in the background, and Leonard looked as if he had just told a joke. His eyes held all the humor his face betrayed. Cain had never seen him like this.

Another image showed his father with a larger group of soldiers, all gathered around a fallen tree trunk, brandishing weapons and with their faces darkened by camouflage paint. His father's eyes were stark white points against his face, piercing, intelligent, filled with a passion that scared Cain because he had never seen it in real life. Not like this, not so pure. The man he had known must have been much reduced by some event in his past.

The next page contained another letter from his mother. It was not a love letter. Time had moved on, and now the two of them were in a comfortable relationship, and she spoke only of news, most of it insignificant. It was a missive written for the sake of it . . . but then the final paragraph made Cain freeze: *Leonard, I have some news I can only tell you face-to-face. I so look forward to Saturday.*

Next page. Cain's parents sat on a cliff-top bench overlooking the sea. Whoever had taken the picture had caught a moment of intense intimacy, one that brought fresh tears to Cain's eyes because he was looking at himself for the first time: his father's hand on his mother's stomach, his mother smiling just over her husband's shoulder, seeing some lost future in the dim distance.

Cain looked across the bedroom at a mirror. He stared into his own eyes and tried to discern a similar future, filled with such hope and potential. But tears seemed to obscure the way, and his pupils were dark and bottomless.

He turned more pages, and the past came at him like a flood of forbidden memories. He had tried to imagine these scenes so often—his parents together, his mother blooming as her stomach grew, the private past that his father would never discuss—that some of them felt like vague memories. It was as if he had dreamed each and every photograph and then forgotten the dreams until now, when the actual images reminded him.

He knew the face of his mother, even though he had never seen her before. So beautiful, so caring, and so naive of what his father would become following her death. Cain knew for sure that there were no such things as ghosts. If there were, his mother would have surely returned to help him by now. He looked around the bedroom just in case. As ever, he was alone.

There were more letters in the album, more photographs, and then Cain saw himself. A small baby, helpless, pink, and wrinkled and staring out at a strange new world with disbelieving, wide-eyed innocence. He looked in the mirror again and his expression now was similar; all except for his eyes, which, instead of innocent, were dark with fear.

His mother was no longer in any of the pictures. His father was there, grim-faced, heavy sacs beneath his eyes, and he seemed to have aged an eternity in the space of one page. His eyes no longer met the camera lens, and whoever took the pictures seemed to have lost all interest in the subject. Some of them missed part of baby Cain, others cut out most of his father, as if the emotions of loss and grief were affecting the images and distorting what they purported to show. These scenes should be all happiness and smiles, but even the baby seemed to be crying in most of them. Missing the breast, perhaps. Missing the warmth of his mother, lying there while his father cried and did not reach out to touch his newborn son. Maybe a simple hand on the baby's head would have comforted both of them and changed everything that followed. But his father looked too distraught and had never been tactile. Cain had grown up without a single loving hug.

He stared at that picture for a long, long time. It said so much. Most of all, it told him how alone he had always been, from the moment of the birth that killed his mother. His father's face was filled with sadness and hopelessness, but each time Cain looked again his expression seemed to have changed. As the night moved on, and Cain glanced back again and again at the photograph, his father's face showed grief, despair, and rage. Most of all, rage.

The idea that much of what Cain had endured was rooted in his father's anger—his need for some form of revenge—was almost unbearable.

There were no more photographs, no more letters. The rest of the album was blank. He flicked the remaining pages again and again, staring at the blank leaves in the hope that something more may appear. A sign, perhaps, that his father had loved him. An acknowledgment that his early years had held some semblance of normality. But the pages remained as empty as Cain's memory of those first few years of his life. A few weak thumps came from upstairs, as if the shadow were trying to help. But even darkness sat wrong in Cain's mind, because darkness implied something to hide.

Cain sat there for the rest of the night, nursing the photograph album and wondering why Peter had been so keen for him to see it. Peter had known his father, but he had never mentioned his mother, and this album was mostly about her. Even that last photograph, so indicative of what the future would hold for the poor baby Cain, was most powerful due to her absence.

Had Peter known her as well? It seemed likely. Whatever secrets he had yet to reveal, however, had been slaughtered by that mad dog.

Cain tried to sleep, but sleep was elusive. Dreams hovered like carrion birds, waiting to sweep in and take him for themselves. His wakefulness kept them at bay.

About four in the morning the birds began their dawn chorus. Cain opened the window so that he could hear better, perhaps discern some meaning in their joyous babble. The singing was wild and loud, as if the birds reveled in this hour when they had the daylit world to themselves, free of humans ruining its beauty with car engines, bustle, and the belief that the world was here to serve them. Birds sang from the front garden, the rooftops, and on the wing, and their celebration of the new day almost made Cain cry. It made him realize just how insignificant he was. It also scared him; there was understanding in the birds' songs, a comfortable knowledge that humanity had it all wrong.

Perhaps this was a secret that Magenta, Whistler, and the others were aware of.

Cain opened the photograph album to daylight and a picture fell out. He had not seen it before. He could have sworn that he'd checked every page, but still this new picture lay on the floor. He remained seated for a while; he had an inkling of what he was seeing, but to move closer would be to fully reveal the truth. He was not certain he wanted that. He could stand and leave the room now, without looking back. Ignore the picture. But he had an idea that even if he were to do that, he would see it eventually. Magenta would force him to look. Or Sister Josephine would appear naked to him again, in a dream or not, and smile as she explained everything. *Here we are with your father*, she would say. *A long time ago now, but I remember it as if it were yesterday*. And she would tell him why she remembered that time so well, and that was something Cain had no wish to hear.

To see the picture himself would be for the best.

He bent and picked the rectangle of card from the floor, something flat containing such depth. And there they were. His father, young and yet with eyes already shaded by the death of his mother. Gathered around him in a protective group were Whistler, Sister Josephine, George, and a short blond woman with piercing eyes that must have been Magenta. His father's hand rested on

Magenta's shoulder. Apart from his father, all looked exactly as he knew them. No younger, no different, no evidence that time could play with them. *Immortal,* Cain thought, but it was an abstract idea and he did not dwell on it. Did not *believe* it.

He sat back, holding the picture at arm's length lest it bite. He wondered whether Peter had been the photographer.

A door opened and the birds paused in their song. The sound of pan pipes struck up from somewhere, inside or outside Cain could not tell, and the chest in his flat began thumping the floor as if the shadow wished to follow. The birds started singing again and Cain cried out, suddenly afraid of the sounds, hoping that the siren would sing in and silence everything for a few precious seconds with its gift of pain and punishment. But the siren stayed away.

Magenta entered the room, the fresh new Magenta ready for the new fresh day. As she sat on the bed and held him, Cain thought of his father touching her shoulder and staring grimly into the camera.

"I don't understand," he sobbed, ashamed of his tears but unable to hold them back.

"You will," she said, hugging him to her. There was nothing familiar or affectionate in the gesture, and it felt awkward, but Cain was thankful all the same. Right then, even though he feared Magenta, he was grateful for the contact.

He cried some more, she rocked him, he glanced up at her face, and she stared away as if distracted.

Suddenly feeling tired, he rested his head against her shoulder and closed his eyes, shutting out the soreness of tears, the sting of revelations from the photograph album. As if to escape the coming day and what it may bring, he slept.

He is in a room he has never seen before. There is no young Cain there this time, it is him as he is now, the new Cain, the explorer Cain discovering his life. This is not a room in his father's house. It has colored pictures on the wall and extravagant furniture. There is a crystal chandelier hanging from the low ceiling. Something nags at him, some troublesome knowledge, but he cannot recall what it is. It remains in the background like a whisper in the night, just beyond the range of hearing.

The voice that screams at him is anything but a whisper.

"Come back!" it screeches. Its panic and volume make the voice unrecognizable and androgynous. Cain does not fear the siren right now, but he does fear the voice. It is insistent, demanding, and desperate, and the implication is that if he does not obey, bad things will happen. "Come back! *Come back!*"

A rhythmic thumping accompanies the voice. It provides a background tempo to the screams. It could be a fist banging on a door, or a head impacting a wall.

Cain thinks that the voice may belong to the Voice, or the Face. They can see the problems he has encountered, and they are begging him to return to Afresh, to find safety and leave danger behind. Come back, they are calling. But that does not sound like them. They would not scream or rage, they would be gentle and understanding.

"Come back!"

Not like that.

The thumping again, and behind the sound is something worrying: the cracking and splintering of timber, as if something is breaking through.

Cain thinks he may be dreaming, but everything feels very real. He walks to the door and tries the handle, but it is locked. He runs his hand across the door's surface but feels no lumps, no evidence that it is being battered from the other side. It is cool and calm.

"Come back!" Pleading and threatening. Cain shakes his head and cringes, as if to instantly lose the memory of the voice.

He walks to the first of the pictures hanging on the wall. It shows a view of 13 Endless Crescent from across the street. The photographer must have been standing with his back pressed against Peter's front door; there is even the hint of a shadowy overhang in the top of the picture. Number 13's front garden is trimmed and well-maintained as ever, but even from this angle there is no hint of what lies beneath the low shrub canopy. The house is bathed in sunlight and the first-floor window is open, revealing a figure standing just inside. The sunlight barely touches the shape, and yet Cain can see that it is an incarnation of Magenta. Those eyes hold no doubt. He looks up at his own dining room window. Though there is a face there, it is not his own. It is a shadow in defiance of the sun.

"Come back to me!" The voice has changed now, become more modulated and thoughtful, as if realizing that blind panic will never work. Cain still feels no compunction to obey its strange command. He does not know exactly *where* it wants him to go, nor even where it is coming from.

The next picture looks like a police photograph of a murder scene. But it is so well-taken, the lighting so perfect, that Cain suspects that it took a while to set up and many attempts to perfect. It shows the landing outside his room, the small attic door standing ajar, Vlad's belongings spilled out like vented guts. Everywhere there is blood. It is splashed up the walls, spattered on the carpet, ground into the inside and outside of the opened door, rich and black in the claw marks slashed into the wood. The door to his own flat is closed, and speckled with blood and viscera. The color is startling, the quantity shocking. *I thought he was killed far from here,* Cain thinks, but then he catches sight of the next photograph and his attention is drawn away.

It is a painting this time, set in his own flat. There is much that he recognizes, and yet he also perceives subtle differences: The walls are too bright, the furniture wrongly organized, as if whoever painted this did so from instruction rather than memory. His coat is flung over the back of the sofa, making the flat his own. The view through the window is blurred, a chaos of colors that seems on the verge of breaking through the glass and flooding the flat, swallowing everything whole. There is something behind the sofa.

"Come back, Cain!"

Cain frowns, moves closer to the painting, and as he steps to one side his view behind the sofa inexplicably improves. He presses his face against the wall, squints, and now he can see what it is. The wooden chest. Or what is left of it.

"Cain, *Cain,* come back! Don't leave me all alone, not here, not forever!"

The chest has exploded from inside. Splinters of wood prickle the rear of the sofa, and several have even penetrated the ceiling, hanging there like stalactites.

"Cain . . . no." The voice speaks this time. The shouting has stopped. And Cain knows it is the voice of the shadow. He had not recognized it before because he was so used to hearing it mocking, sardonic, not like this. Not shouting. Not hopeless and pleading.

Whatever was inside the chest has gone. The broken timber is scored with claw marks, though he cannot tell whether they are on the inside of the wood or the outside. He glances back at the framed photograph of Vlad's murder scene, but these new marks are different. Less violent, more desperate.

"Cain?"

"Yes?" At last, Cain could no longer prevent himself from answering.

"I need you. Not everything you see is true. Don't believe your eyes. Believe your mind."

"You're the shadow," Cain says.

"If that's how you want to view me."

Cain stares at the painting of the broken chest. A

painting rather than a photograph, because it has yet to happen.

"Don't believe your eyes," the shadow says again, "and come back to me, Cain."

"I don't know what you mean. I don't know what to believe."

"Maybe you've just had a bad dream."

Cain runs his index finger across the top of the picture frame and it comes away dusty. He wonders whose skin he has on his. "There was a woman," he says, "and she kept changing."

The shadow is silent for a while, as if considering his comment. But then it chuckles, back to mockery, all evidence of former insecurity now vanished. "Cain, *really*."

Cain turns and walks to the window, looks out, sees nothing at all. It is not simply night, it is *empty*. There is nothing beyond the room. He glances over his shoulder at the door and the banging starts again, but this time its insistence is intimidating rather than frantic.

"Come back to me, Cain," the shadow says in a singsong voice. "We belong together."

Cain shakes his head, sits down, and wakes up.

"Cain?"

Someone shook his shoulder. He opened his eyes and saw the strange woman, but her eyes gave her away. Strange, yes, but always Magenta.

"Is this a dream?" he asked.

"Not this, not now. Come on. You've slept past midday, and we need to talk."

Cain sat up on the bed, groaning and massaging

his limbs. It felt as though he'd run several miles in his sleep, over and above the distance they ran last night. Magenta stood back and waited by the door, but Cain's gaze was drawn to the wall next to her. There were no pictures there and no sign that there ever had been. The room was as blank and sterile as the rest of Magenta's flat. He glanced up at the ceiling, but nothing slammed down demanding his return.

"You look like you've seen a ghost," she said.

Cain laughed. There was no other way he could react to such a platitude. His humor did not last for long.

"How do you feel?" she asked.

He shook his head, ran his fingers through his hair. "Like I've been duped into being myself. Like I don't really belong anywhere. And I'm starting to really believe that."

"None of us belong, Cain," Magenta said. "Why do you think we're all here together?"

"I have no idea! That's what I mean, this is all just so alien, so confusing! And I'm not one of you, Magenta." He shook his head. "Is Peter really dead, or is that another lie?"

Magenta turned away, her eyes downcast. "He's dead. George has never listened to any of us. We all know that we're right and strong and free, but George's fault is that he acts on that too much, not only when he needs to. We told him that you'd discover everything soon enough, in your own time."

Cain thought of the album he had looked through and the pictures contained therein. His father was around him now more than he ever had been while alive. Cain found that comforting, and yet also unfeasibly terrifying, as if the old man could spy on him even now. Magenta and the others were a part of his father's secret past, a past that Cain was never meant to know. Or was he? And there was the crux of his confusion; the fact that this whole situation still felt manipulated and coerced.

"You've known Peter a long time," Cain said—a statement, not a question.

Magenta nodded. Cain tried to perceive a glint of mourning in her expression, but he could not fool himself.

"Aren't you sad that he's dead?"

"Everyone dies."

"Even you? Even Whistler? *He* looks exactly the same now as he did in that old photo with my father."

"Whistler and I know the Way."

Cain waited, but she did not elaborate. "So that's it," he said. "That's an explanation. The Way gives you eternal life."

Magenta laughed. "Of course not," she said. "It just tells us how to live life properly."

"By killing people."

Magenta stared at him, a slight smile on her new, fuller lips. "Your life has changed," she said.

"You think I ever *had* a life?"

"Forget your preconceptions. Forget everything you think you should have, and start thinking about what you need. You're blessed with such a gift, Cain."

"Blessed! Do you know what my father did to me?"

227

"Of course I know." She waved her hand, dismissing such a stupid question. "He was a trifle extreme in his efforts, but only by society's standards. And that's where all concepts of freedom, choice, and free will fall down. Consider yourself a part of society—part of the norm—and you've set yourself down a path from which you will never deviate. It may twist and turn, veer left and right, and sometimes fracture, but it always progresses the same way. *This* way: birth, school, job, marriage, children, death. However many variations of that life there may be, there are constants by which it will abide, simply because of the world it exists in. And those few—those very few—that find the Way are called either mad or criminals. Simply because they follow their hearts!"

"You're not making any sense."

"I'm saying Leonard gave you a blank slate, and still you left Afresh believing you knew what you wanted."

"Of course I know. I want my own life."

"So what are you going to do with it? What does that really *mean*?"

Cain blinked, stared at Magenta's beautiful, bewitching eyes. "I'm going to make it my own," he said. "My father denied me—"

"He denied you the easy route!" Magenta said. "He sacrificed much of his life to make sure you got the best out of yours. He never found the Way himself, not like me and Whistler and the others. He was like Peter—a trickster who had some knowledge, some skewed insight into how things *could* be, but could never quite get there himself.

He only wanted the best for you. For him, that was the next-best thing. You're all he ever wanted."

"He tortured me!"

"You did that to yourself."

"No! He kept me locked in a room, he hurt me, and—"

"How? How did he hurt you?"

"The siren!"

"Every time that happened, it was you that prompted it."

Cain felt threat oozing from Magenta now, a rich, alien sense of menace that flowed around him like her exhalations.

"How do you know so much?" he asked, aghast.

"He gave you everything he could without ruining your life," she said, ignoring his question. "He gave you the chance to start."

"I don't want it," Cain said. "If it means I become something like George, I don't want to know the Way. I want a wife, and children, and a job."

"No you don't!" Magenta scoffed, turning and spitting at the wall. Her saliva sizzled into the plaster and disappeared, and Cain wondered whose imagination was making it do that. "If you do, then you're a fool," she said, "and Leonard and I wasted our time."

"So will you all decide to kill me now?" Cain asked. "Slaughter me like you did Vlad, tear out my guts and leave me in a park somewhere? Set George on me one evening while I'm out walking?"

Magenta looked at him, and suddenly her eyes were filled with something he could not identify at first. It was so far from the anger that had been percolating there that he stood from the bed and backed away toward the window. It was, he supposed, sadness.

"Of course not," she said. "You may think us inhuman, but we're far more human than most." She lowered her eyes. "No intelligence murders its own son."

Cain did not hear the word. He could not. Shock held him cool and heavy in that room, grasping tight as if ready to burst his soul from the weak construct of flesh and bone that betrayed it every single day.

Son.

"What are you saying?"

"You hated your father, Cain, even though he did everything in his power to give you something special. That's all he ever wanted for you. I don't want you to hate me the same way. Go if you want."

"Are you saying you're my *mother?*"

Magenta stepped aside and opened the door. "Nothing will happen to you," she said. "Go back to Afresh. Have a nice life. I wish I'd never bothered. Poor Leonard . . ." Her eyes glittered, though tears and anger fought for the cause.

Cain did not want to move past her. He thought of the group photo loose in the album, his father so much younger and the blond woman he had already assumed to be Magenta, his father's hand on her shoulder, squeezing.

"I'll make it easy for you," Magenta said. She left, slamming the door behind her.

The flat was suddenly empty. Unlived in. Sterile. As Cain sat on the bed and started to cry, his tears gave it life.

* * *

Later, Cain left the bedroom and peeked into the living room. The flat was deserted; he did not need to look around corners or through doors to know that for sure. It was an empty space filled with unused furniture, that was all, and there was not one clear sign of Magenta's occupation anywhere. There were not even any smells—no whiffs of perfume from the bathroom, no stale cooking from the kitchen. He had seen her sitting cross-legged on the living room floor, motionless, as if loath to move and touch, mark this place as her own.

Perhaps she was a ghost. Cain did not believe in ghosts, but neither did he believe in werewolves, or nuns that flew, or musicians that could hypnotize a person with one note. And at least that wild possibility would explain her lack of presence here, and the fact that she seemed to change appearance at will.

Mother? Cain thought. *Can it be that she's my mother?*

But she was no ghost, just as George was not a werewolf, not really. They were people changed beyond recognition by what they knew. Moved on, they would claim, but Cain simply thought of them as changed. If anything, lessened. He did not wish to be like that.

"No way," he said, and the siren exploded inside him, driving him to his knees in the lifeless flat, fingers clawing furrows in the carpet, head vibrating with the volume, eardrums heating and suddenly cooling again as they leaked blood. He screamed but could not hear himself. He cried, but no tears fell. It went on and on, longer than ever before, and though Cain knew it was not really here, he could not convince the siren to fall quiet. With his eyes squeezed shut, there was nothing to see but blackness. A shadow seemed to dance across his negative vision, a shifting blur on his eyelids, but if he turned his eyes in pursuit it jigged away. Always hidden, always just out of sight. Buried in such pain, he could not really see anything at all.

The siren drifted away in increments, not simply snapping off as it had every time before. There were echoes, but none of them touched anything in that room. The violent noise whispered away, hissing angrily in his bloodied ears, but none of the air in the flat vibrated with its memory. It was inside him, hidden away deep in memory and history and the part of him that strove for a life of its own. However convinced he was that it would never come again, it would always be there, waiting. And yet he could still not quite believe that it was of his own making. A cruel, confused memory controlled the siren still: the memory of his father.

Perhaps his mother could influence it also.

Cain sat up and leaned against a wall, panting and sweating as the remnants of agony receded like dusk fading to night. He wiped a trickle of blood from each ear, and when he rubbed his fingers together the blood seemed to disappear. He heard a fast, insistent thumping, and it could have been the chest on the floor above, or his heart projecting its beat. If he closed his eyes, the shadow still inhabited the blood-red landscape of his inner sight, so he kept them open, excluding the presence for now. The thumping lessened as his heart slowed, he calmed, and sunlight shone impassively through the windows.

Magenta had left the photograph album in the bedroom, propped against the unruffled pillows like an offering. Cain would not accept it. He had seen what it contained, and those memories would be with him forever. There was no need to reinforce that secret history. He had rejected Magenta, and whether or not she was his mother, that had felt good and *right*. He had stood up for himself, imposed his own version of life onto the idea that Magenta seemed to have for him. Magenta, and also his father, because the old man's influence was as rich as ever, hanging around him now like a smell that can never be washed away. The siren was proof of that. The two of them together had wanted him to gain Pure Sight, but he had his own visions of what his life should be. It did not involve killing, or flying, or changing into other people. It had nothing to do with seeing past the way things seemed to be, because Cain would be quite happy with that comfortable surface reality. If things ever *seemed* sane, level, and safe again, why should he seek more? The brief glance he had been afforded into their strange world would stay with him, but in time it would fade into a hazy memory to accompany dreams of the basement room, the tortures, his misplaced childhood. He would prove to himself that his own modest aims were pure and honorable, not naive and shortsighted. Magenta's great fault was believing that she was special. The conviction that her strange existence placed her above normal people denied the very reasoning *behind* her existence. In her quest for individuality and freedom, she had discovered ego of the most destructive kind.

This night, Cain would develop his own ego. He would avoid self-importance and embrace humility, because he was right and they were wrong. The Way was a method to get lost within oneself, not found without. He would be silent and secretive on his mission, and by dawn he would have proven to himself that they—George, Whistler, Sister Josephine, even Magenta—were as damaged and imperfect as anyone. Inadequate. Insane. Monsters.

He pushed himself up the wall, feeling the pocket zipper on his trousers scraping the paintwork. When he turned around and saw the scratch in the plaster, and the small shower of shed paint on the carpet, he smiled. It was the single sign of habitation in Magenta's flat. Already he had made his mark.

But he felt alone and afraid, and once on the landing outside Magenta's front door, he crept up the narrow flight of stairs to his own flat. He glanced at the short door to his right and ran his fingers down the ragged grooves in its surface, thinking of the photograph he had seen, the blood that had bathed this painted wooden surface. There was no sign of it now. The door had been cleaned very well. He considered venturing into Vlad's storeroom once again, but there was probably nothing new to learn in there. Nothing comforting, at least. The trapeze artist had denied the opportunity offered him, and now he was dead. That single brutal truth was all Cain needed to know.

If Magenta really was his mother, perhaps they would not be so cruel.

Shaking his head to prevent foolishness from taking root, Cain opened his door and stepped inside. He threw the bolt behind him and went straight through to the living room. He held his breath, fearing the worst, and before entering he peered through the crack between door and jamb. Moving left and right, he could see most of the room. He let out a relieved sigh when he saw the chest pushed neatly into its corner, undamaged and unopened. The painting downstairs was a lie, at least for now.

Sitting on his sofa, Cain already felt weak. He had devised something of a plan and here he was, already retreating to the comparative safety of his abode. He frowned, staring out the window at the roofline and the sky above. The moon had begun to peer through, universal history prying into the day. He began to shake. Any brief sense of confidence was shivered away, leaving him like water evaporating in sunlight. He drew up his knees and hugged them to his chest, taking comfort in the contact, trying to make himself as small as possible so that the world would not notice him. He was angry with himself, but that anger only scared him more. The memory of Peter being taken down by the mutated George hit him, and recollection gave the image a bloody splash as the landlord's throat was ripped out, his scream swallowed whole. Cain wondered where Peter's body was now, and whether there would even be any fuss when it was found. George was removed from society, and Peter had been too. Perhaps his death would go unnoticed.

Thoughts of Vlad's final minutes created themselves in his mind, and the more he denied them the stronger they became. The fear, anger, and pain he must have felt. The denial. *This is not happening!* Would that intense disbelief make such a death easier to accept? Cain thought not.

The sudden image of his living room window shattering inward as something came through made him stand and retreat to the kitchen. He poured a drink but could not swallow. He was hungry, but the thought of food made him gag. He burped up bile and wondered what somebody else's insides would taste like.

Where had that thought come from?

There was a thump from the living room, and Cain saw the chest moving from the corner of his eye. "Not you," he said, denying the shadow a life because it was so much a part of his father, the past, the rotten past that had tried to change the potential in Cain.

He reached for the telephone to call the Voice and Face and tell them everything that had happened. It would be madness to their ears, but that was just what he wanted; they would come and take him back. Back to Afresh, back to the beginning again, but at least there he would be safe in his own little world. And whatever he wanted that world to be, he would be allowed to construct it. The Face and Voice would guide him through his life, and when death finally came Cain would know that he had lived his own way.

At Afresh . . . locked away . . . where madness was understood.

Am I really mad? he thought. *Maybe I am. Maybe all this is me, the mad life I've already created for myself.* He thought not. It was madness, yes, but a complex creation like this was way beyond him. His father and Magenta were responsible for this insanity.

He dialed, the chest slammed against the floor in the living room, the phone rang at the other end.

"It's me," Cain said when the Voice answered.

The chest exploded.

Cain? the telephone asked.

"Me . . ."

Timber rattled across the floor, ricocheted from the ceiling, and something dark seeped from the shattered box and slid behind the sofa.

Cain? Is that you?

"I think so," Cain said, "but it's the last thing I—"

The shadow stood behind the sofa, smiled a smile a little less that pitch black, and darted across the room. Cain could not move. The shadow snatched the receiver from his hand and smashed it down into the phone, cracking plastic and cutting the Voice's final pleading word in half. It continued striking the phone, seemingly enjoying this tactile act of violence. It did not look at Cain, but he felt its full attention upon him.

Cain managed to step back at last, but only a few steps. His hips hit the kitchen sink and there he stood, wide-eyed, watching the shadow destroy the phone. Once finished, it dropped the receiver and went to work on the phone's innards with teeth

Cain could not see. But they were sharp, however nebulous, and wires were shed like slashed bristles across the kitchen floor.

"No more calls," the shadow said. Its mouth did not move, but the voice was clear in Cain's head. Clear, and familiar.

"You're not here," Cain said, breathing fast, hoping to invoke the truth. "You're not real. You never have been."

"You've kept me locked away for so long, have you forgotten me?"

"I dream of you, but that's all you are. A dream."

"Do dreams touch?" the shadow asked, reaching out and running a cool, dark finger across the back of Cain's hand. Cain snatched his hand back and looked at the red line forming there, a scratch from nothing. "Do they taste?" It jumped forward and thrust two fingers into Cain's mouth, working past his teeth and grasping his tongue. He could taste the shadow, like the remnants of a favorite meal, and the taste brought back memories of the times in his father's basement—shadows where there should have been none, and conversation when loneliness threatened to drive him mad.

The shadow stepped back, giving him space.

"I don't believe . . ." Cain whispered, unable to finish.

"Do dreams smell?" the shadow asked, and Cain shook his head, then nodded, because he could smell the faint odor of someone other than himself. "And you hear me," the shadow said. "You hear me well enough."

"I hear something in my head," Cain said, staring

down at his feet. He did not want to look at the
shadow. He could smell it, taste it, feel it, and hear
it. To see it might just make it real.

"That's good enough," the shadow said. "So now
we need to go."

Cain shook his head. "I only want to go back to
Afresh," he said, tears lubricating his wretchedness. "I only want to spend my time as *I* wish to,
not anyone else. *Me.*"

The shadow sighed, and Cain could not tell
whether it was a movement or a sound. "That's all
I want too," it whispered. "But not at Afresh. You
have freedom to explore, Cain. You can't deny
yourself that just because you're afraid."

"If you think Pure Sight is freedom—"

"Oh, for fuck's sake!" the voice said, going from
peaceful to dripping with violence in a sentence.
Cain looked up, afraid that the shadow would be
coming at him, but it had retreated back into the
living room to attack the sofa. It tore the cloth
outer skin from the timber frame in seconds, tacks
flying like bullets and embedding themselves in
walls and ceiling, stuffing pouring out like coiled
guts. The violence was intense and shocking, and
Cain cowered back. But he knew that this devasta-
tion would never turn against him. However frustrated and angry the shadow may be, it was not
there to harm him. It never had been.

"I shut you away," he said, and the shadow
stopped instantly. It turned toward Cain—there
was nothing substantial about it, nothing really discernible other than a shape and a lack of light—
and tilted its head.

"And now you've let me out again."

"I didn't let you out."

"In all but action you did. You need me. You know you do, somewhere deep down, deeper than . . . well, even deeper than me. Pure Sight is just a name, Cain. A couple of words. You have to find what it means for yourself."

"I don't *want* to."

"You have to. You have no choice."

"I need to talk to—"

"You need to act on your fucking *convictions!*" The shadow struck the sofa again, sending it scraping across the room, almost smashed into two parts by the impact of nothing against its frame. "Shit!" The shadow kicked out, rolled, spun, and in a few seconds the sofa was in pieces.

Cain panted, heart racing, wondering whether he could make the front door without the shadow catching him.

"Of course not," the shadow said. "I'm as attached to you as your smell."

"You're my shadow," Cain said, not quite sure whether that was a question or an admission.

"And something a little more," it said. "I'm your potential. Heed me. Find me. Go through with what you decided to do. Follow them, watch them, know from their ways how different your Way can be."

Cain looked around the open-plan flat and wondered whether he could ever live here again. "Do I have any choice?" he asked.

"Yeah, sure," the voice from the dark of Cain's mind drawled. "I'm just your shadow, after all."

Cain sat down on the kitchen floor so that the island stood between him and the shadow. He could not smell it or hear it, and it remained on that side, aware of what he needed. He closed his eyes. But all he could see was that photograph with his father, hand resting on Magenta's shoulder. Cain had rejected her, his own mother, turned away from her ideas of what he needed from life. And now the shadow was inviting him to explore the same thing.

Cain knew that it was right. He knew that what it said was true. It spoke in his mind, and perhaps it was of his mind. And if he could not trust himself, there was no hope left.

As he sat there thinking, the shadow began to hum. It was the tune he had always recognized but never been able to name. It took him back to his father's house, and the sense of peace and safety that tune had once been able to inspire in him, whatever Leonard was putting him through at the time.

"What is that?" Cain said quietly, and the shadow replied, "I'm not quite sure." It spoke the truth, because he had stopped lying to himself.

Cain made up his mind. He could turn away and flee, and never know how life could really be. Or he could stay, go out into the evening, find and feel his way through the worlds the others in the house had created in their own Ways. And thinking that way suddenly felt so right.

Once, Cain had tried to catch his own shadow. He chased it around the room, leaping, rolling, reaching out. But it always remained one step ahead of him. At the time, he thought it was because it was so fast, but later, as he dwelled upon it, he wondered whether it was because he had yet to see the light.

Chapter Nine
Meat

He would hide in the front garden.

On the way out of the house that evening, there was no sign of Magenta, or anyone else. Cain made it past George's flat without being seen—conscious as ever of the peephole in the door and what may be behind it—and approached the front door. The shadow slipped along behind him, sometimes almost touching his heels, other times lagging a few steps behind as if giving Cain space to move. He opened the door onto dusk and cool air invited him out.

The shrubs in the front garden were waist-high and utterly dark. Even now, in the evening, they exuded a sense of watchfulness, as if whatever lived beneath them never slept, only lay there waiting for the next person to pass by.

"Good," the shadow said, and Cain almost told it to keep quiet before remembering it was only in his head. "Good hiding place."

Cain knelt on the path and moved aside several branches. The shadow went in first, emphasizing the darkness. Cain followed on hands and knees, wincing every time his hands touched down. But there was only soft ground beneath his palms, and the long-lost memories of last year's leaves rotting into the soil. He crawled forward, almost having to drop down onto his stomach to pass by below some thicker branches, looking around for the shadow all the while. He found it hunkered down toward what he thought must be the center of the garden. He knew the shadow because it had no texture or substance, not like the other deep shadows below here, those that were merely the absence of light. Knowing where the shadow was, Cain stopped and lay down on his side, propped on one elbow.

That sense of watchfulness remained, emphasized even more by the evening's silence. Cain had the impression that whatever lived beneath here had seen things, heard and known things, that most other creatures never would. He felt a hundred eyes upon him, questioning his presence with interest but no fear. These creatures remained constantly astounded, a living record of the unusual events in the house, and in their impenetrable minds resided so much that Cain needed to know. If only he could reach out, touch a mouse, and know its consciousness. If these watchful worms could talk, or these slugs and snails could explain history in their silvery trails, then perhaps this night would be unnecessary. Because Cain was sure that after tonight, everything would change. His life would be different, and more important, his perception of the lives of others would never be the same again.

"I'm afraid," he whispered into the dark, and the dark listened.

"That's only right," it said.

Cain waited, and the shadow waited with him. Every now and then it would begin humming the tune, breaking off when Cain frowned in an effort to drive another memory down. At first he thought the shadow was doing it inadvertently, but once or twice the tone of the tune changed, as if hummed past a smile. He wanted to ask what it was doing and why, but he also knew that to succeed tonight he had to remain silent. George could be out of the house at any time—if, indeed, he was coming out at all—and to follow him without being seen, Cain could not afford to give him even a slight suspicion of being watched.

Cain hoped that George would not hear the shadow's humming.

He looked up, and between the leaves of the shrub canopy he could see the sky clearing as dusk gave way to night. The moon was waxing half-full, and yet he did not believe that this had anything to do with George. His monstrous transformation came wholly from within, not without. *That's just his Way*, Cain thought, and somewhere nearby he felt the shadow nod.

It was not the most comfortable of places to wait. Cain's arm went to sleep and he had to roll onto his other side, stirring a bush and bringing a few loose leaves down onto his face. Something squeaked and scurried out from under him. The shadow shifted, disappearing and then manifesting again on Cain's other side. It leaned in close, and Cain smelled its odor, like fruit sweating in the sun. He looked from the corner of his eye to see if he could make out any expression. But it was a shadow in the night, darker than the dark. If it was still around come morning, perhaps he would see it then.

The front door opened. Cain held his breath, waiting for the footsteps, suddenly realizing that he would have no way to tell who was exiting the house. "We'll know," the shadow whispered. "We'll *smell* them." And Cain knew that it was right. If Sister Josephine came by, he would know her from her honey-scented skin, magicked up and ready for flight, or perhaps the bees that seemed to like her. If it was Magenta, he would register her lack of odor, cosmetic or otherwise. Whistler would smell of age and must, and George . . . with George, it would be meat.

The front door closed and footsteps came along the path.

"Do you know?" the shadow asked playfully.

Cain was annoyed at its condescension, but he breathed in and closed his eyes. *Oh yes,* he thought, *it's so obvious now.* The rich, bloody red stench of George.

George paused at the front gate, and Cain heard him sniffing at the air. *When's the last time I bathed?* Cain thought. *When did I last change my clothes?* He could not recall. But he had the feeling that George's attention was focused outward into the street, rather than back into the garden. He wondered whether George felt the same way about the garden as he did—unnerved, suspicious, uneasy—but probably not. He was part of the reason the garden was the way it was, after all.

George opened the gate and stepped out into the street, turning left and moving quickly away from the house.

Cain went to move, but something cool brushed his cheek and snagged his ear. "Wait," the shadow said, "not yet. We'll hear him and smell him; don't be too eager to give yourself away." Cain shrugged the shadow's hand from his shoulder and moved forward, away. He hated that touch. Slick, like a corpse's breath on his skin. But he listened to what the shadow said and waited, leaning on his elbows, trying not to move in case he made the shrub canopy shudder with a life it had seldom exhibited before. George's footsteps faded into the distance. Cain went to get up again, felt the shadow's gaze on his back, remained still.

They stayed there for several minutes. "If we can hear him, he can hear us," the shadow said. "His senses could be *changed*." Then, a couple of minutes later: "We'll smell him. And soon we'll hear him."

"How do you know so much?" Cain asked.

The shadow's voice cut in with its sarcastic edge again. "I know what you know but are too afraid to realize."

"Well, fuck this, I'm going." Cain crawled from under the bushes and stood, shaking off the gaze of the many living things beneath there. He was yet another image and experience for them to keep to themselves forever. He walked to the front gate, leaned over to look in the direction George had taken, then lifted the latch and stepped beyond the garden. He set off immediately, trying to move as quickly as he could while making as little noise as possible. His shoes were soft leather, well-worn, and they barely whispered as they touched the pavement.

The shadow joined him, slinking along at the bases of walls and hedges like a cat on the prowl.

They reached the end of the street and Cain inhaled deeply, reminded of George's animalistic sniffing at the garden gate. The faint tinge of raw meat hung in the air—weak to the right, stronger to the left. He headed left, along the road that led eventually to the pub where he and Peter had sat and talked the previous afternoon. The shadow followed without comment.

It was not late—not yet midnight—but the streets were surprisingly quiet. Pubs had already let out and their patrons made their way home. Night shift workers were at work. Police cars were parked up. A couple of taxis cruised the streets, drivers already bored and awaiting their knock-off time. A couple of people passed Cain, keeping their eyes averted and putting purpose in their step. He slowed down each time, glancing down at the shadow where it frolicked at the base of a wall or in a doorway, arrogantly inviting discovery. He wanted to meet their gaze, smile, let them know how lucky they were to be on their way home tonight, a night when there was a mad thing like

George abroad. But he supposed such niceties as conversation took a backseat come dusk, when darkness did its best to unearth primeval fear. So they walked by without acknowledgment, and Cain knew each time that he would never see that person again. They had whole life stories—loves and hates, triumphs and tragedies, successes and failures—and he would never know any of them. They had lived up to this point utterly ignorant of Cain's existence, and their lives would continue on until death in that same state. His torment did not trouble them. There was simply this one minuscule point of contact, when the heat of their bodies had perhaps interfered across a few feet of space, their auras may have skimmed each other, and their thoughts had been slightly stirred by one another. A stranger in the night. That was all he was to them, and all he would ever be. His own story was most important to himself. He strode on with greater purpose.

The shadow loped alongside and marched defiantly through pools of illumination thrown down by streetlights.

"You feel he's near?" the shadow said.

"Do you?"

"I don't know." The uncertainty in the shadow's voice pleased Cain immensely.

"Yes," Cain said. "He's near." In reality, he had no idea at all.

The street came to an end at a T junction, and Cain turned right with barely a moment's consideration. It was not a smell this time, just a feeling. Again the shadow followed, without question or dissent. Cain took that as an indication that he had gone the right way.

The new road turned quickly right, then left, houses valiantly hanging on to its curves. Between two such houses ran a small lane, presumably leading to car parking and garages at the rear. Cain paused at the head of the lane and stared into the darkness. No streetlight probed that far, and tall houses on either side blocked out what little star and moonlight there was. He felt the weight of the unknown drawing him in.

"Here?" the shadow asked.

"What do you think?"

"You're the one with a nose."

Cain sniffed, smiled. "You're the one who seems to know everything." A car passed by, a pale face pressed to the front passenger window, mouth open as if trying to cry a warning.

"I think it looks like just the sort of place George would feel at home," the shadow said.

"I think you're right," Cain said, remembering the alley where Peter had been slaughtered, and the garage where he had seen and heard George ripping something apart. "But I don't want to go in there."

"Do you realize you're talking to a shadow?" the shadow said. Cain glanced to his left where the shadow lounged against a parked car, and he burst out laughing. It was the first time he had laughed in what felt like forever. He had read somewhere that laughter was a natural reaction to outright terror.

"Let's go," Cain said, and George ran out from the lane and straight into him.

Cain fell back under the sudden assault, tried to cry out, but George's hand pressed down over his face. He thrashed beneath the slight man's weight, kicked, clawed at George's clothing, trying to get a grip to haul the madman away before he had his throat torn out. George only pressed down more, crushing Cain's body against the pavement, the contact so complete and intimate that the horrible thought came: *Who's to say he just eats them?*

The shadow leapt at George's back. Cain saw it as a blur against the sky, stars blinking as it passed through the air and landed on his assailant. George shrugged, shook his head, frowned, and looked around. The shadow battered at his head and shoulders with its clenched fists, but George seemed to feel little more than a breath of air. He twisted against Cain, kicked his feet as if to dislodge an annoying child, and the shadow fell away and blended into the night.

Cain screamed in his throat, begging it back.

George was only George. He stank, but his teeth were his own, and the palm pressed across Cain's face was slick, sweaty, and hairless.

"Evening, Cain!" George said. "So I guess Magenta's had at you?"

Cain stared up into his eyes, trying to give nothing away.

"Why else would you decide to follow me? You saw what happened to Peter, you saw what did it. Why else follow, other than to try to make yourself believe? And I know you . . . I *know* you! I've heard your nightmares. You'd only be doing this if you were filled with doubt." He pulled back slowly, releasing Cain's mouth and sitting astride his stomach. He never lost eye contact; the threat of violence was overt. Cain could scream, but it would do him no favors.

"I have no doubt that you're a monster," Cain said.

George smiled, then shook his head. "I'm no monster," he said. "I'm a monster killer. It's just my Way. I need to feed, and I feed on the weak, the meaningless, those with lives of no significance."

Cain thought of the people he had passed in the street, the histories and futures he would never know. "Who are you to judge?" he said.

"I'm something of a miracle," George said. "There are very few like us—"

"I'm *nothing* like you!"

"I'm not referring to you, little Cain. I mean *us*— me, Whistler, Magenta, the Sister . . . even Peter. Poor old Peter. Never quite fulfilled his potential, but he was still better than most in this world."

"You're full of shit." Cain hoped that the shadow was listening somewhere and enjoying this. "And so humble with it."

"You are what you eat, so they say." George looked down at Cain as if examining an interesting animal trapped in a specimen jar. "So what are you doing?" he asked.

"What?"

"What's your choice? Are you going to make Mummy and Daddy proud?"

"Fuck you!" Cain bucked and twisted, but George seemed to be growing heavier, immovable.

"I'm peckish," George said. "It's not my choice,

this hunger. It never was. But once the Way came to me, it's just the route I took. Everyone's different, Cain, and I ended up needing food. Real food. Lots of it. And as I said, I only pick on those with no lives. They work, they eat, they watch TV, they shit, they work . . . Who'll miss them? Who'll miss just a few of the drones?"

"Someone must. Someone knows you're out here doing this, and it's just a matter of time—"

"Time? Come on, I'm sure you saw Peter's photograph album. I've been around for a *long* time. I travel far, and I'm very picky. And besides . . . I'm removed from the petty concerns of society. What I do is equally removed. You think they'll ever find Peter's body? It exists somewhere else now that I've been at it, somewhere more honest. And hidden from most."

"You're so arrogant," Cain said. "You, Magenta, all of you. So filled with your own superiority."

"Not filled with it. *Comfortable* with it." George stood then, his knees crunching like two gunshots. He stretched his fingers and Cain heard them popping, one after the other, *click-click-click*. "Make your choice and live with it." He looked down at Cain. His face had stretched, his jowls dropped, and his eyes seemed to take on a golden tint, though there was no light to be reflected.

"How could I ever want to be like you?" Cain said.

George shook his head sadly, but his eyes glittered. "You have no idea. Tonight, just for you, I won't be so careful. Follow. Witness the freedom of the Way."

Something passed by close above them, swishing through the night and sending a waft of displaced air down at the ground. Cain thought of the shadow, but then he caught a brief whiff of honey, rich and sweet and so filled with memories.

"Must go," George said. For an instant before the changing man fled, Cain saw a troubled look cross his face.

George ran back into the lane. He must have been waiting there for Cain all along. Now, invited to follow, Cain saw no reason to change his mind.

I won't be so careful, George had said. Five minutes earlier, Cain would have taken this as a threat, but not now, not here. George thought himself beyond such pettiness. Once changed, the first person he met would be his food for tonight.

"Thanks for your help," Cain said.

The shadow emerged from behind a fence. "It's all down to you, and you know it. Did you smell—?"

"Yes, I know. That troubled George. I'm going to follow."

"Of course you are," the shadow said, darting ahead and entering the dark lane. Cain followed. He ran blindly, not bothering to put his hands out in front of him to feel for obstacles. Tonight, his own safety was no longer his prime mover. More and more he felt as though he was on the route to discovery.

I'll not live like them, he thought, bitter and defiant. *I won't* be *like them.* But he ran on into the night, and he found a strange excitement growing inside at what may have changed come morning.

* * *

Trying to keep track of the shadow was impossible, so Cain followed George's footsteps instead. They were changing. At first they had thrown back the sound of leather on stone, but now they were softer, punctuated by a sharp, piercing scrape after every impact. Claws. George was changing, or had changed already, and Cain did not have long to catch him up. He had no idea what he would do when he did. *Watch? Am I really just going to watch while he butchers someone?* But he would face that problem when it arrived.

He ran headlong into a garden fence overgrown with rosebushes, cursing as thorns pinned him and stems seemed to curl around his limbs to hold him fast. He struggled, kicked, pulled, and a dog started barking from the other side of the fence. Soon there would be lights and an angry homeowner . . . but then the shadow was there, helping him snap thorns from his clothing and tear his legs free of the offending growths.

"I can't hear him anymore," Cain said.

"Can't you smell him?"

Cain was not sure, but still he ran blindly along the lane. It was much longer than he had expected. Gardens opened up on the left and right, then a row of vandalized garages with doors only half closed, and then a large timber building that seemed to be rotting on its frame. Now that the overhanging hedges and tumbled fences had vanished, he could see more, the landscape silvered by starlight and the weak moon. All colors were washed away. *Blood will be black tonight,* he thought. *Black as the shadow.*

A howl rose somewhere nearby, and a chill of

fear set Cain's hair on end. The cry ended with a chuckle and a cough, and Cain realized that George was doing it just for him. The shadow emerged from a hedge of brambles, giggling.

Cain ran on. He glanced up on occasion, wondering whether it really had been Sister Josephine flying overhead. He could not help thinking of her naked, magicking herself up before him, and the smear of her magic cream on his thigh when he woke up from what he had thought was a dream. If he had enough of that cream, could he—

No! I'm not like them. I'm like me!

"Here," the shadow said. "This way! I think he's stopped." It flowed ahead, turning left and heading across an area of open land toward a house on the opposite side. Though still in the city the house stood on its own, isolated by common land on one side and a huge area of allotments on the other. A light shone in a downstairs window. Briefly, terribly, Cain saw the thing that George had become silhouetted against the light.

"What are you going to do now?" the shadow asked in his mind, and the question was loaded, the voice ready to mock.

"I don't know." He could say no more, because that was the truth. *I don't know.*

Cain ran across the open land. He stumbled once and went tumbling, banging his head on a rock and feeling blood burst across his scalp. It cooled him as he ran on, trickling down his neck and into his shirt. He did not care. *It's only blood,* he thought. And he imagined Magenta saying, *It's only blood, son, only the stuff of the flesh.*

The second he reached the low stone garden wall, he heard glass smash and a short, startled screech. The shadow was already there, lurking at the edge of the pool of light leaking out from the lit window. The *broken* window. It had been pulled completely from its frame, shattered glass sparkling across the ground. He saw George's shadow cast against one of the inside walls, the light swayed and shifted madly, and then there was a roar and the light went out. Another shriek—louder this time, its owner having had more time to *see*—and then George uttered something between a chuckle and a growl.

Cain climbed the wall and paused on top. He could go either way. Let himself fall back and flee across the open ground, leave the city forever, find his way to Tall Stennington and live whatever life he could make for himself at Afresh. Or he could tip forward and go for the window, try to stop George from spilling innocent blood, and in doing so educate himself in another facet of Pure Sight. The shadow hung there with him, smeared across the wall like spilled oil. Cain thought to ask it what he should do, but he knew what the answer would be; this was all down to him. The shadow exuded knowledge and wisdom, but really it was attached so firmly to his own actions that it may as well be his third arm. It awaited his decision.

There was a riot of noise inside the house—someone running upstairs, another scream from a child's mouth, an adult shouting and raging—and then George let out a roar that shook the remaining windows. This one was pure and basic, no longer simply for Cain's benefit. This was George at the height of the hunt, releasing an ecstatic celebratory howl seconds before the kill.

Cain leaped from the wall and ran at the window. He had no idea what he was about to do. Something drove him, a feeling so deep down that he had never felt it before, and as he dived for the window he wondered if it was valor. He rolled across the floor and stood in one movement, wincing at the broken glass that had pricked and gashed his back and head. He was alone but for the shadow. He headed for the door.

"We have to do something," Cain whispered.

"We do?" the shadow asked, pausing on the bottom step of the staircase.

Cain ran right at it, head down, storming upstairs without realizing that the shadow had stepped aside. He thought perhaps he had it draped across his head, some rudimentary camouflage from George. What he would do in the second or two it gave him he had no idea, but he could hear a little girl crying now, and that thing that had risen from deep inside forbade any true consideration of the situation. Valor or stupidity, it drove him on. Even when he reached the landing and realized that the shadow was ahead of him again, he did not stop. The crying came from a room at the end of the landing, pink door smashed from its hinges, George hunkered down in the doorway, growling, drooling as he advanced slowly on whoever cowered on the bed.

Cain glanced through an open doorway to his left and saw the body of a man lying on the bathroom floor. He had been struck across the throat, his windpipe and carotid artery opened up, and he blew bubbles as a puddle of blood spread across the vinyl. His hands were clasped to his throat, trying to press the wound together, fingers buried deep in himself. Cain met his gaze and saw the message straightaway. *My baby. My baby!* He looked away from the dying man and advanced on George.

He passed the shadow and it held back, slouching down at the head of the staircase, expression unreadable as ever. "Scared?" Cain asked in his mind.

"*You* should be," the shadow said. For the first time, Cain believed the shadow had spoken aloud.

He was three steps from George. The man had transformed into something monstrous and yet still so obviously George. There was no gray pelt, no lengthened legs, no extended snout filled with wolverine teeth. He was still a man, but in whatever grotesque manner the Way had twisted his soul, it had also acted on his naked body. His back was arched, ribs pressing against the skin below his shoulder blades. His face was transformed by a hunger that mere food could surely never satiate, and his eyes reflected some inner pain, red and ravenous. Claws tipped his fingers and toes, thickened and sharpened nails curled into wicked cutting and slashing weapons that were black with old blood and red with new. He stood on all fours, the weight of his change pulling him down.

Cain stood there for a few seconds, waiting for George to turn around. But the monster had not noticed him. Whether he was obsessed with the child inside the room or simply unconcerned at Cain's presence, George showed no signs of knowing he was there.

"You're ugly, George," Cain said. He had no idea where he was finding the courage to face this thing, but he had never really been tested before, not like this. Perhaps he had always been brave.

George tried to turn around, but he was trapped in the doorway by his widened shoulders. Cain took the opportunity to glance past the monster and into the bedroom, and he saw the little girl cowering on the bed. She had the blankets pulled up around her stomach, unable to bring herself to hide away completely from the horror. Perhaps her child's logic had already told her that shielding herself would do no good. She wore Barbie pajamas, had long blond hair, and her eyes begged Cain for help. She saw a monster and a grown-up, so it was obvious to her who the enemy and friend must be.

Cain dropped his eyes and backed away. Could he really help? He had run here under the impression that George would not hurt him, but where that idea had come from, who had implanted it in his mind, he had no idea.

Could he really, truly help?

George tried to turn again, twisting hard. His shoulder struck the door frame and wood splintered, architraves falling against Cain's upraised arms. George growled. Perhaps he was trying to speak, but his mouth had become a shape that could never form words. He was built now for killing and destruction, not thought and conversation.

"So ugly I want to puke," Cain said quietly, not quite believing his own words.

"Oh shit," the shadow said in his mind, its voice receding as it fled elsewhere in the house.

George leaped and Cain backed away. He stumbled but kept pushing with his feet, putting distance between himself and George. The mutated man landed on all fours and came closer, jaws dripping, teeth bared and long where the gums had receded. He reached for Cain where he lay floundering on the landing.

"No!" Cain shouted, and the shadow winced in his mind. George sat back and laughed.

Cain recognized the trick immediately. He tried to stand, but the monster was already away, moving quickly back through the shattered door and into the little girl's bedroom. As Cain stood and ran forward, he heard the girl's screams cut off by a sickening tearing sound. Blood splashed and turned the bedroom light red.

A hopeless sob escaped Cain's lips, and tears tried to make the scene unreal.

Someone whined. Cain glanced to his left into the bathroom once again. As soon as the stricken father saw the horror in Cain's eyes, his hands dropped from his throat and he died, his final tears diluting his already thickening blood.

"You bastard!" Cain shouted, running to the room. He did not want to see, but there was no way now that he could turn away. *This is my fault, all my fault!* George had done this to show Cain what he could do, and why, and how powerful the Way had made him. If Cain had not shunned Magenta yesterday, this family would still be alive. If he had taken more time to look into himself, see whether Pure Sight really was there and what it would entail in his form, George may have gone days or weeks without another kill.

"Can't blame yourself," the shadow said from elsewhere in the house. "You didn't kill them. It's just the Way of things."

"Fuck the Way!" Cain shouted. "Fuck it! And why are you so scared? Piece of shit, that's you!" His feet tangled in a length of architrave, and he bent and snatched it up without thinking. The wood was thin, but he might be able to fend off George's first blow, at least.

"Not scared," the shadow said. "You have to see this on your own."

Cain stood in the doorway and took a good, long look at the scene before him, punishing himself with the horror of it all. George was leaning over the bed, blood streaking his bruised and stretched skin, heavy shoulders flexing as his arms ripped at the dead girl, hand falling and rising to lift scoops of meat to his jaws.

"I have always . . . been . . . alone."

The monster turned around and the grotesque, bloody smile on his malformed face brought the rage up out of Cain. Fear hid away, farther than the shadow. Doubt was drowned, smothered by the sense of rightness that rose within him, up from depths he never knew were there. He brought up the length of broken timber and growled like a wolf.

For an instant a flicker of doubt crossed

George's face. He looked left and right like a nervous bird. But then he looked straight at Cain again, threw back his head, and laughed, spitting gobs of flesh that stuck on the ceiling between glow-in-the-dark stars.

"Hey, ugly," a voice said from Cain's left. "Sometimes you go too far."

Sister Josephine was squatting on the sill of the open window, slick hands and feet resting delicately between a collection of model horses. Her habit flowed about her. Honey filled the room, an overpowering aroma that succeeded in washing out the stench of blood and insides . . . but only for a moment. Cain did not look for long, did not breathe in that scent and believe that everything was all right, and if the nun spoke again he did not hear her words. He grasped the moment she had given him—George was still staring at Sister Josephine, his jaws hanging slack and bloody—and thrust forward with the broken architrave.

George screamed. It was an expression of sheer agony that the little girl had never had the chance to utter. As the wood jarred home in the monster's stomach, Cain shouted too, his hands slipping along the snapped timber and picking up a dozen heavy splinters between his fingers. He backed away, aghast at what he had done. The shadow appeared at his shoulder and laid a cold hand against his neck, but Cain shook it off, swearing, backing up to the doorway as George stood to his full unnatural height.

"I'm sorry!" Cain shouted, ridiculous and yet heartfelt. George staggered across the room toward the door, blood spewing out around his hands where he held the architrave protruding from his gut, and Cain wondered whether that blood was all his own. Several bees buzzed at the .wound and, finding it not to their liking, bumbled lazily out the open window. "I'm sorry!"

"Shit," George growled, his voice distorted. "Oh God, it hurtsss!" His body already seemed smaller than it had before, not shrinking but lessening. However the monstrous transformation took him, he could not maintain it in the grip of such pain.

Cain glanced again at the open window. The nun had gone, but he thought he heard a laugh hiding somewhere among George's continuing cries of pain.

"I bet that hurts," the shadow said.

"Of course it hurts!" George shouted. "Pull it out!"

"Sure thing," said the shadow.

"No!" Cain said, and he realized the shadow was playing with both of them.

The injured man fell to the floor, rolled onto his side, and started writhing. Another scream came, rising into a high, keening whine that seemed to go on and on, assaulting Cain's ears almost as much as the siren. But only his ears. This sound could not reach inside his heart, because guilt was quickly being buried by the anger. His newfound confidence hammered it down and told him that George deserved this, every painful second between now and his death had been earned a thousand times over. Cain looked to the mess on the bed and nodded, unable to stifle another sob for the fate of that poor girl.

The shadow voiced its agreement from behind. "We should leave," it said then. "There's nothing more we can do here."

"I can't go anywhere!" George screeched.

"You're not," Cain said, "and there's *plenty* more we can do." He saw confusion in the monster's eyes as he walked forward to stand over George. *Could still be dangerous,* he thought, *could lash out with those claws, those feet, and maybe he's just feigning it.* But he could see a curl of gut squeezing from the wound in George's stomach now, and he knew that this was no sham. "Here, let me." He reached out for the end of the protruding architrave.

George grew still. Perhaps he thought Cain really would help him, find his Way in time to realize just how George was helpless in the face of his own.

Cain grabbed the wood in both hands and twisted, pushed, leaning left and right, and he closed his eyes to the horrible sight of George thrashing and dying beneath him.

The screams, though. He could not avoid the screams. They were rich and loud and filled with the memory of decades of death. Such was their intensity that Cain expected the siren to scream in and punish him for such an experience. But at last, at long last, he believed that he was way beyond its reach. This murder by his own hand had shifted him out of his father's influence forever.

If only I'd been faster, Cain thought. *If only I hadn't delayed out there in the garden. Maybe all this would have turned out differently.*

He had begun to make his own life.

* * *

"How do you feel?" the shadow asked.

"Leave me alone."

Cain was sitting beneath a tree in the park. The shadow moved around him, across the grass, in and out of a clump of bushes, circling like a dog avoiding its angry master. Cain was carefully pulling splinters from his palm and the flap of skin between his thumb and forefinger. There was not enough light to see by, but the slivers were large enough to get a grip on in the dark. Each one hurt more, and he welcomed that. Each extraction brought tears and he let them flow free, hoping that they would distort this world beyond what it was revealing to him. Exactly what that was, he was unsure. But he wanted none of it.

He could still hear the echoes of George's final screams, as if they were haunting the park.

And he could still hear that little girl's final cry. He would hear it always. It had replaced the siren as his tormentor, his punisher, because had he acted differently that scream would have never been uttered. The girl would be asleep in her Barbie pajamas, with her model horses watching over her and the luminous stars on the ceiling giving her sweet dreams.

"We should move," the shadow said.

"Why?"

"Someone may find us here."

"So? What about it?"

"You don't want to be connected—"

"I *am* connected!" Cain shouted, standing and kicking out at where he thought the shadow may be. Darkness slunk away from him, flowing about the tree like water. "I *caused* that! George did what he did because of *me,* to show *me!*"

"Fool," the shadow whispered. "You can't blame yourself for what he did. He wasn't so insecure that he'd need to show you *anything.* Don't flatter yourself with the idea that you could have prevented that."

"But . . ."

The shadow emerged from the dark and stood beside him, more solid and real than he had ever seen. Cain leaned back, eyes wide with a fearful fascination, staring at the shadow and trying so hard to make out any features. There were none; only a consistent absence of light. And yet it held the shape of a human, moved like a man, and spoke with the calm assurance of someone comfortable in their own skin.

"You remember those months and years in your father's basement?" the shadow said. "Those times he tortured you, trying to pry a talent from you that he knew he could not possibly have himself?"

"Pure Sight is no talent," Cain said.

"Whatever the fuck you call it!" the shadow spat. "Shut up and listen. You remember those times?"

"Of course."

"Your father would exclude all sound from your world for weeks on end, making you exist in utter silence. No talking, no laughing, no crying, no conversation. You had to cover your ears when he slid your food tray in, just in case it made a bump and you heard it. You used to enjoy eating so much because you could hear your jaws clicking, the food being mashed between your teeth, and you thought of that as a small victory."

Cain nodded, though he could not recall the shadow being there, not then. And if it had been there, how could it have known what he was thinking each time he chewed, drank, swallowed?

"Whose fault was it when the siren shattered your mind?"

"My father's."

"No, it was yours."

Cain shook his head. "Magenta already told me that. She was wrong, too."

"No she wasn't, she was right. If what George did was your fault, then the siren was your fault as well. You alone are to blame for what it did to you."

Cain frowned, glared sidelong at the shadow that stood beside him. "What are you?" he asked for the very first time.

The shadow only chuckled and moved away. "Think about it," it said. "Think about guilt, and cause and effect. What you did tonight was to stop George, not steer him. He picked his own path, and the Way was his guide."

"They're all fucked up," Cain said. "George, Whistler, Magenta, even the nun. So much potential put to waste! There's so much they could do with what they have! Think of all the *good* they could do! It must drive them bad. Evil. They're evil."

"That's not what they'd say," the shadow muttered. "But I suppose that's something for you to decide."

Cain started walking toward the park gates, eager to leave and get back onto the streets. He had no idea of where to go, but simply moving felt better than sitting and musing on things. His original intention had to been to follow them all, see what Pure Sight made of them, and then reject it totally and utterly. Witnessing them would convince him of his decision. It would strengthen his conviction.

What George had done this evening was more than enough to do that on its own.

But there was something else: the shadow. Cain had no idea what it was, although he knew it had kept him company when he was younger, hidden away in his father's basement and enduring the old man's misdirected experiments. It had come from Cain himself, he was sure, emerging to protect his sanity during those long, awful years when he should have been meeting friends, going to school, discovering girls, playing football, having a life of his own. The shadow had been his only friend. And now that it was back, Cain found himself relying on it once again.

The question that nagged at him was *Why* was it back? It had been locked safely away for so long that he had stopped thinking of it as real. The chest had become a symbol, that was all, an indication that he was attempting to put the past behind him and move on to whatever he could make of his future.

But now that the chest was ruptured and open, and the shadow was out, he realized that it had not been his past contained therein at all. It was something much, much closer to him.

"What *are* you?" he asked of the dark, and the shadow spoke back.

"I'm your help, and your Way."

Cain walked on. He did not understand, but he found himself comforted immeasurably.

Cain had often searched the house for signs of his mother. When his father was locked away in his study, or working in the kitchen or workshop, Cain would wander from room to room. He never found anything: no pictures, no letters, no clothes. He took to imagining where she may have stood, how she could have walked, what she would have looked like gliding down the staircase in a long summer dress. But try as he might, he could never see her face. She could have been anyone.

Chapter Ten
Music

Beyond the park the streets were deserted. Pools of light huddled beneath lampposts, small and nervous against the night. An occasional house light was on, but curtains were always drawn. The night was its own. Cain wandered the streets, the shadow at his side, and tried to decide what to do next.

He should go to the police . . . but somehow that seemed so pointless. The bodies would be found, a reverted George would be discovered with their blood and skin beneath his fingernails, the case would be closed. A terrible murder. Monstrous. George was at the end of his road. Besides, there was nothing that Cain could tell them that would make any sense.

The night felt full and incomplete. Cain kept expecting to find the shadow gone, but it remained with him, dashing off now and then only to reappear minutes later from a different direction. Like a caged animal set free for the first time, it seemed keen to explore yet loath to leave the side of its owner for too long. He wished it could tell him more, but it had already said enough. It had been silent since leaving the park. Whatever happened next was completely down to Cain.

As if on request, the tune waited until Cain had made the decision to return to his flat before making itself known.

"That music . . ." he said, looking for the shadow because it was humming again. But this time there came complete understanding. Cain knew this tune, where it had come from and why, and he experienced an instance of such ecstasy that he sank to his knees on the pavement. He stared up at the stars as the tune played itself out, and it was the theme of his life. The stars twinkled and danced in synchronicity. A shadow obscured his vision, wavering frantically before him, and cool hands grabbed his shoulders and shook. But though the shadow fought hard, Cain could only smile at its concern. It was *not* humming the tune, he realized, not this time. And that only made it more wonderful.

The tune was so new and immediate. Though created now for the first time, Cain knew every note, every twist and turn of the melody, because he had heard it many times before. The shadow had hummed it to calm him down.

Whistler stepped from the shadows beneath a tree, his pipes playing softly, his lips working the tune from their hollowness, turning air into a vibrant depiction of time and all that it promised.

"This one is for you," Whistler said, "the theme of your life." Even though he paused to speak, the music continued.

Cain smiled. "I know my song."

Whistler frowned for a moment, but then continued playing and smiled again. Cain hummed along for the first time and the tune was new in his throat, a taste of great beauty that he had never known. Any other night it would have sounded different; warmer air, higher pressure, a different light quality would have made it so. But tonight it was exactly as he imagined.

Whistler led the way.

There was no sense of being coerced or forced to follow. Cain walked a few paces behind the tall man, studying him properly for the first time. His ponytail was long—almost down to the bottom of his back—and it was held together in several places by metal rings. They shone with reflected starlight and seemed to dance in the night as his hair swayed with every step he took.

Cain saw something streak across the road from his left, the shadow, tangling itself in Whistler's feet in an attempt to trip him. The tall man glanced down but walked on, seemingly unconcerned. It was as if he had walked through nothing more than a cloud of smoke. He dropped a note, but it matched Cain's knowledge of the tune perfectly, and his own hummed imitation dropped the same note.

The shadow came back at Cain and hit him head-on, but though it held weight, it carried no import.

"Cain!" it seemed to shout, but the voice barely registered. He smiled. The shadow had been here for him, and now Whistler was here for him in its place. Cain was following his own path, discovering his own Way, and that was only right. It was his life to lead, after all.

(Whistler led him on.)

His life to lead and *follow,* take himself wherever he wanted to go, and as the Voice and Face had impressed upon him so much—

(Whistler turned left; Cain followed.)

—the route he took was entirely his own choice. No longer was he controlled by his sick father. He was his own man. He did not need that shadow anymore, that strange childhood friend that had helped him when he was young and which hung around still. It had always made him feel like the weak one, mocking him, pouring scorn on his fears and ideas.

The shadow hit him again, striking between the eyes, but it was barely the tickle of a fly.

"Got something to show you," Whistler sang, and the tune from his pipes never faltered. "Something sweet and dear. If you'll spare me a moment, this thing is pretty near."

"I'll spare a moment," Cain muttered, smiling, and starlight kissed his lips with all the power and depth of its implied history.

Whistler walked slowly along the dark street. The lamps here were not lit; it was a minor side road, and perhaps they were turned off after midnight. Cain followed the glint of moonlight on Whistler's metallic hair bands. But he followed the music as well. It steered him exactly the way he would choose, should the imperative be put in his hands. *Here I would go right,* and Whistler turned right. *Here I would continue on until reaching that timber gate,* and Whistler did just that. Cain was comfortable with the idea that he was taking his own direction, not following Whistler's. The pipe player was simply acting as a guide in the dark, finding Cain's preordained route.

"What are you going to show me?" Cain asked.

Whistler turned, and Cain saw the glint of teeth in his smile. "Something sweet and dear," he said. The pipe music continued, ever familiar, echoing from the dark and moving on.

The shadow made itself known to Cain once again, clouding his vision. He closed his eyes and followed the tune, and even sightless he was no less confident in keeping to the right path. His head and neck felt cold, as if touched by frost. He shook his head and the shadow relinquished its hold, flowing to the ground and up the back of Whistler's legs. Cain opened his eyes again and saw it there, like a water stain on the tall man's clothes. And though it thrashed and twisted and spun, its touch was ineffectual.

Whistler's music went on, and Cain hummed the way.

"Cain!" the shadow shouted, floating at his shoulder. Its voice came from very far away, and the more it shouted the more Cain was sure it was simply another unpleasant memory of his bizarre childhood. He shook his head, and the memory receded. He concentrated on Whistler's back, and the shadow faded away. By the time they reached a junction between two streets, it had vanished altogether.

The music filled the night. A row of houses to the left reflected moonlight cast through a thin layer of cloud, and the clouds' slight movements gave the impression that the houses swayed slowly on their foundations. Their occupants would be dreaming sweet dreams. Perhaps in the morning they would not remember, but that did not matter. Memories were just as important unremembered as they were in the light of total recollection.

"Not far now," Whistler said, glancing back over his shoulder. Starlight gave life to his eyes. The pipes remained at his lips, spilling the beautiful music that insinuated itself deeper into Cain's body, his guts, his bones vibrating with each note. It was as if he were slowly becoming an instrument to Whistler's cause, a human tuning fork for his ambition. It thrilled through Cain's body and made him smile.

They came to a street lined with houses on one side and a park on the other. Trees stood sentinel at the park's perimeter. The moon sat behind them, low in the sky, casting their shadows across the road to stroke the houses' facades. Cain and Whistler passed through these shadows, and as they touched each one the corresponding tree shivered, leaves rustling, branches creaking. Cain thought they may be shaking with joy at the music Whistler was giving to the night. It filled the air and made it safe. It touched the trees and the park beyond, and to the left it passed through windows and into the houses, the glass doing little to alter its effect. Front gardens seemed open and welcoming, and he would not have been surprised if the houses' doors swung inward to invite music-slicked moonlight inside. But they remained closed, and Cain thought that it was only because Whistler desired it so.

With music like this, Whistler could do anything. If he wished streetlamps to strobe in time with the tune, they would do so. Should he desire animals to join in their slow march, then neighborhood cats and hedgehogs and foxes would be there for him. If he wanted the dark to give way to an early dawn, perhaps even the sun would oblige. But for now his tune was solely for Cain, and that made Cain feel special.

Cain thought of George, but those events seemed decades ago. Filtered through time, they seemed to lose their importance. A twinge of guilt came, only to be washed away by another reprise of the tune. Whistler had started again, and it was in no way identical to the first time he had played this melody. Yet Cain hummed along, following every note exactly.

Whistler looked back at him, smiled behind his pan pipes, and nodded across the road. "We're here."

There was a house. It stood by itself at the edge of the park, and Cain was sure it should not be there. A moment of doubt confused his thoughts. He frowned, stepped back, and for a second the shadow was before him again, solid and so there that Cain could not see through it. It shouted at him, *Cain!,* and Whistler approached quickly from the left. The tall man struck out with another frantic series of notes, and the shadow slipped away. Cain's doubts melted to nothing

The house . . . it looked like the most perfect place he had ever seen.

"Your new life," Whistler said. "It's daylight." And it was. "You've long forgotten this place." Cain smiled. "You're happy. You've found your Way in life."

And he had.

This was the life he had come here to find. The reason he had left Afresh and all the security it offered. The reason that the Face and Voice were sad, but also eager to see him go. Here, in this house, was the future that had eluded him for so long. Its wonder occluded visions of his past, clouding them out like the troublesome things they were. Standing before the house, he tried to think back to the time in his father's basement, but he could conjure only a general feeling of disquiet—no specific times, no individual images. There was a threat implicit behind that feeling—a promise of unbelievable pain, should he do wrong—but he was not afraid, because his future was bright and assured. Whatever agonies he had been through, he had come out the other side to find himself here.

He stood before the house and examined his future life. It was a detached cottage, maybe two hundred years old. The garden went all the way around, with a small driveway for the new sports car that sat there, roof down, inviting him to take it for a spin. He had never learned how to drive, but that would be no problem here. This was his future, and it was perfect.

Rosebushes climbed the sides of the house, bursting out in gorgeous red and yellow blooms that filled the air with their subtle perfume. Windows reflected clear blue sky, fluffy white clouds drifting slowly across the sun. The garden buzzed with bees and birds. The roof was covered with old slates, some of them cracked and dipped, all of them adding to the character of the place. And yet this intensely hackneyed image of a perfect country retreat was also personalized in ways that took Cain some time to notice. He had no idea how long he was standing there—the tune flowed through his head, echoed in the natural music of the birds and insects—before he spotted the old garden swing. Its arches were rusted red, the timber seat polished smooth with use, the ropes old and frayed and dappled black with moss.

And it was *his* swing, from the time when he and his parents had lived in a house similar to this, their lives uncomplicated and filled with pleasure. Summer days they would spend in the garden, young Cain swinging back and forth while his mother puttered about the planting beds, and his father built a new fence or painted the shed tucked away in the corner. At that moment he saw the shed, hidden away behind an explosion of clematis. He knew the door, the window with the diagonal crack that he had put there with a football. He knew the color—dark green—that was rich and full, but which needed recoating every year. Cain often helped his father with the painting, and each year he commanded control of a larger brush, marking his passage through childhood with the amount of painting he was allowed to do. Every year would provoke complaints from a Cain who wanted to do more, but he realized now that his father had known what he was doing.

This is wrong.

The tune came in again. Cain looked for Whistler, but he must have been around the other side of the house. Bees buzzed circles of eight above flowers rich in pollen, and their wings beat in time with the music. Birds sat throughout the garden—blue tits, sparrows, siskins, coal tits, a wren, goldfinches, and a greater spotted woodpecker high in one tree in the corner—singing their pleasure at its diverse nature. He heard humming from somewhere, and he walked through the front gate and into the garden to investigate. It was only as he moved that he realized the humming was coming from him. He smiled, and continued following that tune.

Here was his future, and yet his past as well, a past he must have forgotten. Dark memories were beaten back by the sun. He saw a tricycle that his father had spent hours pushing him on every day. In his parents' vegetable patch there was a corner set aside for Cain, where he was growing purple sprouting, onions, and garlic. And here, was the future as well, because he would become self-sufficient, growing much of his own food and reveling in the knowledge that he was following what his parents—

This is wrong!

There was a basement door set into the side of the house, down a few worn steps. It was made of rotting timber and corrugated iron, adorned with heavy iron hinges and a rusted handle that belonged in a castle, not here. There were heavy timber boards fixed right across the door, bolted into the frame and almost fused there by time. Weeds grew around the foot of the door. The magnificent rosebushes grew across it, all but obscuring it from view. Cain had a brief, terrible moment when he thought that the door would swing open nonetheless, but then he heard the music again and he turned back to the garden.

Wrong, wrong, this is a lie, a woman's voice said, and he looked around for a memory of his mother. But he was alone there, alone with his future, comfortable with this brand-new past that had been hidden from him up until now. All that wasted time. All those years spent in fear, when he should have been reveling in memories such as these.

They're not real, the voice said, *you never lived like that.* Another, deeper voice countered with words he could not make out.

The tune faltered. A cloud passed across the sun. Cain stumbled and fell, grabbing hold of a thick rose stem and feeling vicious thorns pierce his palm and wrist.

Come out of it, Cain!

The garden wavered as if a sudden heat haze had sprung up, and for an instant he saw the roses dead and the bees changed into vicious flying beetles, clicking mandibles adorned with rotting meat. A few notes of the tune sang in and the garden was back, but nothing would ever be the same again.

Cain saw the roses, but he saw the sham behind their wondrous growth as well, and the fact that none of them could ever be perfect. It was as if their thick old trunks were embedded in rotting flesh instead of pure, honest soil, and their beautiful blooms were at the expense of something dear to him.

Just bring him out, the woman's voice said from a distance, and it held a note of authority that set Cain's teeth on edge. *You know none of this belongs to him, and he's nothing to do with you.*

That male voice came again in response, deep and musical, the words difficult to discern. But by now doubt had infected Cain's mind. He looked around at this extraordinary garden and house—his past as he had so wished it to be, the future he believed he could make—and the images were faltering. Bees buzzed in ever-decreasing circles until they fell to the ground, dead. Their stings were missing, embedded in the skin of the truth. Flowers wilted and turned brown. The sun faded, its light being sucked out of the garden and replaced by an insidious, creeping darkness, oozing out from one place only: the barred basement door. This house was unreal, a place he had never been, but the basement was becoming the one pivot of reality and truth. While the house and garden around it blurred, their colors separating into rotten rainbows, the door remained firm. The roses vanished from across its face, the weeds at its foot slipped back into soil that had never birthed them, and the door changed its appearance to one he knew so well.

Cain, he heard, and then: "Cain!" The voice burst in and shattered the last of the sunlight. A cold light bathed him, cool and impersonal, cast down from a streetlamp and surrounding him in an oasis of cruel truth.

Pan pipes soothed the darkness. Cain blinked slowly, his eyelids still painted with the memory of that wonderful place. He smelled honey, a sudden tang that rested on his tongue and the back of his mouth, and someone let him go.

Falling to the cold pavement, he heard the first scream of rage.

Sister Josephine stood bathed in the light from a streetlamp. Bees buzzed her head, danced at her fingertips, moved in and out of her habit. She was down in a fighter's pose, habit swaying around her as she shifted her weight from foot to foot. Cain caught glimpses of her bare legs as she moved, and they were slick and shiny with cream. She was all magicked up. Her hands were fisted, her lips tight, brow furrowed in concentration. It looked as if she was about to fight the dark, but then Cain saw the shape standing in the shadows. Whistler. He had put his pipes away for now, and he stood casually, arms by his sides, smiling at Sister Josephine as though a spectator of her fight, not a participant.

"Leave him alone," the nun said. "He's nothing for you."

"And is he anything for George?" Whistler said. There was a trace of anger in his voice that belied his benign expression.

"George was a fool and a monster."

"No more a monster than any of us."

"Speak for yourself." The nun shifted sideways, always facing Whistler as if expecting an attack at any moment.

"Are you not a monster, Josephine?"

"It's Sister Josephine to you."

Something about the dream had drained Cain, as if he had left his energy back in that imaginary garden. Maybe he had. Perhaps visions of such an unbelievable past and impossibly wonderful future had the power to kill.

"Sorry, *Sister,*" Whistler hissed. "And would Cain know of your little flights of fancy?"

"They're none of his business." She glanced at Cain as well, and he was shocked at the anxiety on her face. She had seemed so in control.

"The nun magicks herself up and flies through the night, looking for men to rape," Whistler said. A bee darted at his face, and he lifted his pipes quickly, played two short notes, and sent it aimlessly into the dark.

"Shut up! That's nothing to him."

"Really? Cain has lived with us for days, that's all. Already he has broken into my home and disturbed my followers. Magenta has told him the truth, he has been responsible for Peter's death at George's hand, and now George himself is dead. How did you kill him, Cain? How could you possibly kill such a man unaided?" He walked toward Cain, coming out of the darkness and into the light, and Sister Josephine scuttled crablike across the pavement. She stood between Cain and Whistler, her back to Cain. He could see her habit shivering as she shook. He smelled honey. He suddenly wished she would magic him up, strip off her habit, and envelop him with her greased body, enabling him to fly away from all this trouble.

"Just leave it be," the nun whispered. "Please, Whistler. George is gone—why make this night any worse for all of us."

"You're the one making it worse," the pipe player said. "I merely want to show Cain his own personal Heaven." He gestured behind Cain and the nun.

Cain turned, and really he already knew which house stood behind them. Heaven stared down, its windows still boarded, the front door solid and firm, the only leftover from the fantasy that Whistler's music had instilled in him.

"It was no fantasy," Whistler said, "just the truth unrealized."

"There's no truth in the past you showed me," Cain said, and his voice was weak, his throat barely able to form the words.

"If you say so. You obviously know everything. You've chosen your Way, it seems, and that's no way at all. I'm only trying to help you see the light. Your father would have wanted that, and I gather your mother still does."

"*Nobody* can force him to find the Way," Sister Josephine said. "We all know that—even Leonard knew. And yet we waste so much time. He has to find it for himself."

"I don't even want to look," Cain said, but neither of them seemed to hear him.

"She flies," Whistler said, voice raised, "and she

prowls the streets, and when she sees a man on his own who takes her fancy she lands·on him, pins him down, and fucks him. They may not want to fuck, but you've seen what's beneath that habit, the *curves* there, the *wonderful curves*. And you've smelled that stuff she smears herself with, whatever the hell it is. Can you imagine being smeared with that, Cain?"

Yes, he could, he could imagine it.

"Can you think of what it would do to a man?"

Cain did not have to think; he knew. He could smell the honey, he was hard inside his trousers, he looked at the nun where she stood with her back to him, still in her fighter's pose.

"But it's rape," Whistler said, "and sometimes she fucks them to *death*! What a way to go, Cain. Josephine's Way." And Sister Josephine went at him.

Whistler stepped aside, but the nun did not rely on her feet to guide her. They left the pavement and she hit Whistler like a huge bat, her habit trailing and slapping at the air as she made a sudden change of direction. There was a loud crunch as her hands connected with Whistler's face and he went down. Sister Josephine landed on top of him, beating with her fists, the habit waving and flapping like a boiling shadow. Bees buzzed the fighting pair, attaching themselves to Whistler's face before veering away to die.

Cain watched aghast, wondering just what they were fighting over. His future? His past? Or their own?

"Maybe," someone said, and he knew that voice. The shadow squatted next to him, fingers splayed on the pavement before it. It ignored the light from the streetlamp, casually existing where it should not. Cain had never seen it in such detail; the silhouette of its hair was thick and flowing, the outline of its face strong. And though he could still not make out any particulars, it seemed a friendly face. One that he could trust.

Whistler shouted. The nun rose several feet directly above him, screaming as she paused in midair, and light gleamed off something in the pipe player's hand. A knife, short and bloodied.

"Feel good?" Whistler asked, and any pretense at being calm and tempered had vanished. "Feel good being fucked to death?" He thrust upward suddenly, giving the nun no time to rise away from the knife. She screeched as it caught her in the stomach, and drifted higher to lift herself from its keen edge. Blood rained down onto and around Whistler, spattering the pavement with black spots that complemented the dying bees.

"Stop it!" Cain shouted, but they ignored him.

"This is about a lot more than you," the shadow said. "Don't you think? These creatures that have so much actually know so little. They claim Pure Sight, and yet they're jealous of each other. How can that be? Pure Sight is freedom, so they say."

"Selfishness," Cain said, so weak that he could barely answer. He slumped back on the pavement and watched the two people fight. Whistler, his pan pipes long since replaced in his hands by two short-bladed knives, both of them now wet with the nun's blood. And Sister Josephine, the woman who could fly, hovering around Whistler's head and jabbing at him with her bare feet, her long-nailed hands. Blood mixed with the magic cream. The pavement around the fighting couple was wet with both. Metal scraped against bone, and the woman screamed. There was a *thunk* as something snapped, and the man bellowed. Lights came on in several houses along the street but instantly went out again. *I wonder how used to this they really are?* Cain thought, and beside him the shadow shrugged.

"Fuck-head!" the nun screeched.

"Bitch!" Whistler shouted. They went at it again, his blades flashing in the weak light, her feet and fists connecting with his head from above. Sister Josephine dipped and rose like a hawk harrying its victim, but Whistler was giving as good as he received.

"Why doesn't she just fly away?" Cain whispered, and someone answered from the house behind him.

"It's what they live for," the voice said. Cain turned to see Magenta standing before Heaven's corrugated iron doorway. "They've done it before, they'll do it again. Neither of them will ever die easily."

"Magenta," Cain said. *Mother*, he thought. The shadow drew close to him like a frightened child.

"I can hardly see you," Magenta said, and Cain thought it was because of the dark. But then he realized that he was lying directly beneath a street-lamp, and he wondered exactly what she meant. Perhaps the shadow hid him from view? It held his arm, and though it felt cold, it felt right as well.

"Come inside," she said. "Away from this madness. It's not fair on you, not when you have to make up your own mind. Cain? Are you there?"

"Of course," he said.

"We should leave," the shadow whispered into his ear, its breath cool and calming. It touched his forehead in an affectionate gesture, and Cain smiled and shed a tear at the same time. No parent had ever done that for him.

He stood slowly, and Magenta smiled back. She was the same as when he had last seen her. When they met she was the Clown, and then the Savior. Now, dressed against the cool and carrying a bag over her shoulder, perhaps she was his Mother.

Cain glanced over his shoulder at the fighting couple. Sister Josephine's tactics had changed now, and Whistler roared in rage, shouting at her, calling her unclean and monstrous and twisted. She had torn her habit away and floated above him, naked but for her wimple. There were puncture wounds in her stomach and chest, and her hands were gashed from where she tried to fend off his knife blows. But she was smiling. Her skin glistened with the magic cream, the warm honey aroma wafting across to Cain in strong waves, and she opened her legs to Whistler. He struck at her, but bees went for his eyes, stinging, entering his mouth when he screamed. And then she had him, grasping him around the waist with her strong thighs. She forced him to the ground, tipped him onto his back, and laughed as he stuck a knife in the side of her neck. Blood flowed but turned a pasty, pale color as cream slipped across her body to dilute it.

"Feel good, being fucked to death?" she screamed, reaching down between them for his zipper. Whistler bucked and threw her aside, though her ankles remained locked behind his back.

"Get off me, whore!"

"Nothing less than what you do to your followers, you fucking monster!"

"Get your hands away or I'll cut them off!"

"Ahh, see, I knew you wanted me!"

They rolled into the road, cursing and screaming and fighting, and Cain turned away.

"Are they mad?" he asked Magenta.

"Aren't we all?" She turned from Cain and tugged at the corrugated iron front door to Heaven. "You won't find anything good in here, or anything fresh," she said. "I suspect it will only compound those mysteries in your mind. But it's somewhere you'll be able to think."

"Anywhere's better than here," the shadow whispered in Cain's ear, still holding on to him like an infant grasping its parent. Cain could only agree. He heard the terrible fight continuing behind him, and he followed Magenta into the darkness of Heaven without a final backward glance.

He had seen enough madness for one night.

He hoped that he would discover no more inside.

"I can barely see you."

"It's dark," Cain said. "I don't like it in here. This is Peter's place."

"Peter's dead," Magenta said.

"That's why I don't like it. It's not fair. We shouldn't even be here."

He heard Magenta rustling around, opening drawers, tripping over something and cursing as she landed on hands and knees. From outside, the fighting sounded as frantic and violent as ever. *No sirens,* Cain thought. *No people coming to help. Perhaps even if they can see, people want to keep to themselves. Even if it means someone else will die.* The thought depressed him suddenly and totally, and he let out a sob of loss for the Face and Voice, and safety.

"I'll never be safe again," Cain said, and Magenta did not dispute his statement.

"You never were," the shadow said. "Look what you had as a mother." As if on cue, Magenta struck a match and lit a candle. There were dozens scattered around the hallway—in wall fixtures and candlesticks, and standing alone—molded to the antique furniture and floor by melted wax. She lit several more and handed one to Cain. Her movement caused shadows to dance behind her; ironic that the only true shadow was still at Cain's side.

"I see your shadow," Magenta said, and then she turned away and headed for the stairs.

Cain panicked. Nobody had ever commented on the shadow before! It had always been his and his alone. Even his father had never known of it. But as he turned around he saw his true shadow cast behind him, distorting as his gasp of relief set his candle shivering. "She means that," he whispered, but the shadow holding on to his side did not respond.

"Cain," Magenta said. "Follow me. There's a room up here you should see. Peter was a very old man, contrary to appearances. It's actually a terrible shame that he's dead."

"So nice of you to show some concern," Cain said. Magenta looked around the hallway as if trying to place an errant thought, then turned and started upstairs without replying.

Cain followed. There was nothing more for him to do. Magenta was his mother, and he supposed out of all of them he must trust her the most.

"Don't," said the shadow, "you can't choose your family." Its fear seemed to have vanished, and the old bitterness was back.

But trust her he did. She had not changed since the last time he had seen her, and he took that as a mark of her respect for his thoughts. And though they had parted recently on such a sour note, still she had come back to him, his savior again in different clothes. She had taken him away from the terrible, impossible sights outside, and though she must know he had killed George, she had yet to mention that madman.

It's what they live for, she had said of Whistler and Sister Josephine. For the first time, Cain wondered whether George really was dead. Perhaps tomorrow they would all return home and Number 13 would be full again. But he doubted that. He had heard the screams and sensed the change with which the others—Magenta included—viewed him now. Not exactly as one of them, but not as a normal person either.

Magenta talked as though he still had to make up his mind, but he had already changed.

"I'll never be like you," Cain said. Magenta kept climbing above him, but her stance changed. More stressed, tensed.

"Wait until you see," she said.

"What are you going to show me?"

"A room. Filled with dead people, I think. And every one of them knew the Way."

"They're all here, dead, now?"

She paused and turned to look down at him. Her eyes were vacant, as if she were looking into some unknowable distance. The past, perhaps. Or the future, a time quite literally filled with change for her. "The house *is* called Heaven, after all."

"Perhaps Hell would be more appropriate," he said.

"None of us are evil, Cain, not even those two outside. We simply know so much more. How can we live normally with what we know?"

"You can live *morally*."

"Morals are a conceit of society." Magenta looked into the flame of her candle and her eyes swam with fire.

"Someone else once said that to me," Cain said.

"Your father. I taught him that very idea." She turned and moved on.

"Then he was wrong as well," Cain said, but she appeared not to hear.

At the top of the stairs, they turned left and walked along a narrow landing. The carpet was threadbare, the wall finish moist and moldy, and in several places the ceiling had caved in. Its remains had long since been trodden into the floor or kicked away, but the holes left behind stared back with pure darkness. *Could be anything up there,* Cain thought, and he held his candle high to ward off the unknown.

At the end of the landing, they came to a door. It was cracked and warped, as if something had tried to force it open from inside, but it still hung strong in its frame. Several large padlocks secured bolts in place.

"I've always wanted to see in here," Magenta said dreamily. "But none of us are allowed."

"Who doesn't allow it?"

"Peter. He may not have been like us, but he had a job to do. All of us know more of the world than anyone normal, but as you've seen from Whistler and the nun, sometimes we need protecting from each other."

She placed the candle at her feet, reached up, and touched the first padlock. It sizzled and became fluid, re-forming into a metal tankard that clanged to the floor.

"Shit!" Cain said. He should not have been surprised, he supposed. He had seen Magenta change, from clown to warrior to mother. The fact that she could enforce a change on other things was only one step removed.

"I don't do this much," Magenta said, and her voice held a trace of pain. This was uncomfortable for her.

"Don't hurt yourself." He heard the shadow giggle at his shoulder.

Magenta laughed as well. "Concerned for your mother?"

Cain shook his head, but she had her back to him and did not see.

She touched the next padlock and it fell to the floor as a shower of ball bearings. The final lock twisted, flamed briefly, and then dripped down the face of the door, scorching it, drying and hardening into a slick of melted metal. Magenta stood back and sighed, seemed to relax into herself, shook her head. Then she picked up the candle and turned to Cain.

Her eyes were scanning the landing behind Cain as if looking for a missing thought. "I've never been in here," she said, "and I don't quite know what to expect. I think it's just the minds of dead people . . . I think. But they may have a strange effect." She stared into the darkness beyond the candlelight, and Cain suddenly believed that she truly could not see him. "Cain? Are you with me?"

"You're just like me," the shadow whispered, snickering.

"I am," he said. As Magenta pushed open the door, Cain wondered which of them he had answered.

The light from their candles filled the room. Cain was aware of the smudge of shadow on his left, but he did not glance that way. He looked straight ahead. At the glass cabinets, and the things inside them.

"Oh, Peter," Magenta said, her voice surprised more than disgusted.

"Fuck," Cain said. "Monsters. You're all monsters, *all* of you!"

"Don't leap to conclusions," she said. "Who knows exactly what your head would look like were it stripped of flesh and hair?"

Skulls. There were at least forty glass cases fixed to each wall, and in almost every case sat a skull. Cain turned in a circle, looking all around the room, and the movement of his candle gave life to the skulls' eye sockets. Their ghost eyes followed him, and as he paused and stood as motionless as possible, still one or two of them seemed to move. Every skull was grinning. Smashed nose sockets snorted darkness.

"Monsters!" Cain said, and he turned to leave.

The door slammed shut. Magenta was there, waving the candle in front of him, her eyes still distant and uncertain. "You're there," she said. "You're here. Somewhere. And now you have to see." She stepped forward, and Cain stepped aside to avoid being burned by her candle.

"Can't see you," the shadow on his shoulder said. "Your mother can't see you."

"Did she ever?" Cain said.

"What?" Magenta turned, and her beautiful eyes were filled with sadness. Almost as if she knew what Cain had been talking about.

"Nothing."

"See here," she said, waving her hand around as if giving a guided tour. "The remains of dozens that knew the Way. All these were people like us, people with a knowledge of the universe that so surpassed normal understanding that it set them far aside. So superior that—"

"Superior," Cain said, nodding. "That word again. So superior."

Magenta must have heard his sarcasm, but she chose to ignore it. "Peter was our landlord, but he was a caretaker as well. When someone with the Way died, he would dispose of them. Some of them are too . . . different to be left lying around."

"Was Peter left lying around?" Cain asked. "After George tore him to pieces?"

"Peter's body is somewhere apart from the world," she said. "No one will find him."

"And these?" Cain asked. "These freaks? What are these, your brothers and sisters? My aunts and uncles? Mother . . ." He did not feel the need to finish the sentence. Magenta looked right at him, and he shifted his candle to the side. Her eyes followed.

"Here," she said, turning back to the wall. "I knew him. Markus Keene. He was a conjuror of fire. He died from his own gift. Corrupted. Power corrupted him."

"I thought you were all perfect," Cain said, looking at the skull. It had a part-melted appearance, like a wax model left out in the sun.

"Not all, no," Magenta said. "But most of us are."

"Whistler? Sister Josephine?"

"As unique as the rest of us. Look, here's Lockley! I haven't seen him for four decades, not since he was shot. A hunter mistook him for a deer. Such irony." The skull she indicated had antlers protruding from its temples. They had been cut so that the skull would fit into the glass case, but their roots were thick, and Cain suspected they had once been grand.

There were more, dozens more, and Magenta knew more than a few of them. Ashley, with teeth so long that they would not look out of place in a crocodile's mouth. Arthur, an old, old man from ages past who had been killed by the stench of technology. The Twin, two skulls fused together so that they shared a mouth but each had two eyes, a nose, a brain. The junction of their skulls displayed yellowed cracks like the map of a river and its tributaries, as if they had spent their lives going different ways. Angus, a skull with the snout of a bull, replete with a brass ring still fixed against its smashed nasal passage. And more, yet more, and for every five normal skulls there was one with three eyes, two mouths, and other less obvious differences that marked them as so definitely inhuman.

"And here," Magenta said, "is George." She reached into a bag slung over her shoulder. Cain cringed back, petrified at what he would see, but fascinated at the same time.

"Peter should be doing this," Magenta said as she placed George's severed head in an empty case. She adjusted its positioning for a full minute, turning it this way and that, stroking hair from over one eye, finally settling on an aspect that seemed to please her. Then she closed the glass lid and stood back.

George had not reverted to his human form. Maybe he had died before the full change could be complete. His jaws were distended, teeth long and sharp, and it appeared that his top lip had been shredded by his own underbite. His forehead sloped backward, hairless and shiny even in death, and his eyes were buried in shadowed pits. Cain shivered, and his candle gave George flaming yellow eyes, filled with rage and a promise of pain to come.

Cain tried to look away but could not. Is this

why Magenta had brought him here? To watch her place George's head among these other dead freaks? Because he had killed George, and this made him involved. This made him *responsible*.

"I thought you said you weren't sure what was in here," he said.

"I'd only heard. I'm never sure until I've seen something for myself. You've seen so much already, Cain. Aren't you sure? Have you no certainty yet?"

"Don't try to draw me in," he said. "Don't try to involve me."

"You're already involved. With all of us. We're unique, and you're beginning to realize—"

"Inhuman," he said.

"*More* than human. But that's your choice. I believe, Cain, that it's a choice you still have to make, no matter what the signs tell me. Don't let yourself believe that it's cut-and-dried, because I know there's still doubt in you. You'd have gone from here by now if that wasn't the case. I hope that you choose to live for what your father believed in. You thought of him as mad, but he was far from that."

"I can never be what he wanted!" Cain shouted. His movement gave George's head a smile and a burning glare. "Why did you leave?" he asked wretchedly. "Why did he tell me you were dead? I never had a mother . . ." Cain sobbed the last word, unable to finish the sentence and unsure of what he had intended saying.

"I'm sorry, Cain. I told you, you were all Leonard ever wanted. As for me, I found the Way the instant I became pregnant. After that, things were so . . . different."

"You didn't want me? You don't care?"

Magenta looked more uncomfortable than sad, and that was as much of an answer as Cain needed. He held his head in his hands and cried, wanting nothing more than to feel his mother's warm hand on the back of his head, comforting, loving. But all that touched him there was the coolness of the shadow.

"I'm leaving now," she said. "I hope we'll meet again. Son." And before Cain could say another word, Magenta left the room and disappeared into the dark depths of the house.

Her candle remained propped on one of the glass cases. It gave the skull beneath it a quizzical smile, and Cain wanted to smash the case and lose the smile to the dark. But he held back. He could not do that; he had no right.

"Let's get home," the shadow said, and Cain said the same.

"I don't like this place," Cain said, and the shadow echoed his words.

On the way out, they carried both candles.

There was no sign of Sister Josephine, but Whistler was lying moaning in the gutter. His hair was caked with blood, his face a contour map of bee stings and wounds, and his pan pipes lay crushed into the concrete pavement. He would have more, Cain knew. His time was not yet over. For now, this strange man's skull was safe beneath his ponytail hair.

* * *

The front garden no longer held any fears for Cain. He felt changed by everything he had seen this night. The creatures beneath the shrubs were quiet and watchful, and he wondered what they saw when they looked at him. A man with a shadow on his back? Or no man at all?

All the way upstairs to the first floor, along the landing and up again to his own front door, Cain avoided looking to his left. The shadow was still whispering to him, but the voice was deep down inside his mind now, almost incomprehensible, and it may as well have been his own thoughts mumbling away. So he looked to the right, and not because he did not want to see the shadow again, but because he suspected that the shadow had gone.

In the front door, through the bedroom, into the bathroom, in front of the mirror, and Cain finally knew the truth that had been hounding him all night. He had not wished to admit it to himself, however strong the evidence. That way lay madness. But now he could see, and he knew that the shadow had gone forever.

Because Cain *was* the shadow.

His reflection stared back in fear and shock, and he could see himself only because he knew for sure that he was there.

Cain was the shadow.

When Cain first saw the shadow in his father's basement room, it spoke with his voice, but he gave it a stranger's lilt. It bore his shape, but he made it larger. It spoke of mild rebellion and he shied away from its audacity, though it was really verbalizing his own deepest thoughts. He kept it apart from himself.

For the first time in his life, he had a friend. He would do nothing to ruin that.

Chapter Eleven
Shadow

Next day, Whistler broke into Cain's flat.

Cain crouched in the corner of the living room and watched the tall pipe player wander in, through to the dining area and kitchen, out again. Whistler paused to look at the pictures in the hallway, rubbing the glass as if he could erase the traces of color that Cain had put there himself. He went into the bedroom and Cain followed close behind, standing in the corner as Whistler rummaged through his clothes, lifted the bedspread, opened the small wardrobe as if looking for a shadow that never was.

Whistler never saw Cain, because Cain was that shadow.

The tall man sat in the living room for a while, nursing a new set of pan pipes and bringing them to his lips, away, up again. It was as if he could not bring himself to play them. Perhaps he was afraid that they would no longer work, or maybe he feared that Sister Josephine would hear him. His face was bruised and stung from their fight, and he carried himself stiffly, broken bones only too keen to remind him of defeat.

Cain sat next to the window, out of the path of sunlight that streamed through. He did not make a sound, though he was not sure that Whistler would hear even if he did. He watched the tall man, and when Whistler finally stood to leave—pushing on his legs to stand up, an old, tired man—Cain followed him to the front door.

Whistler paused there in Cain's hallway, then spun around. Cain stepped sideways against the wall, hitting it with a thump, and the impact set one of the landscape pictures shaking. Whistler stared at the picture, brought the pipes up to his lips, and played the first notes through this new instrument. Only two notes, quiet and low and quick, but they made the hair on the back of Cain's neck stand on end.

Whistler lowered the pan pipes and smiled. He looked around the flat one more time and, in a voice so low that he must have believed he was speaking only to himself, said, "I only hope he's happy." Then he left and closed the door behind him.

He had not noticed Cain. Even when Cain had been standing right in front of him, Whistler had not seen him. He had suspected Cain was there maybe, or guessed, or known in some obscure way that only those with the Way could understand. But he had not been certain. Because Cain was the shadow, and even on the brightest day a shadow has a home.

Cain sat in his living room, feeling the warmth of Whistler fading slowly from the sofa, and cried bitter tears. Once, the choice had been his to make.

No more.

Cain crept downstairs that evening and waited in the lobby. He approached Sister Josephine's door several times, raised his hand to knock, drew back. In the end, he hid beneath the stairs with the other shadows, waiting for the sun to sink lower and the light to fade away.

As darkness fell, the world was opening up to him. Reality. Truth. Concepts that he used to have on the verge of sleep or in the depths of dreams, rich ideas of change and exploration, all rose up and invited his inspection. Unlike before, they did not vanish with his next breath. They remained, honest and true, and he could not help feeling a spark of excitement deep inside. Sometimes he used to think he had an original thought; now he had many. He had never felt such potential.

He walked to the nun's door and tapped on it three times, stepping quickly to the side. He heard footsteps from inside, and she opened the door, glanced out, holding a gown closed across her chest.

Cain slipped in.

Sister Josephine shivered and slammed the door, backing away from it, staring at the wood as if it would bulge in after her. Cain was a step behind her, walking back as she did. He could reach out and touch her hair, should he so desire. He breathed in and reveled in the honey aroma, a mysterious and exotic mix of sweetness and sex.

She could not see him.

He stepped aside and held his breath as she passed by, a frown on her face. He waited in her hallway for a few seconds after she had moved into her bedroom, gathering his thoughts and hating himself, *hating* himself.

Was this what Pure Sight was all about? George was a killer, Whistler was a manipulator, and if the pipe player was to be believed, Sister Josephine flew across the city seeking men to fuck to death.

Was this what it was all about?

Cain walked to the nun's bedroom, knelt, and looked inside. She was on the bed, her gown thrown open to reveal her full nakedness. There was a pot of her magic cream on the bed beside her, and she was working it slowly into the knife wounds that Whistler had punched into her body. She cringed. She cried. The smell of her tears merged with the warm, rich tang of the cream, and Cain hated himself even more when he felt the heat in his groin.

Had his father wanted this? Is this what his mother had? He stared at the beautiful naked woman—no nun now, for sure, although she no doubt had a whole history that would always be a mystery—and he thought of what Whistler had said about her. She could fly, Cain had seen that for himself. And she could fight. She was like an imaginary superhero, but one with dreadful faults.

But wasn't that the case with all of them?

Her hands broadened their areas of application, passing over the slits in her skin and working through fresh blood.

A bee came at Cain, slow and unconcerned, and he remained still. It struck his cheek and veered away, buzzing in confusion at hitting nothing. The nun paused and stared at her bedroom door, and Cain moved quickly to the side, out of view.

"I hope I see him again," she said. Cain bit his lip and frowned, looking down at his hands, seeing them only because he knew that they were there. A waft of fresh honey came from the bedroom, and when Sister Josephine's groans turned into moans of a different kind, Cain moved away and quietly let himself out.

He returned to his own flat, and as he opened the door the phone on his bedside table was ringing. He picked it up and the Voice crackled at him, asking him where he was, whether he was well, why he hadn't called to tell them how things were. Cain held the phone for some time, listening to the silence that the Voice was expecting to be filled. And then he hung up. There was really nothing he could say.

He found it easy to slip into Whistler's flat. The piper was standing at his bedroom window staring out at the dusk, but Cain was not there for him. He crept into the room named for "The Followers" and closed the door behind him.

The difference was immediately apparent. The creatures still looked dead and stuffed, but there was a subtle sound playing on Cain's ears, almost too low to hear. The sound of movement. Muscles stretching, bones creaking, dried pelts whispering as unaccustomed shifting affected the whole room.

He turned the corner and stared at the fox and chicken, and over a couple of minutes he saw the two of them move a minute amount. It was like watching the hour hand of a clock—movement obvious, yet not visible. The fox's jaws closed slightly, the chicken's head fell more to one side, and the flow of spilled blood widened and spread across the floor like melted wax.

Cain turned the final corner and saw the woman in the chair. She was not Magenta. She seemed to be in exactly the same position as when he had last seen her, but her eyes had shifted to the right as if still following him from the room. He leaned in close and listened at her nose and mouth, but there were no signs of breathing. He waved his hand in front of her face, but of course she would have seen nothing anyway. Even in his new state, he did not wish to touch her.

Cain watched for a few minutes. Her eyes did not change. Her chest did not expand to bring in air. But over that time, her mouth opened and closed almost imperceptibly. Wherever she existed now, she was gasping at something both profound and amazing.

That night, Cain went out. He moved through the streets, flitting from shadow to shadow, listening to people whisper sweet nothings, flicking their hair, a goose walking over their graves.

He breathed on one girl's neck and made her turn around, seconds before she would have stepped into the path of a joyrider. She walked on, unnerved, never to know that her life had been saved.

In a shop doorway he found a mugger, scoping his victims and heading out only when he spied a teenager on his own. Cain tripped the mugger and sent him sprawling. The teenager glanced across the street and hurried away from the man, who seemed drunk. The mugger tried to rise, but Cain sat on his back, whispering into his ear, "I'll be watching, I'll be watching." When Cain finally stood, the man scrambled to his feet and sprinted off down the street, looking around wildly, all thoughts of theft and assault purged from his mind.

In a car park there were a couple having sex in an open-top car. Inviting discovery obviously added to their thrill, but they carried on unaware of Cain standing beside the driver's door. He hated that, but he also loved it. He had become so different.

That night, he followed a murderer home and planted evidence on his clothing. He closed an open window just as a burglar was about to climb through, and gave the boy a shove into a spiky rosebush for good measure. And as dawn began to bring the city to life, Cain's shadow moved across the eyes of a sleeping child, driving away a nightmare that would have marked her day.

Cain had always felt unnoticed, and now that was truly the case. He was a man with a future. He had found his Way, and if he could learn to live with that, the possibilities were endless.

FEARS
UNNAMED
TIM LEBBON

Tim Lebbon has burst upon the scene and established himself as one of the best horror writers at work today. He is the winner of numerous awards, including a Bram Stoker Award, critics have raved about his work, and fans have eagerly embraced him as a contemporary master of the macabre.

Perhaps nowhere are the reasons for his popularity more evident than in this collection of four of his most chilling novellas. Two of these dark gems received British Fantasy Awards, and another was written specifically for this book and has never previously been published. These terrifying tales form a window into a world of horrors that, once experienced, can never be forgotten.
